YO-ELK-064

VIRGO RISING

Tina Borders

Me Myself and I, Inc.

Portland Oregon

Copyright © 2019 Tina Borders

All rights reserved. No part of this publication may be reproduced, distributed or transmitted in any form or by any means, without prior written permission.

Tina Borders (tinaborders.com)/Me Myself and I, Inc.

Publisher's Note: This is a work of fiction. Names, characters, places, and incidents are a product of the author's imagination. Locales and public names are sometimes used for atmospheric purposes. Any resemblance to actual people, living or dead, or to businesses, companies, events, institutions, or locales is completely coincidental.

Book Layout © 2014 BookDesignTemplates.com

Virgo Rising/Tina Borders. -- 1st ed.
ISBN 978-0-578-40241-3

ACKNOWLEDGEMENTS

I would like to thank Brenda for asking me if I write. Amy, for being such a good friend you liked it even when it was a mess. Noramah, for your endless reading and editing, and Debra Hartmann at Pro Book Editor (theprobookeditor.com) for your patience and objective editing skills, with which I could never have given this book its professional polish. Thank you!

For Brett

AUGUST

The sound of Kirsten's father singing the doxology made her want to disappear. As he sang, his lower lip protruded from the force of the sound that emanated from deep within. He was unaware of the part he should be playing. This was not a performance by The Mormon Tabernacle Choir. Most people wanted their voices to blend in, if not be barely audible, but not August.

He was a proud man, who had the self-confidence of a shirtless, steed-riding Vladimir Putin. However, unlike Putin he could rest on his good looks instead of the power that came with being president of a formidable country.

His deeply rugged brow seemed perpetually tan and magnified the blue of his eyes. The slight silver that was beginning to show in his otherwise blond beard and hair only added to his appeal. He was of an acceptable height, but when asked, he would stretch and say he was exactly six feet.

She was mad at herself for agreeing to come in the first place. It was one of the trade-offs of moving to Minneapolis—she'd have to see him.

Trapped as she was, her thoughts wandered back to her journey here. Less than a month ago she was happy living the single career-girl life she'd carefully planned for herself. The blur of the last week swirled with images, voices, and conversations that never would've happened if she hadn't received that one phone call. It only takes a moment to monumentally change a life.

She needed to be alone. She desperately wanted to sit and process. It was all too much; even the seemingly straightforward drive here was determined to be eventful.

She closed her eyes, pretending to be lost in the moment, and found herself back in her old Volvo chugging up the mountain pass. Like now, she'd felt boxed in by the steep mountain of shale on her right and the guardrail marking the edge of a deep canyon on the opposite side. A yellow yield sign warned of possible falling rocks. As a child she'd been a little scared about the possibility of falling and wondered what the chances would be of it happening. This time fate answered. As she came around the next bend she saw a large boulder had crushed the bed of a pickup truck. The already beat-up-looking truck had been on her tail not more than five minutes ago and angrily passed her. Sheer fear gripped her as she held her breath. The damage to the truck was extensive, and debris and rock covered the road, cascading down the canyon. Metal fencing usually saved for corralling horses or cattle lay strewn about and one even dangled precariously on a piece of craggy rock above her head.

How is that even possible? she wondered. Kirsten sat clutching the steering wheel, not sure what to do. She'd taken first aid in high school but never did very well at the sight of blood. She could make out a car stopped on the other side of the road.

Was it hit too?

No, she could see someone getting out of the driver's seat as she heard the rumbling of a semi stopping behind her with its loud squeak and whistle of compression brakes. Before she could find the handle on her door, the trucker jumped out and ran toward the victim in the crumpled king cab truck. Kirsten was forever grateful to Mister Trucker for showing up and taking charge. She got out but hung back a bit as he opened the door and tried to talk to the driver. The truck was bent in the middle where the boulder lay. The glass in most of the windows was shattered. The trucker was trying to wake up the driver, who was slumped over the wheel unconscious. It looked like he had been wearing his seatbelt, at least, since the truck was probably too old to have air bags. The driver started to move, and the trucker told him to take it easy and sit back. It was then she and passengers from a car on the opposite side approached the trucker to see if there was anything they could do.

Kirsten observed a foursome—two girls and two guys—about her age—who appeared to lead a very different lifestyle than hers. They had dreadlocks hanging from under their matted-down wool knit hats and wore a combination of leggings with shorts or cargo pants and jeans. Their clothes were dark muted hues with softer underclothing of t-shirts and socks in bright solids and patterns of greens, reds, and blues. They had an old Subaru plastered with stickers, many of which were peeling off, proclaiming their eco-religion. The lead eco-guy held his cell phone up, saying he didn't have a signal. Kirsten immediately ran to her car, grabbed her cell, and turned back waving her phone, "Yeah, I don't have one either." Mister Trucker said he'd call on his radio and asked the eco-guy to take over, which he did without hesitation. Again, Kirsten was grateful.

More vehicles slowly approached on both sides and people

were getting out to see what had happened. It was a strange and eerie feeling to be up in the mountains with total strangers from different walks of life, the mere thread of a highway bringing them together. The briskness of the mountain air caused her to pull her coat and hat out of her car and put them on as she rejoined the passengers from the eco-car. They had been first on the scene, and despite their outward differences, their circumstances created a sort of solidarity.

Kirsten felt like such a girl while she just stood there watching eco-guy and Mister Trucker take care of the driver. He seemed groggy but was now able to talk. He did have a big gash on his forehead and the bleeding was being stopped by a t-shirt the trucker had brought with him. The girls from the other car had grabbed some blankets to help keep him warm. The trucker was successful in contacting state troopers who were on their way and about a half hour out. As bystanders started to close in wondering if anyone had been called or wanting to know how the driver was, Kirsten was finally able to be helpful by informing everyone about what was going on. One motherly type in her fifties came forward and said she was a medical assistant, then started to take over the care of the driver.

Once she realized the driver was probably going to be okay and it was a matter of waiting, Kirsten's thoughts turned to more practical issues, like how long she was going to be stuck up here. She couldn't call her mother, and if she missed her expected call time, it would create needless panic. She thought she'd get a signal a little farther down the road, another thirty to forty miles ahead. Then she could pull over if necessary and call her. It wouldn't be quite to Billings yet, but about the same time her mother would expect the call, assuming of course, she would be another couple hours max before she'd be cleared to go. *Who knows how long this will take*, Kirsten thought. *It's not like she had the ability to assess this kind of situation.* The second eco-guy who'd been hanging with them and sort of disengaged the whole time got back into the Subaru. One of the girls he was traveling with said he was sick.

Sick or stoned, Kirsten mused.

Eco-guy number one realized he wasn't needed anymore, so hung back with Kirsten and his other traveling companions.

"Hi," he said.

"Hi," Kirsten returned. She felt a jolt go through her upon noticing how cute he was. Somehow she'd missed that detail before. He seemed to pick up on her attraction, which Kirsten found maddening because it wasn't intentional. He gave her a wide-open grin with a mischievous twinkle from a fleck of amber in his otherwise brown eyes. Damn, he was good! Normally she preferred blue eyes, but his were kind and set deep beneath thick black brows. She couldn't help but be drawn in. His hair was an unruly mess of matching black and the stubble on his face gave him a very sexy, rugged look. Kirsten turned toward the girls so she wouldn't confirm he was right about what he saw.

"So, he's going to be okay?" girl with dreadlocks inquired.

"Yeah, it looks that way," he replied. Eco-guy looked at Kirsten and asked, "Where are you headed?" pointing out her Washington state plates with a nod of his head.

"Minneapolis," Kirsten replied.

"Really? Why would someone from Washington want to go there?" eco-guy asked.

"Work," Kirsten said, not wanting to divulge more than

necessary, as she didn't want him to think she'd opened her door to him. She turned it back on them and asked the girls where they were coming from, seeing they too were from Washington.

"Laramie," said the square but cute girl.

"Wyoming," dreadlocks explained. "We're in the MFA program at UDub and are staging the play The Laramie Project; we wanted to go to the place where it happened."

"Cool." It was familiar, but Kirsten couldn't quite remember what it was about. However, she knew it was probably best not to ask. "Not your usual road trip, huh? How was it? Did you get what you were hoping for?"

"Well, it's about getting the truth. We don't go in with any preconceived ideas," said square-cute girl with a surprisingly sharp tone.

"Oh, sure, I'm not an actor. What do I know?" Kirsten laughed, feeling the cut of cute girl's intonation and realizing the meaning. Eco-guy seemed amused at the slight jealousy, which only made Kirsten indignant.

Kirsten wondered how she'd gotten placed in some bizarre love triangle and why everything had to come back to who likes whom and who doesn't. Does it ever stop being like high school? She wished she hadn't found eco-guy good-looking or at least hadn't let him know that. Why couldn't she be more sly?

Before she could make a polite exit to her car, eco-guy held out his hand and introduced himself. "I'm Ryan, by the way."

She relented after a slight pause, then shook his held-out hand. "Kirsten."

"Lauren," said cute girl with a wave.

"Andi," said dreadlocks, reaching out to shake Kirsten's.

"So do you live in Seattle?" Ryan asked.

"Um, well, I did until today. I'm moving to Minneapolis for a new job."

"What kind of work do you do?" Lauren asked a bit coolly.

"Buyer. I'm a clothing buyer. I used to work for Nordstrom and just got a job at Dayfield's Department Store."

"Hey, a friend of mine works there," Ryan said, sounding happily surprised. "Maybe you know her, Michelle Callaway?"

"Yeah, I do know her, really well, actually. She's our BP manager downtown, which is, I mean was, the department I bought for. She's great."

"Her brother's a good friend of mine. We sort of grew up together."

"Really? Wow. What are the chances? I'll have to tell her next time I talk to her." Kirsten saw Lauren's disgust rise out of the corner of her eye.

"This move isn't forever. It's just an excellent opportunity and I couldn't pass it up. I love Seattle and plan on moving back. My parents live there. I mean, my mom and stepdad and all my friends. I've, like, lived there my whole life practically. Except, I did live in Minnesota until I was five, and I've visited over the years since, so it's not like it's totally unfamiliar. Everyone thinks I'm gonna die in some blizzard or something." *Ugh! Stop talking,* Kirsten, she yelled at herself and quickly changed the subject. "I think that's so cool that you guys drove all the way to Wyoming."

Ryan continued to be amused, Andi seemed oblivious, and, just before she could make it worse, the police arrived to save the day with the ambulance not too far behind.

Thank God!

The flashing lights and uniformed men and women with large, unfamiliar equipment only added to the surrealism. There were questions to answer, contact information to give out, and the general business of clearing an accident. This scene had been played out on TV and movies to the point of numbness. But it's not normal. It's adrenaline pumping and emotionally draining. Kirsten was surprised by suddenly feeling like she was going to cry but stuffed it back down immediately. She wasn't the one hurt. She was fine, so why did she want to break down and cry? She couldn't answer and decided to get back in her car where it was more private.

"Hey, Kirsten? I think you dropped this," she heard Ryan call out.

She turned around and saw her glove in his hand. "Oh, yeah, I must've," she said while checking her pocket for the other one.

"Are you all right?" he asked.

"Um, yeah, I think standing outside this long is starting to get in my bones. I'm cold."

"Yeah, it isn't quite spring up here yet, is it?"

"No, it isn't." She nodded, trying hard not to look away.

"Well, it was nice meeting you and good luck in Minneapolis." Ryan could see that something had given way in her and held back what he really wanted to ask.

"Thanks." Kirsten softened at his kindness, which bolstered his confidence.

"So, uh, I'm on Facebook and friends with Michelle. Maybe next time you're in Seattle we could all go have a beer instead of hanging out at the scene of an accident."

Kirsten smiled at his effort. "Yeah, that sounds like a lot

more fun. It'll probably be a while, though. Good luck with your project…play…thing." She stumbled trying to remember the name.

"Thanks." He started to turn, then stopped. "You know there's a lot of Ryans out there? I'm Ryan Walker."

"Swenson," she said after hesitating.

"Kirsten Swenson, huh?"

"Yeah, I know, it's very Swedish—very Minneapolis-Seattle. Whataya gonna do?" She shrugged, trying to be offhand about it, knowing full well the weight of it in her own life. She had her own Kirsten doll by American Girl carefully tucked away in the little U-Haul trailer she was pulling—affirming her own lineage.

"Wow, a real Swede. It's nice to have met you, Kirsten Swenson. Safe travels." He held out his hand, and she willed herself to look him in the eye like anyone else while she shook it: no agenda. No meaning; just a handshake between acquaintances.

The road was finally clear, so Kirsten started her descent out of the Rockies toward her evening accommodations in Billings. Icy rain pelted her windshield—a final farewell to the unpredictable weather in the mountains of the true northwest. As the traffic eased to its pre-accident pace, she fell back into her earlier driving rhythm. Her mind spun, flitting over the details of the last few hours: the sudden braking at the sight of the accident, the trucker rushing to aid, and Ryan. Ryan and his smiling eyes.

She laughed out loud and shook her head. "I know you, Ryan Walker. You're the type of guy who loves the hunt and gets plenty of opportunity because of your obvious charm. But then what? You get bored and restless and move on. You're wrong about me. I don't know how to play those games."

She felt sorry for Lauren. *She shouldn't be mad at me. She should be mad at herself for failing to recognize his true nature.* But girls like that never do. Instead of blaming him or themselves for their bad choices, they blame the girl who becomes the next object of his desire. It's totally irrational, and if the shoe were on the other foot, she knew Lauren would bask in the attention and rub it in. Kirsten had received the vengeance of these types of girls on more than one occasion and refused to be like the Laurens of this world.

She inhaled long and slow, and as she let out her breath, she pressed down harder on the accelerator, leaving her old life behind. Like a salmon returning to its birthplace to spawn, she traveled toward stories she'd heard passed down through the generations. She recalled her rich Scandinavian history. According to her father, Sweden was the only other place in the world where blonde hair and blue eyes were as ubiquitous as in Minnesota. One of the many arguments she decided not to engage in with him, knowing full well that she was not the only blonde-haired, blue-eyed girl who lived in Seattle.

There was the crazy marriage of convenience between her maternal, Norwegian great-great-grandfather to her Swedish great-great-grandmother. Having lost their spouses soon after their arrival in Minnesota, they married. Her great-great-grandfather was a notorious drunk and had splintered the family with his insistence on staying on the family farm and not letting any of his children care for it. It became a well-known family story because of the time he'd become so mad-drunk over this he nearly killed one of his children by angrily firing his gun in the barn to keep them at bay.

His wife, Kirsten's great-great-grandmother, died of some

unknown illness, which she learned about by her grandmother's telling of her father's fear of her dying and praying she'd live ten more years. And she did. He had been the youngest and Kirsten wondered if he'd prayed that prayer so she'd live long enough for him to be of age to leave. The farm fell into disrepair eventually and was foreclosed on; this event made one of his children take him in until he died. But the damage was done and the children had scattered to the winds, one even going as far as Sweden and reconnecting with family that had remained. Kirsten found it hard to believe such violence existed in her line, when her grandmother had been the sweetest, most giving person she'd ever known. She could believe it in her father's family, but not her mother's.

Her phone beeped at regaining its signal, and Kirsten carefully paired her Bluetooth headset with it so she could call her mom.

"Hey, Kirsten."

"Oh, hi, Mark. Where's my mom?"

"Yeah, no, your mom just popped over to the neighbors' place for a minute and I saw you were calling and thought I should answer it for her. She'd hate to miss your call."

"Oh?" She was disappointed. Mark was her stepdad, but her mom had married after she'd graduated from high school, so she wasn't super close to him. It had been just her and her mom for so long it was odd adjusting to a new family member. She knew it made her mom happy not be alone. She sometimes thought her mom had wanted to remarry sooner but didn't want to introduce more change into Kirsten's already stilted childhood. That and the fact she suspected her mom still loved her dad and possibly why she'd felt the need to move so far away from Minnesota.

"The heart does what the heart does," her mom would always say.

Mark was a good man who was always willing to help. He was a tax accountant at a firm in Seattle and loved to road bike and row on nearby Lake Union. He'd never married before or had children and was a couple of years younger than her mom. It was obvious to everyone how much he loved her, which was more than enough for Kirsten. She just wasn't always sure it was enough for her mom, which made her a little sad, adding to her misgivings about there being true love for anyone. It always seemed there was an imbalance. One party more in love with the other or one incapable of sustaining it.

"How's it going? Are you in Billings?"

"No. No, not yet. I hit a snag. There was an accident in the pass, and I got stuck up there for a couple hours."

"Oh no! Are you okay? How bad was it?"

"Yeah, no not too bad. It was a rockslide, but I think for the most part he came away with minor injuries. It just took a while to clear everything and get the emergency vehicles up there and everything. I think it spooked me a little. I've always been afraid of that happening to me."

"Of course, that would be scary."

"It's okay. I'm about ninety miles from Billings but didn't want Mom to worry by calling late."

"Oh. Here she is now."

"Hi, sweetie. Of course, you call the minute I step out the door. Are you in Billings?"

"No. I was just telling Mark that there was a delay in the pass due to an accident, but I'm about an hour and a half away."

"Well, that's not too bad. You seem to be making good

time."

"Yeah, I am, even with the accident. The weather's been good and not much traffic, seeing as how it's still mostly winter." Kirsten felt her emotions bubbling up again.

"You sound tired. Are you okay?"

Kirsten was unable to speak because of the lump rising in her throat.

"Yeah," she said, crying a little. "I think the accident threw me a bit. It was cold and lonely up there, and it was a big rock that had fallen on a truck. The driver is going to be okay, but I've always been afraid of that happening. I don't know, I think it just really hit me that I'm on my own, you know?"

"Yeah," her mother said in a comforting tone.

"I think I'm getting tired and thinking about everything and it's been so busy these last few weeks." She kept crying while talking and wiping tears away so she could see the road. "Interviewing, resigning, packing…it's like my life has been turned upside-down. I just need time to adjust. I mean, I didn't even move away to go to college, so it all seems like such a big deal."

"Well, it is a big deal, but I know you're going to do beautifully, and you won't be totally alone."

"I know."

"I'm so proud of you."

"I know you are. Thanks, Mom. I think I just needed a good cry. I feel better already," she said as her tears started to diminish.

"Good. Just one more day and you'll be there."

"I know. It's hard to believe. Who knew? A month ago, I never would've guessed."

They laughed.

"Okay, well, I'll send you a text in the morning when I leave, k?"

"Sounds good, sweetie. Love you."

"Love you too."

Her mom had never embraced the world of technology; she didn't have to as an English professor. Kirsten remembered when she wouldn't even text. Kirsten had finally convinced her to at least have a plan that allowed her to receive texts at twenty-five cents a pop, so Kirsten could text her on occasion. She'd tried explaining once. "Mom, sometimes it's easier to be able to send a quick bit of information instead of having to call, listen to the message, and then leave a message."

"Okay, as long as you know I won't always text you back. It's too hard on my dummy phone."

"That's fine." Kirsten had smiled at her one little victory. Eventually, her mother did buy a smart phone, and thanks to a very patient Mark was able to navigate it in its most basic form.

Kirsten wondered what technological hurdles her children would try to make her jump when she was older. A lot had changed in the last one hundred years. There is no need for marriages of convenience and what seemed to be a never-ending parade of difficult births and early deaths. Kirsten was glad she lived now as opposed to then and was thankful for the hardships they'd endured, because without them she would not exist and would not find herself pleasantly surprised to be sitting in a Chipotle. She felt a bit of shame at having assumed Billings would be too backwoodsy to have what she considered higher quality fast food.

She recalled the strange starchy and often fried foods held together by various flavors of canned soup she was left to eat

on her visits to Minnesota as a child, and the strange looks
her mother would get for bringing freshly prepared dishes of
fruits and vegetables for the family get-togethers—especially
the time not a soul would touch the black olives that seemed
as exotic as octopus. It'd become a private joke between them.
Black olives were not fancy and cans could be easily bought
at any grocery store, even in Minnesota! Kirsten loved olives
and often took pleasure in her childish habit of sticking them
on her fingers through their pitted holes and pulling them off
with her mouth. Of course, her tastes had matured a bit and
she now preferred the assortment at her grocer's olive bar,
but still...*really, black olives from a can? That is not weird.*
However, times are a-changing for the better; there was a
Whole Foods near where she'd be living. In fact, according to
The Daily Show a few years back, Minneapolis ranked as the
gayest city in the country, outranking San Francisco—always
a sign of good food and fashion, right?

Her reverie was broken when she nearly laughed out loud
at the parody of this being the gayest city in the country.
She smirked as she looked around at all the good Lutherans
dressed in their Sunday best bringing the service to its close
by singing the doxology.

Barely a beat had passed after the last note rang out when
she heard her name. "You must be Kirsten, how wonderful
to meet August's daughter," said a perfectly groomed and
coiffed woman who'd been sitting behind her. Kirsten was
still trying to come back to the present and had turned toward
the back to collect her purse and coat from the pew she'd been
sitting on. "I work with your father over at the university."

As Kirsten smiled and shook her hand, she had a sickening
feeling that this woman had slept with her father. Or was cur-

rently sleeping with him. A wave of nausea moved through her.

"My name is Sharon. I recognized you from your picture. Your father is quite proud of you, you know. This new promotion is big news."

August turned in time to catch the exchange and commented with surprise. "Oh, you've never met my daughter? She's finally moved back home. She's probably a little older than you remember. You remember Sharon, don't you, Kirsten?"

Finally moved back home? Kirsten fumed and screamed inside. *This is not my home and you know I've never met this woman.* She feigned recognition, "Yes, hello." The congested aisle was beginning to ease, so Kirsten made her escape out of the pew.

Kirsten didn't want to be rude, but she also didn't care to continue the conversation. It took a bit of work, but eventually she made it to the car. Her father had attempted praise-filled introductions as he followed. Kirsten knew she was most definitely sick.

Carol was all smiles, waiting for them at the car. She had been absent during the service to teach children's church. She was so happily clueless. Carol was her dad's wife and Kirsten couldn't quite bring herself to call her stepmother. It wasn't like Carol had raised her. Carol was very sweet but seemed rather oblivious and, therefore, the perfect mate for her philandering father. If anything, Kirsten felt a little sorry for her.

Carol was your typical kindergarten teacher and spent her weekdays working part-time at a local elementary school. She had short, thin, layered no-nonsense silver white hair, with clothing to match. Her only nod to fashion was her funky red glasses and an occasional shoe of trendy merit. She'd been married once before and had a son whom she was very close to. He was married and had given her four grandkids to occupy her time. Her first marriage had been difficult and short-lived—the details of which Kirsten didn't know. Only that it had been a struggle as a single mom for many years. Carol had met her dad through mutual friends.

Kirsten never understood the attraction, other than perhaps comfort. Carol did emit comfort and a sweet naivete, which she suspected her father needed—someone who was forgiving and not prone to suspicion. Which, in Kirsten's opinion, was probably why Carol's first marriage wasn't successful, and why she didn't choose wisely for her second either. But if Kirsten was honest she was a little relieved, because it took the pressure off her. Carol was good at taking care of her father. She just knew she could never be married to a man like her dad and was a little disappointed with the Carols of the world for not being stronger and for settling for less. It seemed to Kirsten too many women settled. They'd give tiny pieces of themselves away in exchange for a relationship. Kirsten refused to do that and was okay with never getting married. She'd rather be happy and single than married and miserable.

As they drove away, the discomfort of the whole morning began to set in and Carol seemed to notice Kirsten was looking a bit green.

"Are you all right? You don't look so good," Carol asked with concern.

"I don't feel very well."

"I'm sorry. Would you like an Advil or anything?" Carol offered.

"Thanks, but I think I just need some rest," Kirsten said, hoping to close the subject.

It was a short drive back to her father's house, but she knew she couldn't take another minute. Carol had put a pot roast in the oven before they'd left, but Kirsten was no longer up to it.

As they got out of the car and headed for the house, she heard herself saying, "I don't feel well. I'm sorry, but I think I'd better go home."

Carol was already inside and out of earshot, but her father was only two paces ahead of her and kept walking as if a word had never been uttered.

"Dad!?"

"What?" he said without stopping.

"Did you hear what I just said?" She forced herself to catch up to him.

"No," he replied.

Kirsten shook her head in amazement. "I don't feel well. I'm going to head home," she said decisively and without hesitation this time.

"Oh, really? I didn't know," August said. "Are you sure? Carol has a nice meal planned."

"Yes, I'm sure. Didn't you—" she stopped mid-sentence, realizing that, number one, she didn't have the strength and number two, it would fall on deaf ears.

August gave her a hug and a kiss on the cheek. "Okay, honey. It was good to see you. Do you want to get that table before you go?"

"No," Kirsten replied. "I'll come get it later." She really did want the table but couldn't bear another moment with him. "Thanks for everything. Tell Carol I'm sorry."

Kirsten got into her car, which was parked on the street in front of her dad's house, and let out a long breath as she turned the key in the ignition. Still a little unsure of her surroundings, she was relieved when she found the on-ramp to the highway back to her apartment.

Her father didn't live in Minneapolis. He was dean of the school of Humanities in a small college town about sixty miles away.

"There we go, now we're cruisin'," she said. As she got closer to Minneapolis and farther away from Northfield, she began to relax and the nausea slipped away.

Her new little apartment was in the Uptown Kenwood area of Minneapolis, thanks to her cousin Sten. He was her dad's twin sister's son and a complete Godsend with the move. She'd known she couldn't handle living with her dad for more than a week, so she'd asked Sten to scout apartments for her based on her Internet research. He was a UX designer at a small tech shop in Northfield but had lived in Minneapolis until a few years ago. He'd gone above and beyond by taking photos of not only the apartments but the environs of each one and had advised her on what he thought about each location.

They'd kind of lost touch over the last eight years as they'd graduated high school, attended university, and moved into their lives as young adults. But there had always been an instant kinship between them (more like brother and sister) no matter how much time passed, perhaps because they were the only children of twins. They even shared the same birthday, except Sten was two years older. Fortuitously, it landed in August so they could celebrate together every year on Kirsten's summer visits.

Her new home was in an older neighborhood of apartment buildings and homes built in the late 1800s, if she had to guess. A lot of the houses had been fixed up over the years and her apartment was as cute as a bug for the price. It even had a fireplace, which was unusual. Okay, so you couldn't use it, but it looked good with its beautiful wrought iron grate and painted wood mantel. At least she had a place to hang her stocking at Christmas—very important when considering a residence, according to Kirsten. There was a chain of lakes with bike and walking paths connecting them, and she knew she'd enjoy many a run in the coming months when everything started to bloom. A plethora of trendy boutiques, eateries, and art galleries were a stone's throw away along with the necessary grocers and drugstores. She couldn't have been more delighted. It was the mirror image of home on Queen Anne, minus a few hills.

She hadn't expected to return home this early, so she exited a little sooner and took a turn around Lake of the Isles to gawk at all the beautiful homes. She crossed Hennepin Avenue, realizing it was the street Dayfield's was on and must be a major artery. "Hennepin, Hennepin, Hennepin," she said out loud only because she found it fun to say. She wondered what it meant. Was it a Native American word or someone's last name? Her stomach started to growl, and she decided to head to her apartment; breakfast had been a while ago and rather small.

She found a parking spot across from her building and smiled at the old brick façade. The elevator was a little slow, but fortunately didn't take too long to reach the fourth and top floor of the building.

She'd pre-stocked her freezer with a lot of frozen dinners. Though they were not ideal, she liked to have them on hand in case. She pulled up the corner of the entrée for venting, popped it into the microwave, and hit start while looking over at the window. There sat two new cute chairs she'd found at a secondhand store, facing each other in wait for her new table. *Damn, I really need my little table,* she thought. *Oh, well.* She stood watching the light grow dim as a cloud covered the sun. All was quiet except for the hum of the microwave until her phone rang, startling her. She lifted it up off the counter and saw Sten's face.

"Hey," she answered.

"Hi. Where are you? Are you at your apartment?"

"Yeah, I just got here. What's up?"

"Well, I was just at your dad's. I thought you were going to be there."

"Oh, yeah. Shoot. I'm sorry. I forgot I told you. I had to leave. Sorry, I couldn't take it anymore. I went to church with him this morning and, well, it put me over the edge."

"I told you not to go."

"I know. I know. I just thought I'd get it over with so he would stop hounding me."

"Did you get the table?"

"No."

"No?"

"Ah, I know."

The microwave beeped.

"What are you doing?"

"Eating."

"Eating what?"

"Enchiladas."

"Enchiladas? Did you get them from Diego's?"

"No. Amy's."

"Amy's? Where's that?"

"Umm, you know, Amy's Organics."

"Oh, that Amy's. Nice. What are you eating them on?"

"What are you eating them on?" she mimicked playfully.

"Kirsten, you're too funny. Now what are you gonna do?"

"I don't know. I'll figure it out."

Sten sighed. "If you want, I could bring it to you tomorrow."

"No, you're not. I'm not going to let you do that."

"It's no big deal. I have a meeting there tomorrow afternoon with a client. I could drop it off after."

"Really? You'd do that for me?"

"Yeah, sure. I can't take the sight of you eating on your table-less chairs."

"You're too good to me, Sten. Are you sure that's okay?"

"Yeah, but you owe me dinner at Diego's."

"Oh, fine. I guess I can do that."

"We'll toast to your new job."

"Hey, I like that. That's a good idea. So, what time do you think you'd get here?"

"Mmm, probably 'bout six."

"Yeah, that should work. Thanks, Sten. I'll see you then."

DAYFIELD'S

Kirsten walked toward the grand old building that was about to become her home away from home. Like a hearty Minnesotan, ignoring thirty-below temperatures, Dayfield's had remained strong in the face of so many department stores succumbing to the crush of specialty retailers. It was one of a few remaining independent high-end department stores in the nation.

A mix of apprehension and excitement bubbled in her veins as she walked around the corner to where she'd been told she'd find the employee entrance. This was it. This was the day she'd been working so hard for since she'd entered university eight years ago. She didn't think it would happen quite this soon and felt incredibly fortunate.

Sure enough, she saw people entering through a side door. Unable to contain her enthusiasm, she smiled and made eye contact with everyone she met. To her surprise, she was received with reserve and no smiles. She began to feel stupid and childlike and ached for the familiarity of home. What was she thinking, moving nearly two thousand miles away to a strange, frigid land? She navigated through the makeup and perfume counters in a daze of disappointment and uncertainty and walked to the other side of the store, entirely missing the elevators and escalators that would take her up to the eighth floor where she was supposed to find her office.

She had no choice but to stop and turn around while a wave of doubt washed over her. Hoping no one noticed her coming from the wrong direction, she joined the line going up the escalator and looked for a bathroom on each passing floor.

Kirsten had dressed for the ten-below temperature outside and was getting hot and sweaty. She began peeling off the layers: hat, gloves, scarf, and finally her long down parka. She could barely hold the pile of fluff and felt ridiculous, like the boy in *A Christmas Story*. Her Sorel booties looked clunky and quite unfashionable with her on-trend business attire.

Girl with fancy job can't afford fancy boots, or car and driver to drop her off so she doesn't have to wear fancy boots, she air-bubbled in her head.

She felt like an outsider and too afraid to ask anyone where the nearest restroom was as she continued with the flow of people into the upper office area. Sure, everyone else knew where they were going and exactly what to do; she thought they seemed robotic in their calm, methodical manners.

Was anyone even talking to each other? How strange? No coworker banter? No "what did you do last night?"

Panic seized her upon noticing no one else was wearing gigantic, heavily treaded rubber boots. Women wore stilettos like it was summer, sans scarf wrapped around head like a mummy. They must have thought she was planning an expedition in the Artic instead of balmy Minneapolis. Silly Kirsten stood in frozen fear despite the beading sweat on her brow.

The escalators became narrower the further she climbed, and the floors stopped becoming part of the store and were walled off to contain what she assumed were the many offices for Dayfield's HQ. Having decided not to ask about a bathroom, she was relieved when the escalator rose in line with the glossy marble of her floor and she saw a sign pointing to the restrooms.

There didn't seem to be anyone in the ladies' lounge, so she took her time at the vanity, washing and drying her hands, and carefully patting her face dry of perspiration. She pressed her chipmunk cheeks down with her fingers to appear older. She wished her face wasn't so round and childlike. But with her petite appendages and shorter stature of five feet, three inches, there was no hiding her younger look. It fed her insecurity of not being taken seriously. Her straight long blonde hair was a whiter blonde than her dirty blonde brows, signaling the changing color of her hair as she aged. It was the one childish feature she'd embraced and fiercely fought to hang on to with many a bottle of chemicals. Her eyes, at least, held some mystery. There was a wisdom behind the intense blue— one couldn't help but be drawn in. The black mascara on her lashes widened their breadth; they were striking against the innocence of her other features.

"You can do this, Kirsten," she said resolutely to her mirror image.

She pulled open the door into the offices and was met by a long gray tweed-like cubical wall preventing anyone from getting the lay of the land, but she didn't need to see it to know it was a network of cubicles. It was half the size of one floor in the store and surprisingly dark. The carpet was a typical flat industrial grade, which if it had a color name it'd be called "Hides Dirt." She was reminded that even though she'd come for Couture, it was all about retail and the lavish styling was saved for customer areas. She turned left where Shelley, her HR contact, had told her to and was finally met with a welcoming face.

"Hi, you must be Kirsten."

"Yes, how did you know?" Kirsten returned jokingly and shook her hand.

"We've been expecting you." Shelley responded very professionally, not picking up on Kirsten's sarcasm, she sat back down at her desk. "So, we have some paperwork for you to fill out, and then I'll take you to your desk where you can meet Eric, the assistant for Designer. Michael is in New York and won't be back in the office until next Tuesday."

"Oh? There's an assistant buyer?" Kirsten tried not to sound too surprised.

"No, just an assistant." Shelley answered summarily.

It was odd that her new boss would be gone. What was the point of coming in so soon if he wasn't even going to be here, and why hadn't anyone told her she had an assistant? Her position was slightly elevated by being an Associate Buyer instead of an Assistant Buyer, but she thought that was only because of the nature of Designer Couture. The buyer for this department traveled an inordinate amount compared to the other departments and therefore needed a more seasoned assistant.

It didn't take long to fill out the requisite payroll forms. Should she do one allowance or none? She settled for none, as she didn't have any assets or children to deduct. She shoved the employee handbook, key card, and important passwords into her bag and followed Shelley's small Asian frame out of her office, down the short hallway, and out to the main floor on the left. Shelley pointed to the right as they walked. "That's the mail room over there. You'll want to check it before the day is out as there is probably a lot in there."

"Box 43, right?" Kirsten confirmed.

"Yes." They continued through the maze, which was opposite the HR office, until daylight could finally be seen streaming through the exterior windows.

Kirsten was assigned the last cubicle before the corner office bearing the name Michael Warner, which glinted its bronze finish in the light about ten feet ahead as she followed Shelley into her new space on the right. It was definitely much nicer than her last office, if for no other reason than it had windows. Windows were usually awarded to buyers. Weary of her load, she dropped everything in the far corner, where the short end of an L-shaped desk and a bookcase didn't quite meet. The bookcase was overflowing and disheveled with notebooks from a bygone era, Lookbooks, and miscellaneous swatches of fabric and notions. It was a mini-library of fashion. The computer monitor was placed squarely in the corner of the L so she could enjoy the view, leaving the long side to trail against the cubicle wall to house some office equipment—namely a printer. It needed a homey touch and she knew just the chair she was going to buy to place in the corner instead of her Minnesota outerwear.

"Here you go. This is your new home." Shelley held up her minute finger, then walked across the aisle to the opposite cubicle and poked her head in to summon a small-framed man out to meet Kirsten.

He swept in with an air of arrogance that matched his looks. He was about her age or perhaps a little older.

"This is Eric," Shelley said.

"Hello. Welcome." He extended his hand for Kirsten to shake.

"Hello." He had an unexpectedly weak and clammy grip.

Shelley smiled at Eric and said, "Well, I'll leave you two to it." She turned to Kirsten. "Eric has been with us for over ten years and is very capable. Don't hesitate to call if you need anything."

"Thanks, Shelley." Kirsten wanted to implore her to stay as Eric radiated like a neon sign that said not welcome. Kirsten's default in awkward situations was to be super friendly and talk too much to dissipate the mood, but she cautioned herself sternly not to. She had the authority to exert her position over Eric but hated bosses like that, so she tried to be considerate without seeming condescending.

"So, I guess Michael is out of town until Tuesday? I didn't know he was going to be gone."

"He's mostly gone, which is why it doesn't really matter when you start. Plus, I've been managing the department for the last three months just fine."

"Cool." Kirsten ignored his laissez-faire attitude. "So how 'bout we start with the financials? I usually find that's the best way to start learning a department."

"You'll find hard copies of everything up there in the notebooks. I'm not involved with that part of it." His tone broadcasted disdain for such things. "You may also want to familiarize yourself with the lines, which you'll find in the Lookbooks over there. We're about to transition into spring and I'm very busy booking reps for all the trunk shows. You'll have to excuse me as I don't have a lot of time today."

"Sounds good." Kirsten smiled and pretended not to notice his disapproving once-over of her before he left, his eyes ending on the pile of down in the corner. *Great,* Kirsten sighed. *Is this new job really too good to be true and I've been played?*

She settled into her cube and started pouring over the financials and the Lookbooks, configuring her email and sprucing up her workspace with a few personal items. Even though it felt like a waste of time, this would be the best use of it for the moment. She was surprised to learn that Designer Couture didn't make money and, if anything, lost money. Was she supposed to know this? But before she had a chance to dig further, a friendly voice surprised her.

"Hi, you must be Kirsten."

"Yeah," she said, turning.

"I'm Nicole. Nicole Smith. Michael's old Associate."

"Oh, yes. Hello, nice to meet you." Kirsten rose to shake her hand. Nicole was also blonde-haired and blue-eyed, but the model hot kind with an appropriate American-sounding name.

"Sorry to interrupt. I was gonna see if Eric wanted to go to lunch, but I guess he's already gone."

"Oh, yeah." Kirsten acted like she knew, despite her being unaware, and quickly glanced down at her monitor, which read 12:56.

"Do you have any lunch plans?"

"No, I was just about to head out."

"You wanna go together?"

"Yeah, sure, I'd like that. Maybe you can tell me where all the good places are." Kirsten started to put on her parka and Sorels when Nicole struggled to hold back a laugh.

"You won't need that," she said.

"Oh, are we staying in the building?"

"No, but you still won't need them."

"Oh, okay." Kirsten grabbed her bag, threw her phone in it, and followed Nicole out to the escalator. They stopped their descent on the second floor. Nicole led the way past Men's and out into a Skybridge. Kirsten marveled at the view of all the Skybridges linking the buildings together. "Ahh, yes, this is why I don't need a parka." Kirsten laughed.

"Yes, the Skyway system links about sixty-nine city blocks." Nicole smiled.

"Well, you got me. I guess it's part of my initiation, eh?"

"Well, maybe just a little," Nicole teased.

"Is it always this cold this time of year?" Kirsten wanted to know since flowers were already blooming back home.

"Yes." No explanation or attempt to assure Kirsten about the below-freezing temperatures. It simply was. Nicole was tall and lean, probably about five feet, nine inches if Kirsten had to guess, and her wavy long blonde hair bounced as they glided through the system while she pretended not to notice people looked admiringly at her. It was hard not to.

They found a quiet café since they were a little past the traditional lunch hour and ordered salads.

"So, what is it that you do now?" Kirsten asked.

"I'm the buyer for the Bridge lines."

"Oh, wow, that's awesome."

"Yeah, I was really lucky the position opened up when it did. Working for Michael is an excellent career move. You'll see."

"How long were you with him?"

"Nearly four years. I was starting to think nothing good would open up, and then it did in Bridge."

"That's great, and well, good for me too." Kirsten smiled.

They chatted easily about the job. Nicole was a lot more open than Kirsten had anticipated, making her wonder if she could be a friend. She was sure of herself, but not self-important. She looked like someone who knew how to have a good time—maybe a little too good of a time. There was a bit of hardness around her eyes, accentuated by heavy eyeliner and mascara, with a slight black curl coming out of the corner as a nod to the sixties coming back in fashion. She was slightly older than Kirsten, maybe as much as seven years but definitely not ten.

Nicole had a devilish grin as she divulged office gossip, "Eric has a crush on Michael."

"Does Michael know this?" Kirsten chuckled, still unsure if Nicole was trying too hard to make friends or if this was how she behaved with everybody.

"I don't think so, or he doesn't let on if he does."

"Is Michael gay?" Kirsten asked hesitantly, not wanting to delve any deeper but still wanting to know.

"No, definitely not," Nicole said decisively. "But there has been a lot of speculation." Nicole smiled and her eyes twinkled. "Most people in the office don't know what to make of Michael. Some resent him. They think he gets special treatment because he's in Designer, but he's just a very shy person who travels all the time. When you've been here longer, you will probably go to New York to help with the orders at market. He's actually a lot of fun. We used to go to the museums and shop at all the new boutiques. He spends so much time alone on the road he seems to enjoy having someone to do stuff with. Your biggest problem is going to be dealing with Lillian. She and Michael disagree a lot, and you will end up being tossed back and forth because they will use you instead of communicating directly to each other, which is what I hated."

"Great, just what I need."

"Have you met her yet?" Nicole asked.

"Yeah, she interviewed me."

Nicole shifted in her seat while her eyes tried to be still.

Kirsten pretended not to notice. "Why do they dislike each other so much?"

"Oh, they like each other. They just don't always agree. You'll be fine. I can tell you can handle it."

Kirsten wanted to take advantage of Nicole's openness as she feared she might not be later. "So, I was surprised when Eric said he'd been running the department for the last three months. I just interviewed a little less than a month ago and they were in such a rush that I had to cut my two-week notice at my last job. Did you have to leave sooner or something?"

"No, not really. It's probably because Michael...well, he can be a little particular, that's all."

Kirsten couldn't help but feel Nicole was choosing her words carefully and holding back.

"You should feel lucky he picked you. In fact, don't be surprised if a few people resent you. It's a highly coveted position and hiring from outside is sure to ruffle a few feathers."

Kirsten realized her misgivings might not be entirely unfounded. Perhaps this luncheon wasn't quite so serendipitous and more like a fact-finding mission.

"Great. Like Eric?"

"Eric!?" Nicole was puzzled.

"Yeah, he seems a little bothered by me." Kirsten laughed.

"Yeah, okay, I guess I've just gotten used to it, but he's just being Eric. He can be fussy and is stressed easily. Believe me, he would start cutting himself if he had to do your job."

Kirsten certainly didn't read it that way, but it gave her a little comfort to hear Nicole be so cavalier about it.

"Well, I'd better get back to it," Kirsten said, sensing

things were winding down. "Thanks for inviting me to lunch and giving me the lowdown. I wasn't expecting Michael to be gone when I arrived, so this has been helpful." Kirsten smiled.

"Sure, and don't hesitate to ask me anything. I'm happy to help. I'd walk you back, but I need to run a few errands. You think you can find your way? Just follow the signs for Dayfield's."

"No, that's fine. I'm sure I can make it back. Thanks again for the lunch."

"No problem."

Kirsten took her time making her way back to Dayfield's, stopping to peruse a few specialty shops, and nearly going into one of the ever-present Starbucks when she spied Caribou Coffee. Always intrigued by something new and different, she decided to try the local coffee establishment to keep her warm for the rest of the day.

Caribou proved to be a little too "Starbucksy," giving her a pang for her beloved Caffe Vita back home. However, she knew it was only a matter of time before she'd find the perfect place. It was a good reminder how change required trial and error and navigating the unexpected—not unlike Michael being absent and Eric's prickles. She headed back to the office with a renewed determination to get Eric to like her.

Per Shelley's suggestion, she remembered to check her box from the mail center. It was across the hall from the puzzle of buying offices. It was housed in the old, and probably original, offices of Dayfield's. The temporary walls of the current buying offices were obviously an outgrowth of a bygone era. Sure enough, there was a lot of mail and even a few packages.

She stopped at Eric's cube first and knocked lightly on the metal trim framing the entrance and pushed her head in. "Hey,

I got this package in my box. I don't know, maybe they just spelled your name wrong? It says Are-ic?" She pronounced it phonetically. He turned his chair swiftly away from the computer to see her and stood slightly to reach for the box.

"That's me," he said in a huff, snatching the package out of her hands. She felt defeated in her attempt to make things better.

"Oh, Eric with an A?" She couldn't stop herself.

"Yeah."

"I've never seen that before." She craned her neck around to look at his nameplate: Aric Feyerabend—as if Feyerabend wasn't hard enough. "What made your parents think of that? Is it German?"

"No. I changed the spelling."

"Oh. Cool." She finally relented and walked quietly back to her cube, remembering Nicole's words and agreeing that the boy was indeed fragile.

The next day was a little easier. She had to keep reminding herself it takes time to become familiar. Thinking back to her first day at Nordstrom didn't quite compute because she'd begun with a few others who were also starting out, and it was entry-level, with less responsibility. By the time she'd worked her way up from sales to buyer, she knew everyone and was familiar with the culture.

Her phone vibrated against her desk, and she saw her dad's white bearded face pop up. She didn't want to talk to him. He'd called last night, too, wanting to know how her first day went and to see if they could go to lunch today. She wasn't ready for that. The last thing in the world she wanted was to subject Aric to her dad and God knows who else. She didn't move here to spend time with her dad.

Out of guilt she answered. "Hey, dad."

"Hi. Say, I'm in town and thought we could have lunch together."

"I can't." *Does he not remember my saying I couldn't last night?*

"Are you sure?"

"Maybe in a couple weeks when I'm more settled. I have too much to do with my boss out of town and the learning curve of a new job."

"I don't get to the city very often and won't be able to for a while. I have something I want to give you."

She held her breath for a second. "Where are you?"

"I'm a few blocks away."

"I'll meet you by handbags on the first floor." Maybe he wanted to give her a gift to celebrate her new job and that was enough to make her give in.

"I was kind of hoping to see your new office."

"There really isn't much to see, just a dark cubicle. I'm on my way out, anyway, so it'd be easier to just meet you. How 'bout in twenty minutes?"

"Okay, honey, I'll see you in twenty."

"Great." She breathed out to herself. Kirsten wasn't on her way out anywhere and now needed to occupy herself with something for the next fifteen minutes. She couldn't imagine what was so important he had to give her something.

She'd barely finished replying to a quick email when she heard a rap on her cube and August came beaming in. "Hello!"

Startled, Kirsten exclaimed, "Dad?! What are you doing up here?"

Aric entered as if on cue for impending drama. His radar was impeccable; if only Kirsten had known sooner how to attract his attention. He continued his promenade by whizzing behind August with a suit dangling from his upturned hand. It was for a photo shoot they'd discussed earlier. He made himself busy by carefully hanging it on the bookcase and nitpicking it for invisible lint as if it were a window display. He seemed to enjoy lingering in the tension and adding to Kirsten's rising annoyance.

Forced to make introductions, Kirsten composed herself and pushed her frustration down. "Aric, this is my dad, August. Aric's our trusty assistant."

"Hello," August said, shaking his hand.

"How'd you get here so fast, and how'd you know where I'd be?"

"I was closer than I realized and asked a few people who directed me here."

Who would direct him in here without authorization? Kirsten let it go as August handed her a wrapped package that looked to be the size of a book.

"Here, this is what I wanted to give you."

"Oh, okay, thanks." She didn't really want to unwrap it in front of Aric and gave him a pausing glance. He didn't pay heed, and Kirsten wondered why he chose now to be so amenable. She didn't trust it.

"Well, open it." August seemed like a kid on Christmas morning.

She struggled with the wrap until an impatient August took over and grabbed a loosened end, pulled it off, and crumpled it into a ball. Kirsten was still trying to imagine what it could be. Maybe it was a book of fashion or something similar and was touched by his thoughtfulness. She was actually enjoying a moment with her father. It looked like a textbook of some sort as she flipped it over to read the front.

The Scandinavian Crossing.

"Look." August pointed to the author. "Written by August Swenson."

"It's your book? But I already have one."

"I know, but now it's a textbook. I just came from my agent...this is a first edition!"

Kirsten felt a surge of disappointment as she realized, once again, she'd been had. Nothing was ever about her. It was always about him. And if that wasn't enough, she watched in horror as he shoved the wad of wrapping paper into an aghast Aric's hand. He stood there, looking down at the squashed up brown paper in his palm.

"Throw this away, would you?" August said without an ounce of courtesy or respect. It was abrupt and demeaning and done swiftly so he could thumb through the pages of his beloved textbook—showing Kirsten all his glorious work.

She wanted to fall to the ground and cry.

Aric, still in shock, curtly turned and left with the ball of paper perched on his open hand like it was a waiter's tray. August, oblivious to his actions, continued talking to Kirsten at an excited pace while flipping through the pages. Kirsten fell silent and pretended to look. She could feel Aric's contempt and wondered how she was ever going to mend what had happened. She began to smolder, as her already tenuous relationship with Aric was now even more precarious.

Now she understood more than ever why her mother had felt the need to move so far away. He was hurtful and toxic. It was one thing to do it to your own family, but he did it to everyone. Everyone! How could he be this way and still manage to charm so many women? It was incomprehensible!

A picture of her mother emerged in her mind; she saw her bravely trying to hide a look of concern when Kirsten had left for Minneapolis. She had passed it off as a mother who would miss her daughter. But it had been the same look she'd gotten whenever she'd left for her summer visits with her dad as a child. It had been so long since one of those visits she'd forgotten how it took her days to recover from seeing her father. Oh, how she'd cry, and her mother would just hold her and love her and not say a word. She never once betrayed him. She didn't have to. He betrayed himself.

MICHAEL

Michael had finally returned. It was Kirsten's second "first day." She was more than a little nervous. Michael was going to be the first male boss she'd ever had, and she was looking forward to it. It seemed all the female bosses she'd had in the past weren't necessarily inclined to mentor her. And sometimes quite the opposite. Forget all that "women supporting women" she'd learned in school; everyone has their own agenda—female or not.

Michael hadn't done the typical interview. "What makes you want to do this kind of work?" "Do you know how to calculate gross margin and what sort of gross margin percent is considered good for this type of business?" "What trends do you see?" She'd liked that. He was more interested in who she was. "What was her favorite movie? What was her best vacation?" He'd wanted to know what she loved about Seattle. Kirsten silently agreed with his questions, because she too felt you could tell more about a person by what they liked than what they thought.

She'd liked him immediately, but figured he was too classy for the likes of her and was surprised when Lillian had called to offer her the job. He was different. Kirsten had assumed she'd be too unrefined a match for him. He had an elegance about him that was from a time before rock and roll had changed the cultural landscape.

She'd arrived promptly at seven-fifty to make sure she was there before him. She tried her best to focus on work, but it was to no avail. She kept fidgeting. She decided to bring impossible order to the overflowing bookcase behind her, and then she'd sit back down to rearrange the smaller items on her desk. The clock ticked slowly past nine and she wondered if he'd dare to be as late as ten.

Finally, she heard Aric's voice break through the madness. "Hey, welcome back."

"Good morning," Michael returned as he stopped to chat with him.

She couldn't see them since her cube entrance was past Aric's. She quietly, and as patiently as she could, waited. She was too afraid to join their conversation.

They began to talk about local happenings Kirsten knew nothing about—chatting easily for twenty minutes. Kirsten nearly gave in and was about to interrupt and say hello when Michael stopped. "Well, I'd better get to work. Everyone is screaming for their orders."

She readied herself.

He barely stepped in and unceremoniously greeted Kirsten. "Hey, Kirsten, looks like you've settled in well."

"Yeah, Aric's been a great help."

"Good. Well, I've got a lot of orders to write so we'll talk later."

"Sure thing." She smiled. *That was it? That's all I get?* Kirsten sat confused. She'd had it all planned out: the timing, the pitch and tone of the entire greeting. *Oh, well,* she sighed. *Get a grip, Kirsten. Why are you so nervous? He did hire you, not someone else.* She wondered if perhaps there really wasn't anyone else as Aric's words echoed in her head about how difficult it was to fill the position and how sometimes it was left vacant for months before it would get filled. Maybe they were desperate!

Kirsten started to spiral.

Knowing Aric, he was probably trying to make her paranoid. She refused to let him get to her. Besides, didn't Nicole already allay her fears on that? Still, she couldn't help shake the feeling he really did want her job despite his insistence he'd hate to have it. "Too much political stuff to deal with," he'd said. According to Aric, all Nicole did was resolve problems with vendors and management upstairs. There certainly did seem to be a lot of tension between the high-end divisions and upper management. That was typical in retail, but especially in this business, where every markdown can be a significant financial hit since price points soared into the thousand-dollar range.

By eleven-thirty he still hadn't come in to ask her about anything. No direction. No little departmental speech. No welcome. Nothing. *Very strange,* she thought. They had been communicating via email, text, and a few phone calls—even the interview had been via Skype. But now that he was here, she expected more. She was beginning to notice Minnesotans were somewhat different than what she was used to back home. The slightest hint of getting too personal with these upper Midwesterners and one would think you were asking them to spill their guts about their deepest darkest secrets. Well, she was a Westerner, despite what her birth certificate might say, so she decided she needed to act like one. She refused to be afraid of her new boss and resolved to go into his office and talk to him.

He was bent over the table behind his desk, hunting and pecking at his laptop. Since his back was toward the door, Kirsten stood unnoticed for several seconds and smiled in amazement because she couldn't believe he didn't know how to type—especially in this day and age. She couldn't help but emit a chuckle, which caused him to turn around. She glibly forced her face to be more serious and cleared her throat.

"So, this is why you have so many orders to write. Gee whiz, it must take you, like, all day just to do one order." He chuckled and relaxed his shoulders, letting his arms come down to rest on his desk.

"Yes, I'm afraid I'm a little overwhelmed right now. I have to get these orders out. I'm sorry I haven't come to see how you're doing."

"That's fine. I had a few questions, but Nicole and Aric have been a great help. I can wait until later."

"Nicole?" He failed to conceal his surprise and involuntarily blinked.

"Yeah, she took me out to lunch last week."

"Oh, good," he said masking his disapproval.

"Nothing urgent. I'm going to go to lunch now, so I'll see you after maybe."

"Okay, yeah, go have lunch and then I should be at a good stopping point."

"Great, see you then." Kirsten turned to leave.

Well, that wasn't so bad, she thought. *And it is officially March, so definitely time to get orders in.*

She took the escalator down to the second floor, which was literally faster than taking the elevator in this old department store—especially at lunchtime. The second floor was the level where all the Skybridges were, or "Skyways," as Aric was continuously reminding her. The club where she worked out was only three blocks away or two Skyways. She didn't like to work out first thing in the morning and knew she'd never do it after work, so the middle of the day suited her best. Her life couldn't have been more perfect. She had a great job, a cute apartment. Life was good. She happily daydreamed on her walk to the gym until she remembered she'd better hurry or there wouldn't be any space left in her spin class.

Enjoying her post-workout glow, she returned to the office in good spirits. The nervousness of the morning was forgotten. Aric, however, wasn't going to allow it. He was waving a postcard in his hand and saying, "All wrong."

"How did you not catch this?" He fumed.

"Catch what?"

"The trunk show postcard. It has the same artwork we used last fall. Didn't you do the press check?"

"What press check? I wasn't aware of any press check."

"How come? That's not my responsibility. I don't handle the advertising. You're supposed to." Aric's tone was thick with indignation.

"Yeah, okay, but I didn't receive an email to do a press check," she replied defensively.

"Yes, you did." He grabbed her computer's mouse and began scrolling through her inbox. "See, that one."

"Well, yeah, that's about the trunk shows. I thought you were handling the trunk shows, so I ignored it."

"Not the advertising for the trunk shows. This can't go out because the vendor is paying to be on the front, and we don't have enough money for a reprint. Lillian is going to have a fit!"

"Okay, well, I'm sure we can get it figured out. Where's

the file with the artwork?"

All the while Kirsten wanted to point out that he'd been very clear it was his responsibility to handle the trunk shows, not everything but the advertising for the trunk shows. Besides, how could she even know what the correct artwork was? She'd started her job after it was decided. He was not in a rational state, and it would be futile to engage with him on the matter.

"Have they gone out yet?" Kirsten asked.

"No, I just called the printer and they're holding them."

"Well, that's some good news, at least," she said in an even tone. "When were they supposed to go out?"

"Friday."

"Who is our contact in advertising?" she asked.

"Brian. Randi's in charge of the whole department if he's not around," he said while handing her the mock-up file.

"Does Brian know what happened?"

"No, not yet. The printer usually sends both our departments hardcopies, and there was no time to involve them, so I just called the printer myself."

She opened the email and made sure it looked like the mock-up. "So just to double-check, this is the correct artwork, right?"

Aric looked back and forth between the two images, nodding. "Yes."

She sensed a bit of shame on his face and hoped that meant he realized it was possible for her not to know without him showing her what the correct artwork was supposed to be. Buying some cred with him was more important than pointing this out, however.

"Okay, I'll go up and talk to him personally and see what

we can do, all right?" she said.

"Okay, thanks," he replied. And, for the first time, he seemed genuinely grateful.

Kirsten had been up to the ninth floor once the previous week to approve a small section of a storewide mailer but had only gone as far as the proof room. The advertising department was more cramped than her floor. It was brightly lit and somewhat disheveled with artwork, posters, and various unusual personal items strewn about as if to say "we're different." The Nordstrom ad department had been a lot more sterile.

Half the department seemed to be gone. Kirsten wondered if maybe they took later lunch hours. A few were eating while they worked. She stopped and asked the first person she saw if they knew where Brian was.

"Um, yeah, I think he's here. His office is the second to the end," said the hipster.

"Great. Thank you."

As she neared the door, she read the nameplate: Brian McNeill. She'd never seen it spelled with two Ls before. *Apparently, everything in Minneapolis was spelled differently,* she grinned to herself. As she entered the empty office, nothing moved except for the rhythmic dance of his screen saver.

"Can I help you?" a voice behind her asked.

"Yeah, I'm looking for Brian. I have a problem with a postcard for Couture," she said, turning.

"Oh, you must be Kirsten. I'm Randi. I'm the creative director," she said, as she reached out to shake Kirsten's hand and take the postcard from the other.

"Oh, good. Aric gave me your name too." Kirsten turned

to face the quirky, skinny girl who really wasn't a "girl" at all. She just seemed perpetually young because of her small stature and style of dress: a crisp, white-collared shirt; black, wide-legged dress pants; and black Doc Martin-style shoes. Her wrists were cluttered with various bracelets over short black fingernails. Her hair was thin and dyed blonde with highlights. It was cut to her jawline, with angular layers adding further interest to her already funky appearance.

"The wrong picture is on the front. This is the photo from last fall, and it's already been printed."

Kirsten didn't notice someone coming up behind her.

"Hey, Brian. That trunk show postcard for Couture has the wrong artwork," Randi said.

"It does?" he said, moving between Randi and Kirsten and taking it from Randi's hand. Brian was about six-foot, medium build, with thick dark auburn hair cut close to his head. He wore dark jeans with a fitted lightweight flannel shirt in olive green and gray. He wore it with the sleeves rolled up exposing a smartwatch on his left wrist. His sneakers were super cool, and predominately white with a little black, of a brand she didn't recognize.

"You're right. This isn't the correct photo." He said looking up at her. His lashes were boyishly long and framed his blue eyes. He yelled out, "Will!" Turning back to Kirsten, he said, "Sorry. This went out while I was gone. We'll get it fixed."

"Well, unfortunately, we can't afford to get it fixed. The vendor pays for it." Kirsten explained. "We were able to stop them, but we have to cover the printer's cost. Is there any way it could come out of your department's budget or maybe cut a deal with the printer? Hopefully, they'd be nice since we give them a lot of business?"

"Don't worry about it," Randi said. "It's our fault. We'll take care of it."

"Thanks, I appreciate it. I'm Kirsten, by the way. I'm the new Associate for Designer Couture," she said, holding her hand out to Brian.

"Hi," he said.

"Hello." Kirsten saw something click in his eyes even though he didn't blink and wondered if she'd been too "West Coast forward." Before he could shake her hand, he was interrupted by a short, stocky young man walking up.

"You wanted me, sir?" he asked in a military style.

"Yes, Will, this postcard for Couture has the wrong photo," Brian said.

"Oh, crap!" he said, taking it from Brian. "I must've forgotten to rename the file when I saved it."

She could tell Brian was a little surprised by his mistake and didn't want to make him feel bad in front of everyone. He sent a little uhm-yeah-what-were-you-thinking kind of smile at him, and Will took it as his cue to go fix it.

"Sooo, this was supposed to go out Friday. Do you think we can still make that happen?" Kirsten said.

"Yeah. I'll call the printer right away and get it figured out. I'll send you an email once it's confirmed, as well as a new hardcopy," Brian replied.

"Great. Thank you. Nice meeting you all," Kirsten said.

"Yeah, it was great meeting you too," Randi said. "Next time it'll be under better circumstances. Sorry about that."

"I'm just glad we can change it without delaying things," Kirsten said.

As she rode the escalator down, Kirsten couldn't believe

how easy it had been to rectify the problem given Aric's panic, but decided not to let him know. She didn't want to lose her upper hand for the moment.

She poked her head into his cube and said, "It's getting fixed and should still go out on Friday. Brian's gonna email me as soon as he gets confirmation from the printer."

"What about the cost?" Aric asked.

"Not to worry. They're going to take care of it. So, no Lillian to deal with," Kirsten assured him.

Kirsten was finally able to eat her much-anticipated leftovers lunch from her dinner splurge the night before. She didn't see much of Michael for the rest of the day, although they did talk about a few things that needed a decision. And, as promised, Brian emailed when the postcard was fixed and confirmed it would still go out on Friday. Not bad for what she considered to be her first real day at the office. As day turned to evening, she wished she could spend it hanging out with good friends at a favorite bar. But, alas, she hadn't made any new friends. Nor did she know where the good bars were.

Since she liked Nicole and she'd been friendly, she decided to wander down her way and see if it might casually come up. "See you tomorrow," she said to Aric on her way out.

"G'night," he returned.

As she neared Nicole's office, she saw Michael leaning his back against her doorjamb and felt a strong warning not to continue. She ducked left down another aisle. She sensed all was not right between them, and began to have misgivings about pursuing a friendship with Nicole as she detoured toward the escalator. Lost in thought, Kirsten nearly missed Randi waving her down as she was descending from the escalator above.

"Hey, you heading out too?" Randi asked.

"Yeah," Kirsten replied as she joined her on the next round down the escalator.

"It looks like Brian was able to get the postcard changed in time," Randi said.

"Yeah, I know, he emailed me about it, so that is good news. Thanks for making that happen."

"Sure, no problem. How's the new job going?" Randi asked.

Kirsten could see she was noticing her uneasy mood and thinking all was not well, so she shook it off and responded accordingly. She didn't want to start any office gossip. Kirsten knew she was often unwittingly too transparent with her emotions, and it frequently caused misunderstandings. She hated that about herself.

"Really good," Kirsten replied with sincerity.

"Where are you from?" Randi asked.

"Seattle."

"Seattle? You're a long way from home."

"Yeah, it's a big change, but I actually was born here and still have some family here too."

"Well, that makes sense, I guess," Randi said.

"The hardest thing is suddenly having no social life." Kirsten instantly regretted saying.

"Hey, why don't you join us for drinks?" Randi asked.

"Um, sure. I'd really like that, but I hope you don't think I was fishing for an invitation."

"Naw! We could use some new blood. We'd love to have you. It's not every day that Buying wants to hang with us, especially from Couture," Randi said.

Kirsten's eyebrows jumped in surprise. "Really?!"

"Yeah. Why? Was it different in Seattle?" Randi asked.

"Um, well, actually, no, it wasn't." Kirsten laughed. "I don't know. I never thought about it before. I guess I just lived there so long and knew everyone so well. I've never lived where I didn't already have friends."

"Yeah, I know what you mean. I've lived here my whole life," Randi said.

"Have you ever thought of living somewhere else?" Kirsten asked.

"No. I really haven't. I think about visiting places, but I've never wanted to leave."

Kirsten found it hard to believe. She'd always wanted to travel and see new places. As they pushed through the storefront doors and rounded the corner, a group of unfamiliar faces, except for Will from earlier, were heading toward them and called out to them.

"What's going on? Why are you coming back?" Randi asked.

"It's too crowded. We were just about to text you but hadn't decided where to go next," said a girl wearing a beret, trying to be all hip and different.

"Let's go to Murphy's," someone chimed.

"No, it's too divey," said the girl in the beret.

"Yeah, it is," Randi agreed.

"You guys are so boring. You always go to the same places. How 'bout over in the North Loop? My cousin tends bar over at Half-Time, and I'm sure he'd take good care of us," said Will.

A resounding "no" was chorused by all the women.

"We don't want to go to some sports bar," said the other girl without looking up from texting.

"Hey, you never let us guys decide. And besides, it's a great place to meet men." Pause. "I'll be your wingman," Will said, trying to work his magic.

"Well, okay, fine," said the texting girl.

"You'll see! It'll be great, Amanda," said Will.

"Okay, but I'd better get a date with a hot guy out of it," she said, finally looking up at him with a playful squint.

"How 'bout my cousin? The girls always seem to like him," Will offered.

"No! Bartenders are the worst," said the "beret girl."

"I'll take the bartender, Chelsea," Amanda said playfully.

"Who can drive?" Randi asked.

"I can. I parked nearby," said Will.

Kirsten was about to wonder if she was going to get introduced, when Randi finally intervened.

"Cool. Hey, this is Kirsten; she's the new Associate in Designer Couture."

Everyone greeted her with a friendly "Hey."

They turned back around from where they'd been and followed Will to his car a few blocks away in a parking garage. It was a tiny, dark purple Scion. Kirsten wondered if they'd all fit.

"We won't all fit," said Chelsea, who didn't like bartenders.

"Yeah, we will. We'll just have to squish. It's not like it's that far," Will insisted.

They all piled in, boys up front, girls in the back. A bike was folded up in the way back so no one could use it. Kirsten pondered about how quickly life can change. Less than a month ago she was doing the exact same thing with a different group of people in a different city, except she'd known the people and the city. She felt like she'd been plopped into an alternate universe where everything seemed the same but really wasn't. It reminded her of one of her childhood books, *A Wrinkle in Time.* She wondered if she looked as lost as she felt.

As anticipated, the bar's interior was loud. There was a sea of black-and-white jerseys out of loyalty to the Twin Cities' NBA team the Timberwolves (or just "Wolves," since it was easier to print across the chest). Apparently tonight was an away game in Boston. Not that Kirsten really cared, because like the other girls, she wasn't a sports fan and didn't care for the bright, brash atmosphere that seemed to accompany such places. Fortunately, they were able to find a quieter, large, bar-height round in a back corner. It was still difficult to hear others talk, but better than being at the bar.

"Okay, wingman. Work your magic. Where's my hot guy?" Amanda said to Will.

"Just give me a minute. Oh, wait, there's my cousin." Will pointed to an average height twenty-something, with wavy brown hair. He wasn't quite as stocky as his cousin and possessed a confidence Will didn't have. He seemed well practiced at the ritual of serving Will and his friends and set a tray on the table with a pitcher of beer and empty glasses. "Dude, you're awesome. Thanks, man. Hey, everyone, this is my cousin Brandon," Will said proudly.

"Hey," Brandon said

"Hi," everyone chorused.

"Hey, thanks, man," said Ian, who was now even happier to be at a sports bar as he scooped up a glass for the free beer.

"It's ladies' night, so you get a free pitcher." Brandon said, looking in the direction of the females.

"Thanks." Kirsten took a glass in response and filled it

three-quarters of the way, hoping she wouldn't hate it. It looked cheap.

"Yeah, no problem, thanks for coming. So, you're the ones who have to put up with my little 'cuz all day, huh?" Brandon teased.

"Yeah," they said in unison.

"Ahh, he's not too bad," Randi said, rubbing the top of Will's head playfully.

Brandon laughed in acknowledgment and left to serve others.

Will said, "So, did I call it or did I call it?"

Kirsten and Randi sipped their drafts and nodded agreement. Amanda rolled her eyes and Ian scanned the room, craning his neck to find the closest TV screen, and ignored everyone.

"C'mon, Amanda, you gotta admit, he's good-lookin', and we got a free round of beers. You said you wanted a bartender. I think he liked you."

"Okay, Squiggles, you did good. Set me up later, k?" Amanda said.

Will clapped his hands and laughed, then he took a swig of his beer. There seemed to be deep affection for Will—like he was the kid brother no one could stay mad at even though he was often a source of frustration. He seemed a little embarrassed about his faux pas earlier today and wouldn't look at Kirsten. Amanda and Chelsea were absorbed in their own world of texting, and Ian continued to be consumed by the game and would jump up and yell periodically.

There was a comfortable, familiar coworker camaraderie amongst them, and Kirsten hoped it wouldn't be long until she fit into a group like this again. Maybe it could be this group. Then still, no one seemed to notice they had a stranger sitting at their table. She considered she might be feeling insecure and should ask some questions to get the ball rolling, but before she had a chance, they started trying to get the attention of someone behind her.

"Brian, we're over here," Will said.

She swung her head around and saw Brian coming toward their table, grabbing a chair as he went. He put the barstool in the little bit of room between her and Ian, who was mostly facing the other way, and she moved closer to Randi to give him as much room as possible. Will headed toward the bar to get another glass.

Brian squeezed in to sit and a look of surprise washed over his face when he realized it was Kirsten. "Hi."

"Hi." Kirsten smiled.

"Kirsten is new in town, so I invited her to join us," Randi said.

"Oh, yeah? Where you from?" Brian asked.

"Seattle."

"Really? What made you want to move here?"

"Why does everyone keep asking me that? What's wrong with Minneapolis?"

"Nothing. Minneapolis is great; it's just... well, not many people move here," Brian said.

"Like for work?" Kirsten asked.

"Yeah." He laughed. "Like for work."

"What took you so long?" Chelsea whined.

"Um...I got hung up." He didn't want to say in Kirsten's presence and everyone seemed to receive the message.

"Is everything okay?" Randi asked.

"No, yeah, it's all good. It just took longer than I thought.

I had to wait for them to get it all set up."

Will came back with a glass, filled it with the rest of the pitcher, and handed the frosty mug to Brian. "To the best designer in town, our hero," he said, raising his glass.

The others joined in. "Here, here," everyone chanted.

Now Kirsten really felt like an outsider, making her suddenly homesick. She wished she were somewhere with Sten instead of this noisy bar with people she didn't know, but Sten was an hour away in some other bar, probably with his own friends.

Brian turned toward Kirsten in an effort to include her, and everyone, but Ian, followed suit. "So how are you liking Minneapolis so far?"

"Uh, I like it."

The look he gave her said he wasn't convinced.

She laughed. "I mean I don't feel like I've had a chance to really get to know it yet. This last month has been a crazy time: interviewing, moving, and a new job."

"Sure, that makes sense. This isn't our best time of year, either. It's sprinter, then it's summer." Brian chuckled at his own joke.

"Sprinter? Did you just make that up?" Chelsea asked.

"Hey, I like that. I'm gonna use it," said Will.

"Do you live in Minneapolis or farther out?" Brian said.

"In. I live in the Kenwood Uptown area," Kirsten said.

"Yeah? Me, too. I love living near the lakes and trails. It's a great place to run. Do you run?"

Before she could answer, the whole bar suddenly whooped and yelled at some fabulous move played by the Wolves.

Everyone else decided to see what was going on or at least feign interest. Ian nearly knocked his stool over in his excitement.

"Easy there, fella," Brian said, patting Ian's arm.

"All right, you guys are pathetic. I'm gonna go hang out over by the bar with the real fans," Ian said.

"Oh, fine. Leave us," Randi teased.

Brian was definitely the glue of the group. Beer flowed, food was ordered, and conversation streamed in witty banter for the next hour. Kirsten could've stayed longer because she had no life, but when Brian said he had to go, it was the beginning of the end.

"Why do you have to go, Bri-Bri?" Chelsea pouted. "You always have to go."

"It's that money pit you go home to every night," Amanda said.

"Yeah, she's such a bitch," Randi teased him.

"Hey, I know it's a complicated relationship, but she's worth it." He put cash down on the table.

"So it is a she, huh?" Chelsea joined the teasing.

Randi leaned over to Kirsten and said, "He's renovating his house."

"House? More like a mansion," Amanda exclaimed.

"Well, unlike the rest of you, I don't live in the city, so I'm gonna go too," Randi said, putting her coat on.

Kirsten was leaving as well, because she couldn't see staying with Will and the two "texty" girls.

"Fine. We should go too since our boss insists that we come in early tomorrow," Chelsea pouted.

It was settled and Brian, Randi, Kirsten, Will, Chelsea, and Amanda headed out together, leaving Ian glued to the television.

It was even colder after the sun went down, and Kirsten

wrapped her coat tighter and stuffed her scarf inside it. She looked up and spied who she thought was Michael across the street, with none other than Nicole. They appeared to be entering a nice restaurant together.

"Hey, that's Nicole and Michael over there. I don't believe it. After all that, she's back for more?" Chelsea blurted out.

Kirsten saw Randi and Amanda look at her in rebuke for having forgotten Kirsten was there.

"Sorry," she said sheepishly.

Kirsten pretended not to notice by pulling out her phone to catch an Uber.

"Are you calling an Uber?" Brian asked. "I can give you a ride if you like. It's right on my way."

She was relieved, as Uber was surging and she wasn't happy about the prices. "Thanks, that'd be great," she said.

"I'm just up a few blocks." Brian pointed the way to Kirsten. "Goodnight, everyone. See you mañana."

"Yes. Goodnight and thank you for inviting me," Kirsten added.

They all said their goodbyes, and Will ferried the rest back to Dayfield's.

"So do you commute with Uber?" Brian asked.

"Sometimes. Mostly I take the bus and hope to walk when the weather gets nicer."

"Walk? Isn't that a little far?"

"Well, I'll probably take the bus in, and walk home. I like walking. I don't know; it may not work. I'm still getting to know my way around. You?"

"I have a garage I use on the outskirts of downtown so it's not as expensive."

"That's a good idea, 'cause I checked and some of these

places are $250 a month."

In the approaching darkness it was hard to tell which car he was zeroing in on. He clicked his key fob and a black BMW lit up—a much older model. Perhaps as much as ten years, which, she decided, must be how he could afford it. Kirsten knew he didn't make nearly enough money to buy a brand new one, plus he was renovating a mansion.

"Well, this is it. You can put your bag in the back seat if you want." Brian said as he slung his backpack in the driver's side back seat. Kirsten's bag wasn't very big and normally she would've kept it with her, but she felt the need to follow his suggestion. She sat in the passenger seat next to him. He turned on the ignition and music blared, which he quickly adjusted and hit a quieter station. He brought the force of the fan, which had been blowing hot air on his drive in that morning, down too; it now needed a moment to warm back up.

"Let me know if your seat gets too hot."

"Huh? Oh, okay." Her slight hesitation made Brian a little embarrassed at assuming everyone knew about heated seats.

A wave of fatigue washed over her as she realized it was the first moment all day she'd sat in a relaxed state. She started to regret having gone out on such an emotionally demanding day. She'd even come in earlier than she usually did. A hot shower and bed were the next things in order, she decided. Well, maybe a little *Masterpiece Theater* she'd DVR'd. It was finally completely dark, and she half expected rain to pelt and blur the windshield, but it didn't because she wasn't in Seattle. It was too cold to even snow.

"Why so quiet?" he asked.

"Am I?"

"Maybe a little. Were we too much for you tonight?"

"No. No, not at all. I guess it made me a little homesick. It reminded me of hanging out with my friends back home."

"Yeah, it must be hard to leave everything you know behind."

"I haven't had time to really think about it, I guess, until now." She searched for something to say for a few minutes. "So is being a designer your cover for your real job in the Mafia?"

"Huh?"

"Well, you live in a mansion and drive a really nice car."

"Oh." He laughed. "No, this was my dad's car, and it's not really a mansion; it's actually in horrible shape. I'm kind of a closet carpenter."

"That's kinda cool. I love old houses. Actually, Kenwood reminds me a little of where I used to live in Seattle on Queen Anne Hill. I think that's why I chose to live there. Something familiar."

"Where to?" he asked as they crossed out of downtown.

She told him where to turn until they arrived front and center of her building. He was nice, Kirsten thought. Easy to be around. It wasn't weird or awkward to be alone with him at all. He helped wash some of her homesickness away.

"Thank you so much for giving me a ride. I really appreciate it.

"No problem. It was nice meeting you today. I think you're gonna be good for Couture."

"Thanks," she said, reaching for the door.

"Well, goodnight, then," she said from the back as she reached for her bag.

"Goodnight," he returned as she closed the car door. He pulled quietly away.

Good for Couture? She wondered what he meant as images of Nicole and Michael entering a restaurant together replayed in her mind.

LAKE MINNETONKA

Summer had finally come to Minnesota, and Kirsten was staying cool indoors by staying at her dad's for the weekend. The house was quiet except for the ticking of a grandfather clock in the hall and the occasional drone of an appliance motor kicking on. She stood in front of the mantel looking at a picture of her father, no doubt taken a few years earlier at some awards ceremony. She wondered what she would think of him if she didn't know him. He was certainly a complex man. From the outside, he was handsome, confident, and charming; that is, of course, if you hadn't known him for too long. Still, there were those who'd known him a long time and thought of him that way, mostly superficial and/or naive women, in Kirsten's opinion. She realized it would be too hard to really be objective because their relationship gave her a unique, close perspective of him.

I don't understand him, but I know him. I know what he will say and how he will respond. Yes, I'll probably always be astonished by it. Does that qualify as knowing a person—being able to predict his behavior?

She wandered through the silence of the house—not exactly snooping but observing how they lived—noticing the positioning of the furniture and the objects of affection. Carol's basket of knitting waited for her to resume from its spot tucked neatly between a side table and rocking chair. A reclining wingback chair sat next to the fireplace, accompanied by a dark wood end table adorned with reading glasses and magazines. Each publication had pages neatly folded to indicate the next article August would read, and they were all stacked precisely as if for someone who didn't like to be disturbed. Kirsten tried to shrug off the memory of his frustration at being interrupted by her as a child while he had been trying to read them. She wondered if it wasn't a bit of a relief for him when she'd left home and no one was around to bug him any longer—no more need to worry the pile would become strewn or the glasses misplaced from a child playing.

She sat on the couch as a melancholy began to fill her. She didn't exactly want to cry, but felt like she was arriving at some sort of truth and couldn't quite grasp it. Or maybe it was a place—a place of peace which had always eluded her. She could never be calm when she was in her dad's presence. He was constantly pushing her buttons, causing her nothing but anxiety, making their encounters nothing but an emotional drain. How she longed to be rid of all those feelings. She wanted to be able to detach herself whenever she was around him, so no matter what he did or said it would have no effect on her.

She pulled her knees up under her chin and wrapped her arms around them, then stared into the empty fireplace. Images of her father in all his humanity, how God must see him, hung in her mind like strands of a wind chime. *Is he really that blind?* She had difficulty reconciling what she saw without addressing her own humanity. *I know I'm not infallible, but I'd like to think I can see who I am. Do I not see myself?* "Know thyself." The old adage was about questioning our inability to see ourselves as others see us. She didn't want to be that kind of person, but worried she couldn't help it.

The afternoon light dimmed toward evening, making her aware she'd been sitting longer than she'd meant to. Snickers, the big fluffy cat, must've noticed the same thing and disrupted her contemplation by hopping onto her lap, nudging her for affection. She mindlessly caressed her furry head, thinking she should get up and feed her. Snickers was the reason, after all, she was here. Her father had insisted she take care of her over the weekend while they were out of town. Like a cat required a live-in caretaker, she'd protested privately, and wondered what he had been doing for the last ten years without her to care for the cat. She'd yielded to his unnecessary and insistent request, as always, rationalizing at least a change of venue would be nice, and then she could hang out with Sten. Sten, however, was unavailable tonight. She suspected he might have a new love interest and was determined to get it out of him tomorrow.

She no longer had the desire to finish her tour.

"Would you like some dinner, Snickers girl? Huh? Would you like that?" she cooed at the cat. She fired up Spotify on the TV and chose a classical music station to go with her mood, taking Snickers into the kitchen to feed her.

She'd picked up a gourmet dinner at the fancy grocer by her apartment on her way to Northfield and looked forward to eating it. She poured a glass of sauvignon blanc from her father's wine fridge and ate in the partially screened sunroom off the kitchen. The heat of the day had evaporated some, but the stifling humidity was still hard for her to get used to, and it wasn't even August yet. But she liked the sound of the evening bugs. She turned the lights on low and lit a few candles—they created a lovely scene. Her dad always did have good taste. It was a beautiful old home probably built during the earlier days of the town being founded. It had a large lawn framing the house on the end of a dead-end street. The sunroom was the same level as the main floor and was made of a blue-gray flagstone with the palest of matching blue-gray walls and white trim. The room was divided into two separate spaces: one was a sitting area made out of whitewashed wicker and teak furniture. The floral printed cushions were in a beautiful art deco pattern. The predominant color was like pistachio ice cream with accents of coral, white, and a steelier blue-gray. It was welcoming and serene. The other half was a place to dine. A round, wrought iron table with a glass top was centered under a metal lantern that hung from above. Four matching chairs were arranged around it. She sat and sipped the crisp cold wine, which interplayed well with her Niçoise salad. Snickers came in and purred against her legs, probably wishing she could eat tuna like that. Kirsten listened to the evening chatter with Paganini wafting in the background. She felt too old to be in her twenties. How many people her age ate dinner by candlelight and listened to classical music? She wagered not many. She wondered if it was because she'd been an only child. Did the lack of sibling rivalry and the presence of only adults in her home make her enjoy mature pursuits more than her peers? She wasn't sure she'd ever know the answer, but no one was here to watch and judge her, so she was able to enjoy the freedom of being herself.

The next morning promised to be even hotter, but she mustered the strength to go out and meet Sten. He had already arrived at the Java Café and placed his order. He waited for Kirsten to choose her coffee libation and, at the last moment, she had it put on ice. It was too hot. It was good to see him again, and there was something comforting about sitting in a coffee shop on a weekend morning. The workweek was done, and the atmosphere reflected the mood.

"Well, how is the professor's house?" Sten goaded his cousin.

"Fine, except for the cat," Kirsten replied. "I never would have guessed he'd be a cat lover. Old age, I guess."

"Gus, old?" Sten said. "Never!"

"So how was your date last night?"

"What date?" he replied, without a telling emotion.

"The hot date that came up at the last minute because suddenly you couldn't see me." She smiled mischievously.

"It wasn't a date. You think only a date would make me cancel my plans with you? I have a life of my own, you know."

She detected a little anger. "I know you do. What's wrong?"

"Nothing. How's the job going?"

"Fine. Sten, something's wrong. Spill it."

"Nothing. Really, I'm fine," he insisted.

"Okay." She put both hands up in defeat and resumed sipping her iced latte.

They sat there for a few minutes not speaking, turning to watch passersby outside and customers inside ordering and conversing. They didn't know what to say. It worried Kirsten because they'd always been so close. Now the one person she thought she could count on in her new life was acting strangely. He looked at her again like he was contemplating what to say and started to open his mouth to talk, but instead looked down at his hands wrapped around his latte.

"Sten!? You're killing me. What is it?"

Silence.

"Oooh, this is familiar. I'd forgotten this about you. You get in these moods, and you won't talk about it. You'll talk around it, but you will never just come right out and say it. It's so infuriating!"

He sulked further into himself.

"You know what? I'm not gonna cajole you out of it like I used to. It's time to grow up." She gathered up her things to leave. "I was really looking forward to spending time with you. This move hasn't exactly been easy for me. Leaving all my friends, my life, everything I know, and to come to a place where there is nothing for me. I hardly have a life outside of work." She rushed out and started walking down the main drag, to where she did not know.

Sten caught up to her, and they walked side by side in silence for a while.

"I am not nothing, Kirsten."

She stopped and turned toward him. "I know that. Why would you think such a thing?"

"You left."

"Left?"

"You stopped coming for visits. You stopped calling. You left."

She was stunned. "You left first. You were older and went off to school. That first summer after you went to college, you didn't come home, and I was here all alone. It was hell."

"Hell!? What about my hell? Couldn't you see through it? You can be so selfish!"

"I loved her too, Sten. She was my little sister too."

"But she wasn't. She was my sister and I'm the one who had to live it every day in that house. My parents were so grief-stricken, it eventually destroyed their marriage and any sense of family I had. You were the only family I had left."

"Oh, Sten, I'm so sorry, I didn't know. I was just a kid myself. You have to see that. I thought that's what you wanted, that you needed to be away to heal, and I did the exact same thing. I stayed in Seattle, then went to school and, well, it was just easier to stay away, I guess. I'm sorry."

They fell back into silence for a while, continuing to walk side by side.

"Well! Congratulations, Sten, on finally being able to articulate what you're really feeling. It was a little scary there for a minute, but I'm glad you finally told me."

He smiled a little and put his arm over her shoulder.

"You're welcome. You know, those summers on the lake were some of my best memories. I was always a shy kid and didn't have a lot of friends, so school could be tough, but summer was different. I felt like I could be myself. You always had that Swenson confidence I never had, except for the asshole part—you had enough of your mom in you to temper it."

Kirsten started to tear up. "Oh, Sten, you were my rock. What confidence?" Kirsten batted him lightly with her hand.

"You know they still own the lake house, right?" Sten said.

"They do? I figured I'd at least have heard if they'd sold it."

"Yeah. My mom is really a mess, Kirsten, and I think even your dad has given up on her. They still have someone care-take it, so it's probably not totally falling apart. She just can't seem to bring herself to go there, and I don't think your dad ever liked it, but she can't sell it, either."

"Have you ever gone back?" Kirsten asked.

"Not for a long time. I did once, maybe about five years ago, but not since."

"I wanna see it. Do you think you'd be up for it?" Kirsten was hopeful as a wave of nostalgia came over her.

He looked at her while trying to decide. "Yeah, let's do it. Wait, what about the cat?"

"Screw the cat," Kirsten said, and they burst out laughing.

They took Sten's old, slightly rusting, dark green Land Cruiser and sped north on I-35. The increasing heat created a mirage effect across the passing scenery—wavering like an old glass window, muting the familiar landmarks and passing towns. Kirsten opened the car vents, releasing blessed air conditioning. She angled them directly on her, as she couldn't stop the sweat from beading up on her skin. A sense of anxious anticipation rose up within them as they traveled to the place of their childhood dreams, where innocence had been lived and lost, their old solidarity emerging under the weight of what they were doing. Perhaps they shouldn't be so spontaneous. But one can never know the full effect or consequences of an action until it's completed. Would they wish later they'd left it alone? Is it necessary to visit the past in order to move forward? It had been nearly a decade since that fateful day on Lake Minnetonka, and though they couldn't fully know why, they knew it was time to open the doors and windows and let life back in.

Lake Minnetonka was the nearest large lake to the Minneapolis metro area and therefore the most popular for water sports. It drew crowds from thirteen different municipalities along its shore. The lakeside retreat had once been the family farm, but hard times had forced most of the land to be sold to wealthy city dwellers for survival. The Swenson homestead was surrounded by beautiful old homes built in the early twentieth century, further dwarfing the simple farmhouse. Hard work and education by subsequent generations helped keep it alive, but eventually death and disinterest funneled down to one or two siblings per generation, the most significant being their grandfather, who had done a major renovation in the early nineties. Kirsten often imagined her lost relatives who'd once lived there. Where were their descendants now? She wondered if she'd bumped into them somewhere along the way. She wanted to tell them they shared the same great-great-grandparents and it was here. Here they'd lived.

The car grew quieter with each turn, as if it knew it needed to ameliorate the stress of the journey. Sten, practically stopping, finally signaled left into the enclave of homes surrounding their family lake house. Kirsten recognized the little neighborhood general store on the corner, known to locals as Melvin's. Memories of afternoon ice-cream cone runs and last-minute trips for milk, butter and eggs flooded back. Apprehension seeped in as she wondered what she might find and whether they should have come. She looked over at Sten and surveyed a similar mien.

They came to the lane on the end, where the house sat all the way down to the right. They descended the narrow hedge-lined drive and watched the old homestead come into view. There it was, dappled in sunlight beneath the canopy of large deciduous trees. The lake glinted in the background and there was a partial view of the dock, the beginning of which was hidden by a slight rise behind the house. The car came to a slow stop and the gravel made its final crunching sound. It was exactly as she'd remembered it. Old lap siding painted a soft pink with white trim and a wraparound porch. It was a basic, two-story prairie farmhouse with double rectangular gabled boxes teed into each other. It was primarily a summer house, the back section of the porch, facing the lake, was screened in for outdoor living. The grass was patchy underneath the trees and therefore required less maintenance. The beds circling the house were filled with overgrown hydrangea bushes.

"Wow, it still looks the same. Maybe even a little nicer. Looks like it's being well cared for," Kirsten said.

"Yeah, it looks better than when I was here last. It must've gotten a new coat of paint in the last few years."

"And roof," Kirsten added.

"Yeah," Sten agreed. "Much better than the old one."

They continued to sit in the car, afraid to move or speak anymore.

"Well?" Sten said, breaking their quietude.

"Well?" she said.

They simultaneously grabbed their door handles, stepped out, and walked in silence back to the front door. The driveway ended along the side of the house, ignoring the front entrance altogether. The hydrangeas flanking the stairs to the porch spilled out over the path, almost meeting the tall hedge walling off the nearly nonexistent front yard and acted as a fence to the neighboring property. The lot was pie-shaped and set on a slight point, giving it a sense of privacy. Sten wiggled the loose finial at the top of the stair rail, thinking it might've gotten fixed along with the new roof and paint job, but it came off as always, revealing the key to get in.

The door opened with a familiar creak, and they carefully stepped in like trespassers. It felt smaller than Kirsten remembered. It was barely a foyer, with a powder room on the right and the stairs, ascending straight up, to the left. The living room was past the bathroom and spanned the middle of the home. The main seating was to the right to allow for enjoying the fireplace on the outside wall, while the left side afforded a small reading/gaming nook tucked into the stairwell wall. Beyond the living space was the dining and kitchen area. The furnishings were draped with sheets.

"Oh, my gosh, the brown shag is gone!" Kirsten exclaimed.

"No way! You're right. What happened?"

"I don't know, but I think I like it. Definitely a huge improvement."

"Who knew these were under that nasty old thing?"

"I know, right?" Kirsten bent down and touched the wide plank flooring that had been lovingly refinished.

The dining area revealed a large rectangular table. The top was also covered with a sheet. Window seating was built into the corner walls, while the opposite sides of the table were filled with old country maple kitchen chairs that matched the finish of the table. Kirsten assumed the window seat cushions must be stored below the hinged top seats. She recalled the classic blue floral upholstery she used to stare at as a child as she'd run her finger along the winding stems and out and in around their flower heads. She could still feel the texture of the fabric. She opened the lid and saw them wrapped in plastic. The house groaned its age as Kirsten moved to the tiny kitchen and lifted the handle on the faucet to the sink—nothing came out.

"They must have the water turned off. I can turn it back on," Sten said.

She looked out toward the lake through the screened-in porch and heard the noise of watercraft just beyond their little bay.

The old wooden cupboards were painted white with matching ceramic knobs and a classic blue Scandinavian flower painted on them. The linoleum flooring was a traditional white tile pattern accented by matching blue diamonds. They quietly shuffled around, peering into nooks and crannies. Kirsten spied the ink smear on the light blue Formica and tensed at the memory of her father's rage for her having been so stupid as to use a pen anywhere near the surface—like she knew the pen would leak. Sten picked up on her gaze and averted her attention, saying, "We should go upstairs."

"Yeah," she said, without regard to what it meant as she followed her cousin up the stairs.

There was a bedroom immediately across from the landing at the top, which had been her father's writing sanctuary, as it had the best view of the lake. Her aunt and uncle's bedroom was to the left. The one bathroom was to the right and the remaining two bedrooms were down the hall, past the bathroom. Sten's was on the end and had once been a large closet. Sunlight was streaming through the doorway of her and Sofie's room. Sten walked past, into his old bedroom. She opened the door carefully. Using only her forefinger and middle finger, she gently pushed in. It was as she remembered it. There were two wrought iron twin beds with peeling white paint and a window centered between them. Their spring-filled bottoms looked lonely. No mattresses or bed linens to receive the dust of time. Pictures still hung in the room and faded drawings littered the wall above Sofie's bed. Kirsten's bed had fewer drawings left. It was hard to make out the crude stick figures, but they were there. Sten, Sofie, and Sissy all holding hands in front of the lake with a bright sun in the corner—its rays shooting out to them. Kirsten reached out and touched her name—Sissy. She was always and forever her sister, never her cousin from Seattle. Here they were as close as any family could be. Aunt Anne was the responsible one, trying to make up for her brother's lack of parenting when they were here. Sten walked in to find her fingering the drawings.

"I'm sorry. I know she was your sister too," Sten said.

Kirsten started to cry and sat on the empty bed. The tiny springs squeaked and bounced. Sten sat next to her, put his arm around her shoulders, and held her as she let it all out. It was a roaring river finally unleashing its fury. All the years of trying to bury it and leave it behind had merely delayed the inevitable. Sten kept holding her, sometimes wiping a few tears from his own eyes. As her sobs began to subside, she dabbed her tears on the bottom of her shirt.

She moved to the dresser and peered into the mirror; her skin was blotchy and her nose was red. She tried to slow her breathing back to its regular pattern.

"Ah, forget it!" She took off her shirt in frustration, revealing a sports bra underneath, and blew her nose in the t-shirt, then dried her tears.

Sten laughed.

She laughed.

They kept laughing. "Fuck! I'm such a mess. I don't even know who I am anymore or where I'm going. I'm twenty-six years old and I'm still a virgin!"

Sten's eyes widened.

"Don't look at me that way. Yes, there, I said it. I'm a virgin. I can't get close enough to a guy. I scare them all away, and then, when I do have a boyfriend, I pick someone who I only really like as a friend. When it starts to seem odd that we haven't had sex yet, I break up with them. I mean, I haven't had a 'boyfriend' "—she made air quotes—"in like three years."

Sten sat there, not knowing what to say.

"It's okay; you don't have to say anything. I don't know why I said all that. Am I weird? Is there something wrong with me? I mean, do you know any girls like me?" Kirsten asked.

"I don't know. I'm sure I do, I just don't know it," he said evenly.

"How many girls have you slept with?"

Silence.

Kirsten eyeballed him sternly.

"What?" he said defensively.

"I guess we're back to that, huh? You never telling me anything of merit. I thought I was your rock?"

"Guys just don't really talk about that sort of thing unless we're measuring our dicks, and even then, you never know who is telling the truth."

"I'm not a guy or your girlfriend, Sten. I'm your sister-cousin."

"Sister-cousin? What is that?"

"Your sister-cousin is the one you can tell everything to."

"Oh, I didn't realize that. Hmmm, even if she's a crazy virgin?" She hit him playfully.

"Yes, even if she's a crazy virgin."

"It's not like I've been real successful with my personal life, either. I don't know. Relationships are hard. Look at our parents. Look at most of your friends' parents. Is anyone really happy? Now we can have sex with whomever we want, gays can be married and have kids, women can have kids without having sex. Gender is fluid. There's no stigma, no rules, and still the divorce rate climbs. Maybe it's evolutionary and you're ahead of the curve and resetting the clocks. Maybe virginity is the next big thing." He smiled.

"Hmm, I don't think so, but nice try. I think we like sex too much. And I do *like* sex. I mean, I'm attracted to men. I like making out with them I just can't go all the way. I stop like some cosmic force steps in, and I can't do it. Then I think, what if I do meet someone and really fall in love, then I'll be able to do it, but what if I can't? I have friends who just sleep with some random guy or some old boyfriend from college or high school just to get it over with, like it's something we have to check off the list, because we don't want to get caught with someone we really like and have them find out we're a virgin. Would you think less of a girl who was still a virgin?"

"No. I wouldn't think less of them, but I'm not sure I'd have sex with them."

"Why?"

"I don't know; it just wouldn't seem right. Losing your virginity is a big deal, and I think more so for girls than guys."

"See, that's what I mean. Why is it a bigger deal for girls than guys?"

"I don't know. You're more emotional, I guess. I don't think you realize what it's like for us. We pretty much want to have sex all the time, and every morning when we wake up, we're reminded of that fact."

"Nice, Sten."

"Well, you asked."

"I'm so tired of that excuse. It all comes down to biology. There's no rationale."

"No, it's not, and we're tired of not being understood, too. *We can't help it!* It's not our fault that's how we're made." He could see he was making it worse and felt bad. "Look, Kirsten, we aren't animals. If we really like a girl, we're not going to care if she's a virgin or not. Yes, I'm sure there are some guys out there who wouldn't put up with it, and they're losers you shouldn't be with, anyway. You are a smart, funny, and beautiful woman. I have no doubt when you meet the right person it'll happen."

"Thanks, Sten."

"You know, I'm not surprised, actually."

"You're not?"

"No. You have always been a pain in the ass when it comes to what you want."

"I have?" she said surprised.

"Yes. Remember the time we all went boating and you were starving, but didn't like any of the food and refused to eat? We were too far out to go get anything else, so you just sat there hungry—watching everyone else eat."

"Yeah." She smiled sheepishly.

"You're just particular, and you've never really cared what people think of you even if you're being ridiculous. That's what I mean about your confidence. I never had that, and I admire that about you. Don't let society pressure you into being someone you're not. And if they do, shame on them, because they'd be doing the exact same thing they've been trying so hard to get rid of—and that's being judged for their sexual behavior."

"I know. It's actually harder letting my girlfriends know. It's like I'm breaking some sort of girl code. Our foremothers worked really hard to get us to this place where we have a say about what we want our life to look like. We aren't bound by ridiculous rules and mores, and I know most of the women in the world still don't have this kind of freedom, but I do. I know I'm lucky, but I can't help but feel we've lost part of the essence of who we are as women. Like you said, we're different from men. So why do we feel we have to act like them and have sex with whoever is willing?"

"Because men are always willing, women aren't."

"Exactly. We're more particular, so why aren't we being more particular?"

"I think most women *are* still particular. It's not like I'm having all this sex," Sten said.

"Okay, fine, but we're acting like men, like we have to prove something. Are we trying to prove we can be as unemotional as men, and if so, why? I don't think our foremothers would approve of how we wield our sexuality. I don't think that's what they had in mind. They wanted to be able to marry for love and not be so saddled with children they couldn't do something besides mothering or teaching. They wanted the same choices as men, to become whoever they wanted to be and still have a family, but I don't think they wanted a society where there was all this casual sex, and perpetual engagements that rarely lead to marriage and family. And you're right, we do have all the power; because if we don't consent to it, then you're not having it."

"Great. So are you saying women should make it even harder for us to have sex?"

"No. How do we bridge the gap? Most people are heterosexual, but the goals are different. I mean at least in homosexual relationships they approach sex the same. I have a friend who told me that if a guy wants to have sex with another guy, they just nod at each other, ask your place or mine, and they go."

"Sweet! I'd like that."

"Yes, I'm sure you would, but it would have to be with a man. Is that what you want?"

"No. I definitely like women."

"Right? I think ultimately we're both going to have to compromise."

"We are? Because I feel like I'm compromising all the time."

"Who is this pathetic creature you keep referring to?"

"No one. Continue."

"Fine, but I'll get it out of you eventually. I admit women have this ridiculous dichotomy of needing, sometimes desperately, to be wanted by a man—and we know we hold this power over their desire and it's a turn on for us—but that doesn't necessarily mean we want to sleep with them. We just need to know they want to sleep with us more than any other women in the room, so sometimes we're not nice, we're a tease, or sometimes, more often than not, we don't know that they really want us until we sleep with them and a lot of times that's too late. I see this with my girlfriends a lot. They don't realize the guy just wants to have sex, and once it's over, the guy doesn't want them as much anymore. It's a powerful drug—to feel a man wanting you."

Sten perked up. "It is?"

"Yes, it is, if we're attracted to the guy, but no if we're not."

"How do you know?"

"Well, that's the trick, because there are those mean girls who just tease and, well, most men can't see through it. Sorry, but we're far too complex for you sometimes."

"Yes, you are. For a virgin you sure do seem to know a lot about sex." Sten laughed at her.

"Are you making fun of me?"

"Maybe a little. I just don't think it's ever going to get solved, Kirsten. Men and women have been loving and hating each other since time began and I don't think it's going to change."

"Why not? We've come so far. We're almost there."

"I think that's just part of the attraction."

"Great. So do you think there's someone out there for you?"

"Yeah, I do, but I think women idealize it too much, and we can't live up to that expectation. Sorry, but we're not all Superman. You think you're judged all the time for your beauty, but you do the same thing to us, just in a different way."

"I never thought of it like that, but you're right, we are hard on you. I'm sorry."

"Unlike women, we're not nearly so complicated and don't need much, but we live in fear of not being able to meet your expectations. I think for a lot of guys, that's what their fear of commitment is really about—not wanting to be with one woman. It's the responsibility of being with one woman."

"Really? I find that hard to believe. You're too visually stimulated; if a cute skirt walks by, all that goes out the window."

"Sure, but it's not that she's cute. It's that she's a clean slate."

"Yeah, you want it to be easy, but we're not easy. See, we're right back where we started."

"No, you just need to be easier," he said, laughing.

Kirsten gave him a sharp look.

"Hey, you said we're both going to have to compromise, and I think you should be easier."

"Okay, fine. We'll be easier, if you'll be faithful and want only us."

"Deal. I'm hungry, let's go see what's at Melvin's."

"K."

They both stood up, took another look around the room and ambled out and back downstairs. They retraced the route they'd come in on. Kirsten suddenly felt old and burdened by the weight of what they'd lost in Sofie. She reminisced walking this way, with her, on many a summer day. She'd been a constant chatterbox, flitting from one thing to the next, asking if they could do this or that and why not—pulling on her and Sten the whole way. Kirsten imagined her looking back at them, running a little ahead with her hair glinting in the sun's golden rays, her bright twinkling blue eyes, the sprinkling of freckles across her nose, and the slight overbite in her smile— the perfect picture of joy and life. She tried to remember what her laugh had sounded like, but it wouldn't come. It'd been too long since she'd heard it. Kirsten brought her hand up to the lump swelling in her throat. Sten took one look at her and pulled her in tight to squeeze the pain away.

Melvin's was quiet on their approach. The hot afternoon whimpered at everyone to stay away. But Sten and Kirsten were unaware. They were lost in the past, living their own rhythm and were not in sync with the current world. Melvin's appeared unchanged to them. It was a simple gable-roofed building, the slope of which was not very steep, more like a barn. The siding was a grayed white clapboard with matching trim. The roof had been replaced with shiny rippled metal. The wraparound cement porch was cracked and uneven, with either broken off or chipped corners, its surface stained from ground dirt and years of mess spilled out. It housed firewood and lawn fertilizer—items you'd find at a hardware store. Rusting red metal letters spelled out Melvin's in the gable end with a large silver light hanging out from the peak above. The entry had double doors; the one on the right was entrance only, while the one on the left was exit only. The top half was glass, their forest green paint chipped and chewed from a century of use, and a bell jingled as you walked in. The interior had old wide wooden floorboards smoothed over time from all the foot traffic. The freezer and cold cases, along with the deli counter, were the only acknowledgment of the present. They were shiny and new.

The deli case had bowls of cold salads like chicken, tuna, coleslaw, and the classic macaroni. Large rounds of meat and cheese—like ham, turkey, provolone, Swiss, cheddar, and a little prosciutto—sat alongside waiting to be sliced for sandwiches. Behind the counter, the floor was made of durable linoleum tiles, alternating black and white, with commercial metal counters and sink used for preparing the food. It was spotless and utilitarian. Kind of like a Minnesotan, Kirsten was realizing. She'd never noticed before how clean this state's residents were. She tried to remember if it'd always been this clean. Old buildings back home were usually messy and dirty. Kirsten was surprised at her newfound knowledge. Minnesotans weren't extravagant or fancy, but they took care of things. She liked that. It had always bothered her that old seemed to mean unkempt and falling apart. It didn't have to.

She found herself rummaging around in a novelty section

geared toward kids. "Hey, look at these," Kirsten said, holding up a little packaged toy of some sort.

"What is it?" Sten asked as he walked over to her.

"It's one of those Chinese lanterns. You light them and let them float up into the air like a hot-air balloon. I've always wanted to try one. Let's get some and send them up on the dock tonight in honor of Sofie. She would've loved them."

He looked at her for a few seconds. "Yeah, okay. That'd be nice. What are you gonna get? I think I'm gonna get a sandwich."

"Mmm, yeah, I'll get one too."

"There's some in the case already made."

"Mmm, I think I'll just order one."

Sten chuckled. "Yeah, of course you will."

"Sorry, that's how I roll."

"Well, hurry up, 'cause it'll take longer," Sten said.

"Are you in some sort of hurry?"

"No, just hungry."

"Well, then eat, don't wait on me. So, should we get something for dinner? Are we going to stay the night? What's the plan?" Kirsten asked.

"I don't know. Should we? I mean, I guess we could."

"Let's!" Kirsten said.

"Okay."

Kirsten looked in the case, ordered her sandwich and a salad for later, as well as picked out a rotisserie chicken from under the hot food lights. Kirsten loved rotisserie chicken. "Oh, and some wine," she said, grabbing a bottle of red and handing it over for Sten to carry. "Oh, and some ice cream too. We gotta have some ice cream." She walked back to the freezer case and picked up a half gallon of ice cream, then grabbed a two-and-a-half gallon bottle of drinking water on the way to the cash register, in case they couldn't turn the water on at the house. As she was checking out, she got the sense the cashier was looking at her like she felt sorry for her but trying not to let it show. Kirsten smiled and pretended not to notice, then realized she shouldn't be buying everything before she had lunch. The ice-cream would undoubtedly melt.

"Would it be possible to keep the perishables in a refrigerator and freezer while we eat lunch?" she asked the cashier.

"Sure," the cashier happily answered. "We have some in the back where I can put them, and I'll keep everything else here behind the counter."

"That'd be awesome. Thank you so much! I didn't think everything through very well, did I?"

"No problem!"

They sat at one of the wooden picnic tables on the side of the old general store, under a large weeping willow, and ate their lunch.

"I think the cashier recognized me," Kirsten said, watching Sten eat his ready-made sandwich.

"Yeah?"

"Yeah. I think she remembers what happened. I hate that; nothing worse than pity. I guess that's why your mom hasn't come back. Maybe she's waiting for the day when everyone forgets so she can come in peace."

"I don't know if there will ever be any peace for her."

Kirsten reached out and touched Sten's hand. "I'm sorry. I should go see her. Is she still in Madison?"

"Yeah."

"And Uncle Bill? Where's he now?"

"He's in Saint Paul. He's been there for about five years

now. Remarried."

"I did hear he'd married. What's she like?"

"She's great, actually. It's strangely easier to be around my dad now that he's married." Sten popped his soda can open and took a big gulp.

"Really?"

"Yeah. It's like a distraction. Before we just didn't know what to do or have anything to say to each other."

"I'm glad."

Sten was finishing up his sandwich as Kirsten's arrived, and she smiled at his annoyance.

"Why does this bother you?" she said taking a bite. "Mmm, this is really good. Much better than yours, I'm sure," she teased. Sten rolled his eyes and decided to relax into the afternoon.

They headed back carrying their heavier load. Sten had the bags of food, and Kirsten carried the water. "I can get the water turned back on, you know," Sten said, watching his cousin shift the water from one hand to the other.

"I know, but stuff happens. It's just in case."

Back at the house, it continued to be blazing hot as the day crept to its zenith. They decided it'd be wise to make sure they'd have everything they needed to stay the night. Kirsten rummaged around for bed linens while Sten got the water turned on. They agreed to sleep downstairs on the couches and used the excuse that it'd be much cooler, ignoring the fact that it was mostly the ghosts upstairs they feared.

They didn't need much, but the worn furnishings made from medium blue tweed were scratchy, Kirsten recalled, particularly on a hot day. Hand-crocheted blankets in coordinating Charlie Brown chevrons were revealed when she lifted off the dust covers. They lay folded over the arms and backs. Images flashed in her mind of blanket fights on cold nights by the fire and fort constructions. She washed the scenes away by the flick and unfurling of a fresh bedsheet and tucking one around the seat cushions of each couch. She placed a second one on top should they ever get cold. She quickly pulled the remaining covers off the end table lamps and coffee table and rolled them into a continuous ball. The tables were made of the same maple as the dining room with blue spongeware lamps placed strategically on the end tables. The thin varnish was worn and slightly scratched in places as her finger traced an unwelcome line on the coffee table. It reminded her of the underside and she quickly bent down and rolled under the low table to see if it was all there. She laughed out loud at the sight of their childish graffiti. Their secret code looking like gibberish. She tried to remember what the sprawling letters and characters meant. "Sten!" Kirsten called. No answer. "Sten!" she called again.

"What?" He came into the room from outside. "Where are you?" he yelled.

"I'm under the coffee table. Remember our secret code?"

"Huh?" He came further into the room and saw her lying partly under the table.

"You know our secret language?"

"Oh, yeah! Is it still there?" Sten lay down opposite her. "Oh, wow, this is too funny. Hey, this was my computer language I was writing."

"It is? I thought it was for our secret club."

"It was. But I was also trying to create code."

"Huh? I don't remember that."

"See, this meant boathouse. It's where we kept all our secret stuff."

"Oh, yeah, sure, boathouse." Kirsten laughed sarcastically. "You were ahead of your time with that old computer your dad gave you. I wonder what you would've become if there hadn't been personal computers and the internet?"

Sten laughed as he affectionately surveyed his childhood writings. "Yeah, I don't know. It's hard to say." They lay in silence for a few more minutes reminiscing. Eventually, the smell of dust and must and the hard floor moved them back up to sit on their freshly made beds.

"Now what?" Kirsten asked.

"I don't know. How 'bout a swim? I'm dripping in sweat."

"Yeah, let's! I think I can make my running shorts work; they have a liner."

"I saw a pair of my dad's old trunks upstairs."

"And I found some towels," Kirsten offered.

Sten came downstairs wearing a pair of faded red swim trunks in an unfashionably short length mid-thigh and a densely gathered waistband from too much fabric.

Kirsten started laughing. "Nice!"

"What? Not cool enough for Miss Fashionista?" He struck a pose, attempting to vogue.

"Um, no, but I'll let it go this one time."

They made their way down to the dock, stopping at the boathouse for some flotation devices and brushed off some old canoe cushions mired in time. Kirsten felt herself breaking back to her childhood. She ran down the dock and screamed as she cannonballed into the water.

Sten followed suit.

"Oh, my gosh, this feels so good," she exclaimed as she popped her head out of the water.

Sten smiled as the water ran down his face, replacing the sweat. They swam and played like it was yesterday until the sun lowered in the sky and the water became like glass. "I love swimming at this time of day. It's my favorite. They call it the gloaming hour. I don't know why it's always still when the sun is right there, but it is." Kirsten pointed at the horizon with wonder. Sten was sitting on the dock drying off and started to get a little impatient with his cousin.

"I'm hungry. Get out."

"Fine," she said reluctantly.

They sat in the screened porch at an old foldout game table and chairs Sten had found and ate their simple supper of rotisserie chicken and Caesar salad. The sun set and the moon rose and the lake lapped the shore. It felt like an evening lullaby except for the occasional disturbance of boats reverberating across the water and the intermittent yell or idle conversation that could only be heard because of the lake acoustics in the still evening air.

It was still quite warm, but Kirsten felt refreshed from the swim. She ate her chicken ravenously.

Sten looked at her in surprise.

"What? I'm hungry. Swimming always makes me really hungry."

"Hmm, I can see that. Save some for me."

"I will, plus we still have ice cream—peanut butter chocolate…your favorite. At least I'm not one of those girls who's afraid to eat."

"Eating, yes. Pigging out, no—not sexy. Maybe that's why you're still a virgin." She playfully squinted her eyes at him.

"Okay, I'm done." She pushed away from the table and sipped her wine while staring up at the crimson sky. "Wow, it's so beautiful here. I do miss this."

Sten finished eating in his own silent reverie and poured more wine into both their glasses. She could see him staring at the big tree stump in the yard, a self-made memorial of Sofie's death. Kirsten still remembered the fresh jagged cut that had splintered when it fell. Time and weather had grayed it, but a few rough shards remained erect, making it an uninviting place to sit. It had been their climbing tree. Never before or since had there been such a tree, nor did she want there to be. Climbing became a cruel form of play.

No one will ever forget hearing her scream as she fell from her forbidden height and the guttural cries of parents losing a child. It was swift and final.

Kirsten wished it was still standing. At the time, it seemed to be the necessary response to such evil, but to look at the sad, empty stump, devoid of life, made the memory worse. She wanted to remember the tree in all its glory. The three of them laughing and swinging from its branches. It would've been better to let it live.

"That stump needs to be blasted out with dynamite and replanted with a new beautiful tree. I can't stand looking at it."

Sten remained quiet.

"You know there was no way anyone could've prevented it from happening," Kirsten said. "She just wanted to be big like us. She was such an old soul. I always felt like she knew things, like she held the secret to the universe. She always knew when I needed consoling, when Gus would stay holed up in his room writing, or, more often, just leave. She'd always come and get me to play with her or just give me a hug, seeming to always know when I was sad. She believed in the mysteries of the unknown and was always telling tales.

Remember how we'd always say 'that's impossible, you're lying,' and she'd say, 'No, I'm not! It's a miracle.' And I'd say, 'Yeah, it must be a miracle because I don't believe you.'?"

"That's why it's called a miracle because no one believes it's true," Sten finished for her, and they both smiled at the memory.

"Let's light the lanterns." Kirsten got up and cleared the table.

They found a lighter in a kitchen drawer and headed down to the dock. Kirsten had to hold the lanterns while Sten lighted them. One, two, three, four, five, six, seven, eight, nine, and ten—one for each year of her life. They traded after the first two so they could each have a turn at lighting and letting go. Up, up, and up the lanterns floated. They sat on the end of the dock dangling their feet in the water, willing the moment into perpetuity.

"Oh, look, there's one still." Sten pointed up over the tree line to their left.

Kirsten laid her head on Sten's shoulder, and they sat until the last lantern's tiny flame blinked out.

"Goodnight, Sofie Anne—sending you our love," Kirsten whispered softly.

MIDSUMMER GALA

So, this is where he lives. Kirsten was surprised. The girls had been right, it was a mansion. But how could he afford it? He must come from money, she thought. Merely owning property in this neighborhood was expensive. The house was old and beautiful. To most, it would seem like too much work, but the craftsmanship and woodwork were exquisite. It truly was a work of art. Not gaudy. It needed a lot of TLC but looked like it was starting to resemble its former glory.

Kirsten walked around the downstairs peering into every nook and cranny while he went to make some coffee. She ascended the first part of the staircase and stopped at the window seat on the landing. Surrounded by a bay of leaded glass windows, it was the perfect place to sit and read—she liked that very much.

Kirsten loved looking around old houses and couldn't help proceed upstairs to check out the second level. Protocol may have warned most people otherwise, but she was feeling too adventurous to pay heed. Not quite as impressive, but the second floor was also full of potential. It looked like it was last on the list to be remodeled, as most of the living appeared to be downstairs. Or was it? The door on the far end of the hall was ajar; she carefully pushed it with her forefinger, opening it another couple of inches. It was gorgeous. It had windows about two feet square around two walls of the room with a bit of stained glass in each. The wall to her right had another window seat with windows going up to meet the squares of stained glass. The walls were a heavy cream, almost yellow, with the wood encasing the windows stained the color of mahogany. There was a beautiful chair molding that circled the room level with the base of the windows. Sunlight streamed through the glass, momentarily blinding her when she crossed. It was then she noticed the neatly made bed in the middle, footboard facing her. It wasn't an obviously masculine room, but then she didn't expect that from Brian. It was decorated simply with the utmost taste and lack of pretentiousness she'd come to admire in him.

Wondering what else she would find, she pushed toward what appeared to be a master bathroom off to the left.

Brian entered with two cups of coffee. "I see you found the bedroom."

Kirsten nearly spun around, trying not to act embarrassed at being caught. She walked back to the doorway. "Yes, I hope you don't mind my snooping. I just love old houses. It's beautiful. I guess I got a little carried away." She flashed what she hoped would be a smile and wondered if he found it odd she would be so bold. She didn't want to send him the wrong signals.

"No, not at all. I did tell you to take a look around. Here's your coffee," Brian said, handing her a mug with just the right color from the cream.

"Thanks."

"Well, there's still a lot to be done." He kept talking, but Kirsten wasn't listening.

She suddenly felt self-conscious about standing in his

room, which she hated to admit. What an idiot! Of course, she shouldn't be in here. She genuinely loved the house and was only curious but knew she should have stopped herself. Some women would do that on purpose, and she didn't want him to think of her in that way. She needed to figure out a way to leave as gracefully as possible.

"...so as soon as I get that done, I'll be able to finish the ceiling."

Kirsten smiled as if she'd heard every word with the utmost interest. "Well, let's go back down. I haven't seen the kitchen yet." Kirsten made her way past him and out the door. "Again, I'm sorry for being such a snoop. I'm afraid my curiosity gets the better of me."

"No, that's fine," Brian replied, perhaps a bit awkwardly, Kirsten wasn't sure and inwardly groaned.

They made their way back down to the kitchen, which was a mash-up of super old and somewhat old. It was a big open square with a dining nook tucked into a bay on the outside wall where a round oak table sat with matching oak pioneer-styled chairs. The appliances and most of the cabinets were on the opposite wall with a long island running parallel. The stove looked to be from the fifties but having stayed so long it was back in style. The other matching white appliances were not-so-cool yet. The cupboards had been painted too many times and the remaining taupe was drab. The countertops were a worn white Formica, and the floor remained charming with its small hexagons of white with a coordinated taupe sprinkled across to look like flowers. It was very functional, but Kirsten wouldn't call it pretty. They sat down at the table, and a sleepy-headed guy meandered in from stairs coming into the kitchen from the basement. He was tall and thin and had hair with a wild 'fro. He had a light sprinkling of freckles across his nose and cheekbones and a complexion the color of milk chocolate.

"Good afternoon," Brian said.

"Afternoon? It's not even noon yet," the guy jokingly responded.

"Kirsten, this is my roommate, Derek. Derek, this is Kirsten. She works with me at Dayfield's."

"Hi, nice to meet you," he said, reaching out to shake her hand.

"Hi." Kirsten was glad she'd kept her exploring to the upstairs hall. She hadn't expected roommates, and with a house this big, he might have several.

"You'll have to excuse Derek; I'm afraid he's not much of a morning person."

"Well, I can relate to that," Kirsten replied.

"Really? I thought you were like the army and had a whole day in by noon," Brian teased.

"Ha, very funny. I'm only organized and efficient on the job, so I have more time to relax in the rest of my life."

"Oh, is that why?" Brian's tone signaled he was shutting up now.

Did she say that too sharply? She hoped not. She really was teasing. He hadn't hit a nerve, but Kirsten was anxious to be gone so she could enjoy some much-deserved downtime.

"I really appreciate your working on this over the weekend. I'm afraid Michael is insistent it's changed." Kirsten left her mug on the end of the table and stepped out into the foyer to retrieve her handbag. Upon her return she found Derek on his phone and sipping coffee on the window side opposite where she and Brian sat. She pulled out her laptop, and a file folder made of heavy recycled paper with a letter-pressed label spelling "Important Stuff" in matte black on the front.

"Cool folder," Brian said.

"Thanks." Kirsten wasn't used to guys commenting on the style of her file folders and found it amusing. "Here's the paper we'd like to have it printed on. I wanted you to have some to see because it's kind of dark, but I think it will still work. The printer has it in stock. This is the shot he wants in the ad." She opened up her computer to bring up the image.

"What's that?" Brian asked, seeing her desktop photo.

"Oh? Uhm, that's the gum wall in Seattle."

"Gum wall? That's all gum?"

"Yeah. I know. Sorry, I guess it's a little gross. I don't know why I put it up. I think because it reminded me of home. It's this brick wall in an alley at Pike Place Market, and I don't know how it got started, but people started putting gum on it and, well, as you can see, it has gotten a little out of hand. Last time I was there, they were power washing it off. It's getting in the windowsills and around the doors of these businesses. Kinda crazy."

"Derek, look at this," Brian said, grabbing her laptop and turning it for him to see.

"Wow! That's disgusting. Where is this?" Derek asked.

"Seattle," Brian and Kirsten said in unison.

"When were you there?" Derek asked

"I'm from there. I just moved here a few months ago."

"Really? Why?" Kirsten and Brian laughed.

"What?" Derek asked, looking like he didn't get the joke.

"She moved here for work," Brian explained.

"Oh, okay. Cool," Derek replied, still not sure why his earlier question had been so funny.

Kirsten took her computer back and pulled the artwork up for Brian. "Here it is. Okay, there," she said, turning the screen for Brian to see better. He looked down and scrolled down using the pad with his fingers.

"And he'd like the typeface to look more Gothic than this," Kirsten said, pointing at the screen while he scrutinized the picture, "but still maintain a clean look. This is all in the email I sent, but since I'm here, I wanted to make sure."

"Yeah, no problem, that's what I'm here for. Although he really did want this image originally," Brian said defensively.

"Yeah, I know, I know. But you know how he can be." They exchanged a discerning look. "Well, I have to get going, but if you have any questions, just call or text me. I hate to have to be under such a time crunch, but if you could email it to him by tomorrow morning, that'd be great." Kirsten closed her laptop and stuffed it back in her bag along with her now-empty file folder. "Hopefully, he'll approve it so we can have it ready for the deadline on Monday morning." She stood up to leave, and Brian took the cue to lead her back to the front entrance. "It was nice to meet you, Derek."

"Yeah, nice to meet you too. Hope you find Minneapolis dirty enough for you. We don't like to put gum on our walls here." Kirsten laughed.

"Yeah, it's gonna be an adjustment, that's for sure." She smiled. "But if you start seeing gum show up on the buildings downtown you'll know why." Kirsten playfully put her forefinger against her lips as she followed Brian out of the kitchen.

"Well, thanks for coming by and giving me the paper. It'll make things easier," Brian said, reaching out to shake her hand. It seemed a little awkward to Kirsten, shaking hands after they'd already been working together for a while, but she didn't want him to feel bad, so she took it.

"No, happy to. I'm not that far away, and I was out running errands anyway. Oh, and if you wouldn't mind cc'ing me on the email when you send Michael the proof, I'd be forever grateful," Kirsten added quickly.

"Yeah, sure. No problem."

"Great, thanks, Brian. Again, I really appreciate this, and I hope it doesn't ruin your weekend."

"No, not too much, I guess; no more than yours."

"Well, I guess that's why I make the big bucks." Kirsten gave him a wink and a smile as she reached for the door, but the knob wouldn't engage. It turned but wouldn't open. Brian jumped to her aid. "Hmm, perhaps it's not so nice after all, eh?" she teased.

"Uh, well, Grandma wasn't big on home repair."

Grandma, huh, she smiled at having found out why he had such a house. "There you go"—he pushed and turned the knob, then pulled the door open—"you just have to push in a little while you turn."

"Ah, I'll have to try that next time. Thanks." She headed out the door, then turned back and yelled as she hurried to her car, "Oh, and thanks for the coffee."

She didn't know why she was in such a hurry. Perhaps she was anxious to be done with work on a Saturday morning. Brian must think Michael was working her like a dog, but ironically, it was him who'd be working like a dog. Kirsten sighed and wished she hadn't rushed out of there so fast. Brian and Derek seemed like the kind of friends she'd like to have. They probably have a lot of fun living there, and perhaps the main hangout for their gang of friends.

No sooner had she realized her regret when she heard Brian calling after her. "Hey, Kirsten?"

"Yes." She stopped and turned.

"Say, we're having a little barbecue here this evening. Just my roommates and some friends. You're welcome to join us if you'd like. You know...barring Michael needing more changes, or your first child or something," he said with a teasing twinkle in his eye.

Kirsten laughed at his humor. "Sure, I'd like that. What time?"

"I don't know...around five or six."

"What can I bring?" she asked.

"Um, your favorite side or drink...whatever's easy."

"Okay, thanks. I'll see you then." How serendipitous.

Kirsten was glad she'd come despite the earlier social misstep in Brian's bedroom. It seemed like it had been forever since she'd felt like she had friends to hang out with. Sure, there'd been drinks after work, but so far, no significant connections.

To her relief, Brian was busy barbecuing when she arrived, and Randi and a few other colleagues from Advertising were there along with Derek, whom she'd met earlier. Derek welcomed her over to a small gathering he was conversing with, and she enjoyed being able to laugh and joke with ease.

"I hate to talk shop." Randi sidled up to Kirsten. "But those invitations are going to be ready to go out next week, aren't they?"

"Yes, I promise." She nodded her head in affirmation.

"Good, 'cause it's not just about Couture. It's all of Minneapolis."

"No, I know. Believe me, I know, but I only have so much

power," Kirsten said in her own defense.

"I know." Randi smiled, acknowledging her plight.

"So what's with these invitations?" Derek asked.

"Oh, it's for the Midsummer Gala," Randi answered.

"The what?" Derek asked.

"The Midsummer Gala is an annual fashion show fund-raiser Dayfield's hosts along with other corporate sponsors, and the money is donated to a different charity every year. This year it's Habitat for Humanity," Randi explained.

"Oh, yeah, I think I saw an ad for it on TV. Isn't Cirque de Soleil going to be there or something?"

Kirsten laughed. "No. No Cirque de Soleil, but it will have a bit of that feel with acrobatic dancers, jugglers, and stilt-walkers. The guest designer is Christian Lacroix, who is known for his bright and festive style. My boss is the buyer for Couture and is being a little, well, protective of how the invitations look."

"Or territorial, depending on how you look at it," Randi added.

"Or territorial," Kirsten teased in agreement.

"Ahhh, okay, now I understand the urgency." He feigned belief.

"Yes, it is." Kirsten played into his sarcasm. "So what is it you do to make rent every month, Derek?"

"I bartend."

Kirsten wasn't surprised. "Isn't this a big night for you? Shouldn't you be working?"

"Well, yes, normally I would be, but gotta be here for the big barbecue. Actually, I'm leaving in an hour to do just that."

"And that's why you sleep in so late," Kirsten said.

"Yes, unlike whatever Brian may say," Derek replied, finally able to defend himself.

"He's being modest," Randi said. "He's actually finishing up his last year of law school this fall."

"Law school?" This did surprise Kirsten. "Wow, that's impressive. What kind of law do you want to practice?"

"Intellectual property," he replied.

"Intellectual property? What is that exactly?" Kirsten asked.

"It's like patents, copyrights, anything that is created from the mind," Derek said.

"Hmm, that's very specific. What made you want to do that?" Kirsten asked.

"The internet," he said bluntly.

"The internet made you do it?" Kirsten laughed.

Derek chuckled. "Yeah, the internet made me do it. It captured my mind and is controlling me. Take me to your leader." Derek mimed walking like a zombie robot.

Kirsten and Randi laughed while sipping their beers.

"There is this whole new world where thoughts and ideas are given and shared freely, and a lot more easily, but ultimately greed creeps in when there is money to be made, and the complexities of origination get muddled. I think it's fascinating. The digital age has ushered in a whole new set of problems the old laws couldn't anticipate. It's gotten far more complex and a lot more interesting. I don't think I would pursue this part of the law if it weren't for the internet. The power has been given back to the people instead of some lab in corporate America where they sit on their fat research grants."

"So basically, you like sticking it to the man," Kirsten teased.

"Right on," he said with a swill of his beer.

"It's like when you could start downloading music instead of having to buy CDs, and there was all this copyright infringement. The same thing is going to happen again with 3D technology," said Derek.

"Oh, yeah?" Kirsten said.

"Well, these 3D printers can replicate any object and could become as ubiquitous as ATMs."

"Really?" Kirsten was intrigued. "That blows my mind."

"Right? I know. There is a lot more anonymity than there ever used to be too. You have all these DIY users creating and posting ideas for download, which may or may not have a patent. It makes it difficult to find infringements, and therefore, nearly impossible to prosecute because you don't know who is stealing it. And if it does become popular, internet users can create a stink with what is known as the Streisand Effect."

"Never heard of that." Kirsten was very engrossed by all that Derek was saying.

"It's when someone tries to suppress something, and instead, the act of suppressing it actually publicizes it. It was coined after Barbra Streisand tried to quash photos of her home, and in so doing, only made people more curious about it. It went viral, and the media got ahold of it," Derek said.

"I can't believe I've never heard of that. I'm just a user when it comes to technology, I guess."

Brian joined the group and proceeded to open his bottle of beer with the bottom of his flip-flop.

"Nice." Randi laughed.

"You like that? I just got these, and I swear I didn't know it at the time, but they happen to have this handy little bottle opener built in."

"And you've been waiting to show them off, haven't you?"

Randi teased.

"Well, yeah, of course." Brian chuckled.

Kirsten shook her head and laughed. "That is such a guy thing."

"I think it's pretty awesome. I want a pair for work, but I don't think anyone would notice since I'm behind a high counter," said Derek.

"Yeah, they'd probably start to wonder what you were doing down there all the time." Randi's eyes glistened.

"Ha ha," Derek said when he caught Randi's meaning.

"So did you get my email with the artwork?" Brian looked at Kirsten.

"Yeah, that was fast. Thanks. But you didn't send it to Michael?" Kirsten questioned.

"I know. I want him to sweat a little longer. Don't want him to think it's okay to keep changing everything at the last minute," Brian quipped mischievously and took a sip of his beer.

"Well, I already forwarded it to him. Sorry."

"No, that's fine. I figured you would."

"A little passive-aggressive, are we?" Kirsten teased.

"Maybe just when it comes to Michael," Brian confessed.

"Yeah, if he's not careful, we're going to lose Brian sooner than later," said Randi.

"What!? You're leaving?" Kirsten asked.

"No, no, it's way too soon. I've only been here barely a year." Brian gave Randi the evil eye.

"But you are planning to, it sounds like?" Kirsten pressed.

"Well, sure, at some point. I want to work at an agency."

Kirsten scrunched her face up in a confused look, so Randi explained. "Most young creatives like Brian move on to a design firm once they get some experience under their belt."

"Oh?" Kirsten still didn't understand why he'd want to leave what seemed like a great job to her but was unable to probe for a better answer as a crowd had formed behind them and was getting louder.

"Chrissy! Chrissy!" and "Tia! Tia!" were being simultaneously yelled at two girls racing to drink their beers first while people made bets. When Chrissy won, cheers went up from all the winners and then Tia barfed all over the grass, which is exactly what Kirsten thought she'd do if it were her.

Are we still doing this in our late twenties? Kirsten wondered. She'd always felt like she was waiting for her peers to grow up and stop engaging in what she considered stupid behavior. She'd never been a big drinker, nor did she understand why people felt the need to be so uninhibited. She didn't dare voice her feelings on the subject for fear of being laughed at. Somehow she'd missed that part of being young.

As Chrissy made her congratulatory rounds, Derek and Brian gave her a specially choreographed handshake only they seemed to know—signaling there was a long-held bond between them. Kirsten found herself standing alone as everyone at the barbecue converged into one large group of old long-time friends laughing and talking their own language. She had met so many new people in the last four months she didn't have the desire to meet any more, and yet here she was—alone again.

How long until she felt like she belonged?

The memory of the barbecue faded over the next several weeks while Kirsten worked tirelessly on the Midsummer Gala. It seemed to default mostly to Designer/Couture since it was their department bringing the celebrity designer. There was a brief moment of panic when Lacroix nearly bailed at the last minute, but Michael worked his charm, even though he loathed working on the event. He liked to stay in his protective bubble. It wasn't ego that drove him, but the safety of staying within the realm he loved and understood. He was talented and persuasive when he needed to be and therefore easily got what he wanted. What he didn't like was having to pander to executives and CEOs outside the world of Designer/Couture. That he left to Kirsten, with which she happily complied. She felt the need to act as Michael's personal buffer. It was no secret how important this event was to Dayfield's board members and executives, and Kirsten found herself in the role of ambassador as she made sure every VIP in Minneapolis knew they were the most important. 'Yes, you can have six tickets instead of four. You are definitely invited to the private cocktail party with Lacroix. I'm so glad you're coming.' These were the promises she handed out at a rapid pace as the event drew closer.

She didn't know why it didn't bother her more that she did this for Michael. Lillian would be disappointed because she knew they'd rather have the cachet of talking to him instead of his lowly associate. Kirsten felt like she understood him in a way most people didn't and could see, even though he'd be unable to say it; Michael secretly appreciated her ability to see him as he truly was and was thankful she did not pass judgment. He was softening toward her, and she liked that.

Kirsten felt immense pressure to look designer stunning for the gala, but even with a hefty Dayfield's discount, she couldn't afford her own Couture. She vacillated on what to wear months before the event and finally came up with what she thought was a brilliant solution. She remembered the beautiful green *Atonement* dress one of her classmates in school had made for their Showcase, which Kirsten had modeled. All the girls in her class had loved the movie *Atonement* and ogled over the flowy emerald-green 1930's styled dress the lead, Keira Knightley, wore. Kirsten contacted Lisbeth, the girl who had made it, and asked if she could borrow it. "Sure. It just sits in my closet collecting dust. It's gorgeous on you. In fact, you should just have it. It's not like I'll ever wear it." Kirsten detected a bit of wistfulness in her tone while children whined in the background. Kirsten felt bad and remembered Lisbeth had married right after they'd graduated and turned down an opportunity to intern at Warner Brothers in their costume department. She was really talented, and Kirsten felt her pain.

"Lisbeth! I can't do that. You must always hold on to it. It's the reason why you won The Showcase. I will definitely return it, well pressed and laundered."

"Thanks, Kirsten. I know you'll take good care of it. At least get a photo with Lacroix and you in it for me."

"I will for sure," she promised.

Kirsten stood in front of her floor-length mirror wondering if she'd made the right choice as the lightweight silk swished around her delicate silver Mary Jane pumps. It was indeed stunning on her and a lot more revealing than she remembered with its spaghetti straps coming up the sides of the backless dress and over her shoulders into a V-shaped, slightly blousy bodice, the cool emerald-green further illuminating her creamy white skin. They'd been just a bunch of girls with a dreamy-eyed love for British romance. This was going to be a room full of colleagues and Minneapolis VIPs. Perhaps she'd overdone it. She didn't like to attract inappropriate attention. This was not any party, but a work party she'd helped organize. Maybe she should've picked a simple black cocktail dress. But this was a black-tie affair. Girls all throughout the office had been planning what they'd wear for months as if it were prom. She'd even carefully picked a backless bra instead of the crisscross tape job they'd done across her breasts in college, which had caused a painful red rash for weeks after. She wore various kinds of backless bras around her apartment on the weekends preceding the event to make sure it was comfortable and she would feel confident it would stay in place. She wasn't as flat as the lovely Keira Knightley.

She took a few more turns in front of the mirror and made sure the faux sash that came around the hipline of the dress was knotted securely in front. She'd had to do a little repair upon its arrival as the sewn-on knot was coming loose. It dropped elegantly down, mimicking the neckline above, and deftly covered the slit up the middle of the skirt. The dress was fitted through the hips and wrapped in the back by a series of dainty asymmetrical pleats. The bias-cut skirt flowed out from there, with a slight train behind. Kirsten twirled gleefully like a little girl and watched the fabric dance like dandelions in the wind. It was too fun and what else was she going to wear at this late hour? She looked squarely in the mirror one last time to cement her decision, grabbed her clutch, and met her Uber.

She needed to arrive early and hang out at the guest relations table in case there were any hiccups with the VIPs. Across from Christine's on the top floor was a large ballroom from a past generation. Dayfield's rented it out for special events and occasionally for their own. It was aptly named The Mallard Room. Like most ballrooms, it was a big rectangle. The floor was a classic parquet pattern. A stage was set with a catwalk teeing out of it on the far end. Successive rows of gold-painted Chiavari chairs, the kind you see at fancy weddings, filled both sides of the catwalk. VIPs had the best seats in the front row, which were reserved via six-by-nine white cards sitting faceup on the chairs, their name or company printed in matching gold. The rest of the seating was open. Tall table rounds were to the left of the entrance with a two-drink minimum bar in the corner behind. Wait staff from Christine's wandered around with trays of appetizers. Aerial dancers performed above the stage set with rock band instruments. The lighting was dark and moody, providing a neutral backdrop for the dancers as they moved above with their brightly colored swaths of silk in hot pink, yellow, and apple green. Guests seemed to be enjoying the scene as the dancers appeared to precariously fall and barely miss the instruments below. To further enhance the carnival feel, performers were walking around on stilts, jugglers juggled, and more aerial dancers twisted and turned along the edge of the room.

Kirsten stood quietly behind her colleagues, mainly Aric, who was taking tickets and welcoming guests. She was relieved it was going well so she could relax and enjoy the atmosphere. Michael finally arrived and nodded a hello to Kirsten as he passed. She didn't want to shrug her responsibilities and risk upsetting Aric, but it did seem a little silly for her to be standing there doing nothing, and she really wanted to mingle a bit and find Michael. She bent down and whispered to Aric, "Looks like it's going well. Is it all right if I leave you? You can always text me if you need me."

"Yeah, no. I'm fine." Aric seemed to come alive in this environment and was slightly annoyed to have to stop and listen to her question. He commanded the table with a professional authority and didn't appreciate having to momentarily give up his stage. It amused Kirsten as it gave her permission to go. She grabbed a couple of mini-shrimp kabobs and a glass of prosecco. She knew she'd need to down some protein to get through the evening, despite having pre-eaten as a precaution. She nearly ran into a pair of stilts and let out a laugh, which no one could hear under the cover of the music and chatter. She was beginning to wonder if she'd be able to find Michael when he suddenly appeared behind a walking juggler. He was talking to a small group of VIPs. Kirsten caught his eye briefly, which indicated he was drowning in small-talk and looking for an exit. Kirsten swooped in to save him. "There you are," she said.

"Yes. I was wondering where you were." Michael turned back to introduce Kirsten. "This is my Associate, Kirsten. This is Juliet and Arnav."

"Yes, hello. Juliet and Arnav Das, right?" Kirsten reached out to shake their hands.

"Yes," they returned.

"It's so nice to meet you in person," Juliet finished.

"I'm so glad you were able to come," said Kirsten.

"Yes, so are we. Thank you for switching the tickets for us," Juliet said.

"No problem." Kirsten's eyes glanced toward a middle-aged gentleman filling out their circle, who seemed a bit out of place with his ill-fitting tux. His girth was too much for his shorter stature, and the button on his jacket seemed about to burst from the pressure. No one seemed in a hurry to introduce him, which Kirsten wasn't sure if she should think was odd. But before the silence became too long, a very handsome gentleman came from behind and sidled up to Michael.

"Good evening, Mr. Warner."

"Greg! How are you, man?" Michael said, giving him a manly hug and pat on the back.

"Good. Yeah. Just got back from Colorado. Wish you could've been there."

"Yeah?" Michael asked. "Next time. Next time."

A beautiful woman in a red gown was not far behind and stood next to Greg, who said, "You remember Valerie?"

"Yes, of course. Good to see you again." Michael said, reaching out his hand.

"Hello," Valerie said. "Thanks for getting us tickets. I love Lacroix."

"Sure. Anything for Greg." Kirsten's mind started to piece them together as she recalled Michael making sure she had tickets for a Greg Vohs and a Valerie Moschetti. The Vohs family owned some oil refinery in the state, which Kirsten surmised must make a lot of money. Michael wasn't introducing them, leaving Greg to do it himself.

"Hi," he said, reaching his hand out to Kirsten.

"Hi. Kirsten."

"Yes. This is my new Associate," Michael finally jumped in to finish.

"New Associate? What happened to Nicole?" Greg asked.

"She got promoted."

"Oh. I didn't know. I just saw her a few minutes ago. She didn't say anything."

Greg glanced at Michael in concerted surprise, making Kirsten feel a bit self-conscious and her bare back all the more vulnerable.

"Your dress is just gorgeous. Who designed it?" asked a wise Valerie, changing the subject.

"Thank you. It's actually a copy." Kirsten thought she'd sound too young if she said it was from school and wasn't sure why she felt the need to cover it up.

"A copy of whose?" Valerie continued.

"Uhm, of a costume designer, actually. It's from the movie *Atonement*."

"Really? Ohh, that dress! That was quite a scene, wasn't it?" Valerie said with unthinking amusement, and Kirsten nearly blushed. *Please, tell me no one here has seen that movie, most of all Michael!*

Fortuitously, Lillian interrupted, changing the subject. "Hello, there you two are. I'm sorry, but I need to borrow these two. Oh, Bob, I'm so glad you came," she said, acknowledging the man in the ill-fitting tux and kissing him like the French, on both cheeks.

"I wouldn't miss it, Lillian. It's fabulous as always."

"Good. Good. Glad you're enjoying yourself. And Arnav and Juliet. Lovely to see you."

"Thank you, Lillian," Juliet said.

"Hello, Lillian," Greg said

"Ah, Greg, Michael's partner in crime," she said, wagging a finger before giving him a kiss on the cheek. "Okay, now we must go," she said, as an obedient Kirsten immediately fell in line behind her and a reluctant Michael followed suit. "Kirsten?" she said, turning her head back. "I need you to do me a favor and check and make sure the Carmichaels are not next to the Emisons. I don't care where you put the Carmichaels, just not near them."

"Sure. I'm on it," Kirsten said as she turned to leave. She couldn't remember where she'd put the Carmichaels but did remember where the Emisons were and didn't see Carmichael anywhere near them, assuring herself all was well before she conveyed this back to Lillian.

Kirsten found them easily enough in another circle of VIPs. She quietly approached and nodded to Lillian with a smile of confirmation. Lillian was a striking woman who looked exotic with her radiant olive skin and eyes like onyx. Her hair was upswept in a French knot, and the deepening silver only enhanced the beauty of her complexion. She was tall for a woman, about five feet, eight inches, and slender. She was the kind of woman who wore Carolina Herrera well, demonstrating the elegant sophistication of gowns inveterate to the first ladies of America.

Michael made room for Kirsten and introduced her as his new Associate. His hand lightly brushed her lower back as he brought her forward for the introduction. It felt accidental until he whispered, "*Atonement*, huh?" as his eye darted out the corner and down her back. Kirsten's skin prickled into an amalgam of fear, shame, and excitement. She looked up and saw Lillian take it all in. Her eyes darkened into a black hole. Kirsten was mortified and did her best to convince Lillian she was the model Associate by conversing with all the VIPs like the good little professional she was. It really was the *Atonement* dress. However, she soon realized Lillian hadn't been disapproving of her, but of Michael. She noticed Lillian quietly communicating to Michael like a stern mother to behave. Was Lillian worried she'd be another Nicole? Kirsten was determined more than ever to learn the story.

Someone who looked familiar, but no, maybe not, was coming toward them. As the figure drew closer, Kirsten felt strange. Her heart began to pound, and she started to feel simultaneously sick and excited. *What is wrong with me?* She began to panic.

Whoever he was, she couldn't take her eyes off him, and she hated feeling so vulnerable.

What the—? It's Brian! Brian? This is Brian? Hello, what's going on? He was wearing a suit and tie and looked unbelievably handsome.

This is ridiculous! she exclaimed inside. It's Brian she said to assure herself.

She had to say something because their eyes met, but she found herself at a loss. She was afraid he could read her thoughts. Terrified, she looked sharply away.

His shoulders immediately fell, and he quickly aborted.

Kirsten was horrified at her behavior. *What have I done?* She quickly whispered "Hi," trying to undo it, but it was too late. *What must he think? How am I going to explain,* she wondered.

She looked around to see if anyone had noticed her indiscretion, but no one seemed to—not even Michael. Thank God! She slowly regained her composure, pretending to be intently listening and laughing at the right moments while her thoughts raced.

"Was that Brian who just went by?" Michael whispered in her ear.

"Umm, yeah, I think it was," Kirsten replied casually.

"We should've nabbed him. He probably would've liked to have met some of these people," he said.

"Oh, yeah, you're right, he would've." Kirsten's voice trailed off as the knife of regret twisted further into her gut. It was even worse than she'd thought, he wasn't approaching her for personal reasons, he was coming to schmooze and her staring at him must've seemed like an engraved invitation.

The rest of the evening took on a dreamlike state; she watched herself as if from a seat in the back of the room. During a few carefully chosen moments, she tried to see where Brian was; refusing to contemplate her sudden attraction, she decided to figure out how to reverse her unforgivable behavior.

It wasn't until after the show when people were milling around she spotted him in the back with his advertising buddies. She came up with a scheme to meander by and offhandedly engage him in conversation, taking every opportunity to make eye contact with him and compliment him on the program. She would atone for her meanness by being incredibly kind and thoughtful. He'd have no choice but to assume he'd misunderstood.

As she headed toward him, Michael foiled her plan by greeting Brian first. She smiled inwardly. She too preferred to hang with creative types rather than heads of corporations. This probably felt like the only safe place at the event for Michael. As she got closer, it didn't seem appropriate to crash their happy banter, so she diverted to nearby Chelsea and Amanda and feigned interest in talking to them. They were a little surprised, but Kirsten adeptly mollified them while keeping her ear sharply tuned to Brian and Michael. It seemed to take forever, but eventually more people congregated around them, widening the circle of chatter.

Brian was receiving a lot of compliments on the program, providing Kirsten with the right moment to deploy her plan. "Yeah, Brian, I was just telling Michael earlier how great everything looks. Thank you for all your hard work." She looked directly into his eyes with all the sincerity and softness she could muster.

He paused, convincing Kirsten she'd worried needlessly, but then he dismissed her compliment and looked away. "Thanks, guys."

Nothing. He gave her nothing. He was Switzerland.

Ack! She wanted to scream.

She hung around for a while after Michael left, waiting for another occasion to talk to Brian, but it never came. Some started suggesting going for drinks, but Brian showed no sign of joining them, and there was no other reason for her to stay. Perhaps she'd have better luck tomorrow. She left in resignation, saying her goodbyes and looking at Brian one last time in hopes of eliciting a response.

He didn't reciprocate.

"Great," Kirsten muttered under her breath as she headed down the corridor to the elevator.

The next day at the office, things were more quiet than usual. Everyone was recuperating from the night before, Kirsten surmised. She was thankful for the lax atmosphere as it was impossible to focus. She opted for more mindless tasks and was glad Michael must've felt the same, as indicated by his showing up at 10:30.

Unfortunately, there was no advertising needing immediate attention, and Kirsten so wanted a reason to go up to the ninth floor. Her anxiety increased as her mind couldn't stop being on auto-replay.

She kept seeing Brian recalibrating his course and turning away at the last moment. She shuddered at the memory of his shoulders dropping while he tried to pretend nothing had happened.

Was that real? She asked herself. Am I attracted to Brian? What if I am? I don't know; it's all so weird. I've never even thought of him in that way. Why would I, all of a sudden, change how I feel? It was that damn suit!

Kirsten was a sucker for a man in a suit. Nobody her age wore suits unless for a wedding, and not always even then. If he really looked that good—good enough to affect her this much—then it was just lust, not necessarily a sign of a love potential. Her mind started to spin, and she didn't know how to make it stop. Her desire to go up to the ninth floor would not abate. She needed to know if what she had felt for Brian was real or imagined, never mind seeing if he was still mad at her.

Kirsten began pawing at her desk looking for anything she could use as an excuse. Nothing.

Well, I could just go up there and act like I have a purpose, then by chance maybe run into him. If I get stuck, I'll fake it. I'll pretend I left something in the proof room and was coming up to find it. Feeling triumphant, she headed up the escalator to the ad department.

As she walked down the hall an even quieter hush permeated the floor than down in buying. Fewer people were hard at work than down in the buying office. Maybe they were all taking a late lunch after their late arrivals or, probably more accurately, didn't come in at all.

Kirsten had nearly entered the proof room when she ran into Sara, the production assistant. "Hey, Kirsten, I was just about to email you. I've been cleaning out some old files and found some stuff that you might want for your records."

The proof room was where print media was viewed by all parties involved in the piece. For example, if there was a mailer involving several departments, an email would be sent out when the proof was ready, and everyone had a window within which to view and comment and make sure the copy was correct as well as the color and content of the photography. This proof was the master and was used in producing the final when it went to press.

"Oh, okay. I'll swing by on my way out and take a look," Kirsten replied. Sara's desk was all the way in the back, past Brian's. She now had the perfect excuse to run into him.

Kirsten turned into the proof room and made a quick sweep so she could "find" what she was looking for, then came right back out and headed straight for Sara's cubicle. As she neared Brian's space, she could see he wasn't there. Kirsten was annoyed but continued on to Sara's office.

"Where is everybody?" she said, poking her head into Sara's cubicle. Kirsten noticed how neat and tidy it was. The one person in the ad office who was paid to be a grown-up.

"Where else?" Sara smiled. "Sleeping off last night. I guess it's the price you pay for being artistic."

"Randi doesn't mind?"

"No, she's gone too," Sara said without looking up from the files she was organizing.

Kirsten bravely pressed further. "Even Brian? He doesn't seem like the type."

"Oh, he's on vacation for the next couple weeks." Sara stopped and looked up to explain.

"Oh, that's right. I forgot." Kirsten nearly kicked herself as she recalled something about canoeing the Boundary Waters with friends.

Sara handed Kirsten the file of artwork. She took it and returned to her office, frustrated she wasn't going to get any answers anytime soon. Aaaa! She screamed silently to herself and called it a day, to which not even Aric seemed to mind. She chose to drown herself in a chick-flick and her favorite ice cream.

She spent the next two weeks obsessing over Brian. She checked out his Facebook page, trying to get to know him a little better. She went over every meeting, look, and exchange of any form between them over the last four months. She drove by his house looking for a sign he might be back, unsure if she'd have the courage to knock on his door should he be there. What would she say? She knew she couldn't do it. It would seem strange and inappropriate. At moments, she convinced herself it hadn't happened and she'd imagined the whole thing. He'd come back and all would go back to normal.

But what if it doesn't? What if? What if? What if he hates me? She couldn't bear the thought. She was driving herself crazy with her newfound feelings and the fear that came with them. She ran more often around the Lake of the Isles, knowing he liked to run there too. Knowing how ridiculous she was to even hope to see him. But no, she yelled at herself, I don't need to see him, I need to exorcize him. Instead, she kept improving her run time. Maybe I should finally enter myself in a marathon, she joked to herself.

She knew not even a marathon would wash it away. She felt his presence everywhere and in ways she'd never noticed before. She recalled exchanges between them that at the time seemed insignificant, but now she deemed them all important. Those memories were all she had to keep her company as she ticked the days off until his return.

She remembered a moment she'd had with him early on and had forgotten. It was during her lunch hour workout down at the Y, back when she'd first started at Dayfield's. She'd been stretching near the entrance when Brian walked in. He was across the room, too far to talk, so instead of waving hello or nodding to each other, it was more like they sensed each other as if in a dream. Their eyes met briefly, but there was no acknowledgment. It was strangely intimate.

That wasn't the only odd interchange at the Y that day. Later, when she was lifting weights, she'd thought she saw her old boyfriend, Kevin, from Seattle, which was absurd. Like a reflex, she'd walked toward him and then stopped when she realized it wasn't him. Maybe she'd been attracted to Brian all along, but only now was becoming aware of it.

How had she forgotten this? Is it possible to be in love with someone and not even know it? Was her brain having a delayed reaction?

It was finally the Tuesday of Brian's return, and she found it nearly impossible to contain her anxiety. She felt like she was twelve and looking forward to going to school to see her new crush. Tuesday, however, came and went without incident, which only made her more restless. She made excuses like she shouldn't have expected to see him on his first day back from being gone so long. The first day back is always busy. But why hadn't she at least passed him briefly in the building?

By Wednesday afternoon, she tried to accept she might never resolve what had happened and eventually she'd get over it. She'd lived through enough of life's uncomfortable and awkward moments to know this too would pass. She let out a little laugh at her silliness while riding the escalators back up from a late lunch. She would be okay, and in time Brian would become one of those awkward, private teenage-like crushes.

Standing taller, she looked up, only to have her legs nearly give out. Her heart caught in her throat. Brian, texting on his phone, was coming down the escalators. They were about to pass each other. She tried to switch gears. "Brian! Hey."

He didn't respond.

Kirsten felt stupid and hoped no one noticed. Maybe he was too absorbed in his phone? Regardless, it wasn't definitive enough to make a judgment of his attitude toward her. It was maddening and her illusion of peace fell away.

The next few days were crazy busy as Michael asked her if she would go with him to New York for Fashion Week—the unveiling of the spring collections. What an opportunity! She was thrilled and relieved to have a distraction and worked frantically to get everything in order before they left. It quickly became apparent nothing could distract her. Her thoughts constantly wandered toward Brian. He lurked incessantly in the shadows of her mind.

It didn't help she had to work with him, either. She needed to get the fall trunk show ads finalized before she left. He'd mostly been communicating with her via email or text, which wasn't unusual in their busy working relationship, but Kirsten couldn't help being a wee bit suspicious. Either she was having incredibly lousy luck reaching him over the phone and in person, or it was more than a coincidence.

Up until now, she hadn't paid attention to how often she saw Brian or had face-to-face contact with him. She had no gauge by which to measure. The evidence was mounting though; he was avoiding her. Even the tone of his emails and texts were more business-like and less, well, flirty. *Flirty? Had they been flirty?* They used to be fun with a few clever puns sprinkled in them, but now those were gone. It was like their correspondence had been neutered.

While diligently working at her computer, she weighed his

behavior and remembered the gym. She almost exclaimed out loud, "That's where I can find Brian!" Pacing her office, she checked the time on her phone and tried to remember when he usually went to lunch. It was one o'clock, but she had no idea when he went. She decided he could still be there. It was not too late. Standing on the down escalator, she willed it to go faster and watched anxiously as the Skyway entrance came into view. As she left Dayfield's, she couldn't believe her luck when she spotted Brian at the other end of the Skyway, gym bag in hand, walking toward her. When he got closer, she noticed his jaw clinch firmly and his gaze lock straight ahead. Walking past, she said, "Hey!"

Nothing. He didn't even look at her.

He's mad at me. He's mad at me! The little jerk! What, are we seventeen? Even if I did deserve it—couldn't he show a little maturity and at least try to find out why I treated him that way? Can't he see I'm trying to make it right? Kirsten feared she was never going to be able to make it right. *What does he think? We still have to work together.* She decided it was a good thing she was leaving town. Maybe he needed time to cool off. This week was almost over, so by the time she got back it'd be nearly a month since the incident—like time healed all wounds.

NEW YORK

New York was even stickier than Minneapolis. The remnants of summer still hung in the air—something she couldn't get used to, having lived in the arid West. The hotel was very Michael. It was masculine chic; modern in its choice of simple clean shapes finished with cowhides and leather to accent the walls and furnishings. It was as if the designer had spent some time on a cattle ranch in Texas but opted for a subtler form.

The lighting was dark with soft wall sconces and oil-burning votives in burnished bronze bowls centered precisely on matching bronze coffee tables. There was something quiet and illicit about the space despite the low drone of people enjoying their happy hour libations. It made her a little uncomfortable. Small groups of two or three talked in soft tones with the occasional single using their various devices while sipping hard liquor in bar glasses that wouldn't quite clink as anticipated on the worn metal tables. Everything about it seemed designed to muffle the sound of the city. Even the front doors were solid, heavy wood with no windows. Roman columns flanked the entryway like a piece of the past that should have been artistically done away with but was instead kept for nostalgia. It was a well-orchestrated symphony of fashion perfection.

She felt a little out of place. *Stepford Fashionistas,* she coined. East Coast fashion was always a bit more gilded with heavy gold metal and silver accents on the wrists and bags. She preferred her fashion to be less formal, like Martin Margiela, whose style had forged the term Deconstructivist.

Kirsten was finally able to wade through the happy hour crowd to reach the registration desk and check-in. She took the elevator up to her room and instead of the same masculine browns from downstairs, she was happily greeted by cool blues and grays. A calm washed over her. She dropped everything on the floor and flopped onto the plush white bed. "Okay, now, I can do this," she said. *I will have this slice of refuge.* She turned her head toward the soft light filtered by an organza curtain, took a deep breath and exhaled slowly while closing her eyes. *Just a few minutes.*

An hour later, she awoke with a start. Apparently, she'd been more tired than she'd realized. The clock on the nightstand read six-thirty-seven. Kirsten had to meet Michael at seven-thirty, leaving only enough time to get settled and freshen up—so much for her planned walking excursion. She'd wanted to walk the city blocks and see some of her favorite haunts, but it would have to wait.

Kirsten tried not to look wide-eyed and juvenile when she came into the lobby to meet him, but knew Michael was somewhat amused by her slight naivety. She tried to disguise her inexperience, but it was useless against Michael's ten-plus years on her it. She was thankful he had decided not to hold it against her. He chose a casual brewpub, which was not what she'd expected, but it offered a breezy coolness to the heat of the day. She'd had visions of something more trendy but felt it was best not to notice. Somehow, she knew anything more would've been too much.

"I'll have the mushroom burger with a salad instead of fries and a Hefeweizen, please." Kirsten watched Michael's face while rattling off her order. "What? Am I supposed to order the Cobb salad or perhaps a chicken Caesar and a glass of chardonnay?" she playfully responded to Michael's quizzical look.

"No." He laughed and fidgeted with the silverware. "You really aren't like, um…"

"Um what?"

"Most assistants," he said with certainty to close the subject.

Kirsten knew he meant like most women who work in Designer Couture.

"Well, this is a brewpub and you did hire me."

"I know, but what's with the Hefe-a-what?"

"Oh, Michael." She playfully rolled her eyes. "I hate to say it, but you really are from Minnesota, aren't you? Ever been to the Northwest?"

"No."

"Well, if you had, you'd understand the Hefeweizen. You know it's not like Minneapolis doesn't have brewpubs. I'm sure most Minnesotans know what a Hefeweizen is."

"Okay, I'll take your word for it," he said, admitting defeat.

Kirsten looked at him with distrust. "You don't like beer, do you?" she said, realizing why he'd ordered a whiskey.

"No. I mostly like hard liquor." Kirsten didn't know what to make of that. She thought it was strange someone would only enjoy hard liquor.

"Really? Not even wine?" she asked.

"No. I'll drink red wine when I'm at a nice restaurant where there's good wine." Interesting, Kirsten thought. Sounded more like he drank wine because protocol demanded it, not because he liked it.

Silence fell between them and Kirsten, not knowing what to do, looked about the room. She wondered if she'd thrown him a bit. Had she been too familiar with him? Did she shake his reserved Midwestern ways? She didn't mean to. Was an attraction developing? She didn't think so and didn't want it to be. Kirsten liked him as a colleague and mentor, maybe somewhat like a big brother, but nothing else. She decided this was the moment that always seemed to happen in new relationships. The point where assumptions start to give way to truth. The surface gets a little scratched and first impressions go out the window; you adjust your thinking and wonder what else you were wrong about.

The waiter broke their lull in conversation and sloshed her beer on the highly varnished table. He quickly apologized by setting down some bar napkins to mop up the mess and carefully placed Michael's whiskey in front of him as neatly as he'd ordered it. Kirsten wiped down her glass.

"There's a lemon in your beer?" Michael said.

"Are you teasing me again?" Kirsten wasn't sure if he was serious.

"No. Why? Is there supposed to be?"

"Yes." Kirsten fished out the lemon with her fork and squeezed its juice into her beer. "Here, try it," she said, holding it out to him.

Michael relented, not wanting to be further harassed over his apparent lack of beer knowledge, and made a face as he sipped from the frosty mug.

"Still don't like beer, huh?"

"No." He smiled this time.

"It's a little effervescent, but that's why I love it. It's perfect on warm days like this. Very refreshing. I tend to like the extremes. In winter, I switch to Guinness, but only Guinness. I've tried other dark beers, but so far nothing is as good. Well, I take that back. Once I came close when I was visiting a little Danish-style town on the coast of California."

"Do you not like wine?" Michael seemed almost concerned.

"No, I do. I love wine too, just not chardonnays—too oaky. While we're on the subject, I also like vodka. See, you're not the only one who likes hard liquor." He laughed at her effort. "That's about it. I do like a good cosmo. See, now, that is very girly. Does that fit better?"

A faint tremor went through her like a warning, and she pulled the conversation back to more pertinent matters.

"So…you said things were going well. What have been some of your favorite lines?"

"I don't know. I tend to like the Italian designers best," Michael said.

"Yeah, I know what you mean. They're more understated. Simplistically ingenious." Kirsten said.

"But, of course, that's not what we're here for," he said, while pushing the side of his chair out from the table to face it diagonally and crossing his legs. He flicked a small thread off the elevated knee of his impeccably tailored suit pant.

Michael was like Richard Gere to her, his mysterious darkness fracturing his otherwise perfect exterior. His beautiful dark hair could become unruly from its slightly wavy texture and his dark eyes were piercing.

Kirsten thought about her mother and pondered the incongruous relationship between the attraction of darkness and perfection. Her mother loved Richard Gere, which was why

Kirsten had seen a lot more of his movies than most of her peers, not that she wanted anyone to know this about her. But she felt Richard's persona was helpful in dissecting Michael.

She wanted to compare Michael to her contemporaries and would sometimes land on describing him as a hipster, but it didn't quite fit. There was something older in him, even older than his own generation. She wasn't sure he came from money, but she had a sneaking suspicion he did. Old quiet upper Midwestern money. It was the glove he'd been born into, and he didn't know there was any other way to be.

The conversation was becoming stilted, and not knowing what else to say, Kirsten moved to business. "Anything I should know for tomorrow? I mean, I mapped everything out and created our schedule. Did you get a chance to see Lillian's latest budget with a slight decrease?"

"Yes." Michael uncrossed his legs and moved them back under the table at seeing the waiter bringing their food.

She hadn't wanted to make him retreat, but somehow felt she'd discouraged any further conversation. She'd learned quickly he didn't explain much and frequently pivoted from open to closed.

Disappointed, she was glad the food arrived, making it more difficult to talk. The meal took on more of a business tone, and Michael let an incoming text distract him. "Sorry, I've been trying to get ahold of this person."

"No problem." Michael asked for the check before they'd finished and got it signed precisely at the close of the meal. He said goodnight out front and hailed a cab. Kirsten stood on the sidewalk, looking lost and wondering who Michael was off to see. She finally turned and walked aimlessly down the street in the direction of the hotel. Spying a little bodega, she went inside and got some staples for breakfast.

The evening had cooled to the perfect temperature, beckoning Kirsten to stay out. She Googled "gourmet ice cream" and serendipitously found herself in a most charming gelato shop.

The next morning, Michael met her in the lobby right at 8:45. Their hotel was near the Garment District, which ran from Thirty-Fourth to about Forty-Third between Fifth and Eighth Avenues, making it easy to walk to their first appointment. The vendor's offices were much nicer than working in Junior's, but still more utilitarian than you would expect for designer wear—as always, the focus was on the clothing. People were everywhere as buyers met with sales reps and rolling racks of samples were moved to and fro. Michael seemed to be well-liked by everyone, but then buyers are usually well-liked by sales reps. Kirsten kept silent and only spoke when spoken to. Michael never wrote anything down, so she made a point of making notes in the Lookbook about what he seemed to like; for her own amusement, she marked what she would buy.

The day flowed at a quick pace, and they had to forgo lunch because Ralph Lauren moved up their appointment. They finished their day at Tory Burch. It was all very classic American.

Exiting the coolness of an air-conditioned building for the final time that day made the hot afternoon hit Kirsten like a steam shower. Michael waved a cab over and they climbed in. The cab wasn't much better. Its windows were rolled down in lieu of air conditioning, signaling its age. She was surprised cabs without air-conditioning still existed. The turban-wearing driver seemed indifferent, which confounded Kirsten because the last thing she wanted in this heat was anything on her head. Michael loosened the knot in his tie but otherwise showed no acknowledgment of the heat.

She looked at the cabbie and wondered where he was from, feeling self-conscious in her above-the-knee dress and heels. He could be from Pakistan or India, she thought, but not all women in those countries wore burkas. Yet she couldn't help wondering if he looked down on her for her immodesty. Perhaps he was a chemical engineer or in some other highly educated field, and this was the only job he could get in America. She didn't want to assume he was happy enough just to be in America, or maybe he was a terrorist? Being in New York, one couldn't help but let those thoughts lurk in the back of the mind. Ridiculous, she chided herself. She didn't want to be guilty of prejudice and felt the need to show extra kindness to prove not all Americans were self-absorbed capitalist pigs. Like that was her job?

Really, Kirsten, what are you, the American Ambassador for equality? Well, America is the flagship of freedom, is it not? Maybe he escaped a life of oppression and/or poverty, like her ancestors had. She smiled at her ridiculous thoughts and wished more than anything she could spread her legs open to vent more air under her clothes, but that *would* be immodest.

***

"What?" Michael asked bemusedly at seeing her smile.

"Nothing," Kirsten said with a shake of her head at being caught.

They turned their heads toward their respective windows, viewing the loud, irritating traffic.

Michael turned back and watched Kirsten, wondering what she was thinking. He'd had many assistants throughout his career and only recently had learned the hard way to keep clear lines between personal and business relationships. Lillian felt the need to help Michael keep within these lines, which he found aggravating.

He'd finally caved at her insistence and hired Kirsten, despite his misgivings. She was too vulnerable for the likes of him, or so he'd thought. Actually, he could never decide, which was another reason why he'd relented to Lillian's advice on the matter. He really needed someone who could run the business on their own since he had to travel so much, and increasingly he hated the responsibilities of the home office.

Kirsten was proving far more capable than Nicole had ever been. But Nicole was beautiful and unrelenting in her pursuit of him and he wasn't strong enough to avoid her advances. It's true she was not his first assistant, and it's not like he had gotten personally involved with every assistant, but he'd blurred the lines for far too long, and it had nearly cost him a legal battle.

He could never prove it, but he suspected Nicole had taken advantage of their sexual relationship by crying sexual harassment. She had been the one who'd come on to him and said, 'This is just sex, okay?' Regardless, he never should've allowed their relationship to go beyond professional.

Lillian had seen the truth of her right away and never liked her, but in the end she'd given her the second most coveted buying position, in Bridge, and miraculously, the lawsuit went away.

Kirsten didn't know it, but she was to be the one to atone for his sins. The years were ticking by, and as much as he hated to admit it, he wondered if Lillian was right. Was his penchant for women getting out of control? He hadn't done anything illegal, but if he were judged on a purely moral plane, he knew he held most of the blame. He was the boss, and he never should've allowed it. He still believed he could and would settle down and get married—even have a few kids— but as he approached his forties, it seemed less and less likely. He felt an increasing prick in his heart about his inability to stay with one woman. It was getting harder to ignore. He was feeling guilty and glanced again at Kirsten, who was continuing to look out her window. What was she thinking? Why did she smile? He suddenly wanted to know. Oblivious Kirsten, who didn't deserve any of his hardness, who chose to ignore it and remain unruffled while doing an excellent job. He suddenly felt the need to extend an olive branch.

"There's a party tonight being hosted by Cotton Incorporated if you're up for it," Michael offered. "There'll be a lot of industry people there."

"Sure, sounds like fun," Kirsten replied casually. But secretly, she was thrilled.

***

What to wear? Kirsten wanted to look fabulous, but without looking like she'd tried. A party for fashionistas would be a tough crowd. She couldn't afford designer clothing, but did have a few pieces thanks to Aric, of all people. He'd shown her where to find returns from already altered garments they couldn't resell and suits of mismatched sizes that unfortunately went unchecked upon their sale or return. She'd finally landed on a pair of silver strappy wedges and dark rinsed skinny jeans. She topped the look with a halter-style top in a beautiful, flowing floral silk à la Prada in greens and blues. It'd been washed instead of dry-cleaned and was a rumpled mess upon its return. Why the store took it back no questions asked was beyond her. Some people have all the nerve to insist it was the manufacturer's fault. Kirsten, however, was very skilled at reworking fabric, and painstakingly ironed it with a cool iron and water. It wasn't quite the same, but in her opinion, better than the original. All the manhandling of the fabric gave it some much needed street cred.

She gave herself a once-over in the mirror. No visible female parts showing, but still attractive. Looking at the clock, she realized she was two minutes late. She grabbed her clutch and rushed to the elevators.

Michael was running a bit behind, too, and arrived a few minutes after Kirsten, who was waiting in the lobby. He took a minute to observe her before he tried to get her attention to leave. She looked so happy, young, and fresh. To know he was the main contributor to her present disposition renewed his resolve to be a better man. He'd forgotten what it was like to be unknown and inexperienced.

He didn't have to be the one to crush her with the truth— at least for now. Tonight, they would enjoy the magic of the evening by attending a fabulous industry party, surrounding themselves with artfully made clothing and conversing with like-minded people; no spreadsheets or budgets to contemplate. As they stepped out the hotel doors, a perfectly timed cab pulled up for a drop-off and swept them away.

It was a short ride to their destination, and Michael held out his hand to help Kirsten out of the cab and onto the sidewalk. They stood facing what looked like a hole in the wall on a dark street with a dirty dark door illuminated by a lone light above it. The only light on the short block. It was exactly what you'd expect from a movie set in New York. The door opened to a dimly lit but short corridor leading to an elevator—one of those grungy metal, warehouse-like elevators. There was a security guy operating it, and only after checking invitations carefully would he let you go up to the fourth and final floor.

Wow was all Kirsten could think as the heavy elevator door opened to reveal a huge brick-walled space with old worn floor planks and a roof terrace beyond, lit with sparkly lights and scattered with bar-height table rounds. There was a DJ, a large hosted bar, and Cotton Incorporated was tastefully woven into the décor. Michael was waved over by someone he knew and Kirsten followed. She smiled politely and shook hands, wondering how hard she should try to remember names. She should try, but her brain was fried from a long day filled with everything new. She was overwhelmed. She smiled and nodded periodically, faking participation in the conversation, which was easy to do as Michael's shadow.

Kirsten was about to slip away, as she felt she was no longer needed, when the rep from Calvin Klein, who looked more like she modeled for Calvin Klein, intently asked her, "How do you like working for Michael?"

Her name was Kyra, and she was the perfectly natural-looking waif with a slight strawberry tinge in her otherwise long blonde hair.

Caught off-guard, Kirsten quickly gained her composure and realized as soon as Kyra opened her mouth she'd never make it as a Calvin Klein model. She lacked the requisite sexualized child-like innocence. Her sexuality beat like a hardened rocker chick. "What, I'm supposed to *like* working for Michael?" Her timing and tone measured the perfect balance to come across as professional teasing.

Everyone laughed, and Michael had no choice but to go along.

Kirsten sensed he was concealing surprise, thinking "what was that"? Maybe he even had a wee bit of admiration for her quick wit. Feeling relieved, her nerves eased, and she finally relaxed into the evening.

Eventually, most of the assistants to both buyers and sales reps—mostly women and gay men—gravitated toward each other, and she found herself chatting easily among her peers despite not having met any of them before. There seemed to be more than the normal curiosity about Michael, giving her unexpected notoriety, while others seemed maybe a little too familiar with him.

When things started to wind down she looked around for Michael to see if he was ready to go. She heard female laughter and an, "oh, Michael, you better be joking," behind her. She turned around and saw him in the elevator with Kyra, who was pretending she wasn't excited to be leaving with him. Kirsten's and Michael's eyes caught briefly in acknowledgment before the doors closed. She was on her own. What if she hadn't turned at that moment? Would he have just left without a word? Yes, she believed he would have. She must've seemed a little lost, as her eyes grazed across the bartender while she scanned the room. He'd been staring at her. Suddenly she felt bare in her carefully styled outfit and looked for the bathroom to freshen up and figure out what came next.

It was such a beautiful night and she didn't want it to end, but people were starting to couple up, and that wasn't something she was going to do. Effects of the alcohol she'd consumed during the evening were making the thought possible, and she considered getting rid of her virginity in one fell swoop, quietly and out of the way. She scrutinized herself in the mirror, but all she could see was Brian looking back at her. Every moment was captured into a slideshow on a continuous loop. It was like Google had invaded her internal camera and organized all her photos without asking. 'Thought you might enjoy how we stylized these pictures for you.'

'Thank you, Google-brain, but please leave me alone,' Kirsten wanted to scream.

That first night at Half-Time, at his house, at the gym, in the office; every exchange meticulously cataloged ad infinitum. The time their hands brushed or they were close enough to touch. She felt the electricity of those moments for the first time. It was all there, but it wasn't until that night, that one night, when she finally saw. Why had she not seen it before? How could she have not known? Her core melted again at the memory of how handsome he'd looked walking toward her the night of the gala. How vulnerable she'd felt, and how, out of sheer panic, she had looked abruptly away. The ensuing sag of his shoulders as he changed course. She squeezed her eyes shut, clenched her fists, and shuddered at the pain of him feeling rejected.

A woman walked into the ladies' room, ruining the privacy Kirsten needed. She pulled herself together, then found her way out and down to the street, where she hailed a cab and asked to be taken to Washington Square via Fifth Avenue. She suddenly needed to see the arch lit-up against the dark sky. She got out a few blocks early so she could see it in its entirety. The breezy warm evening rustled her blouse and blew through her hair. She stopped to lean against a tree growing out of the sidewalk along the street. She closed her eyes and focused on her breathing, in and out, long and slow, trying to free herself from the weight of the day. She felt her pulse begin to slow.

Inspired by the beautiful glow of the arch, she pulled out her phone and took some photos, walking closer and moving out into the street and then back onto the sidewalk again. She used the foliage of the trees in the foreground to create a frame for the arch. The photos were for her, not Facebook or Instagram. Here she was able to enjoy the moment; there was no contemplating Brian, no work demands, no trying to figure out Michael.

She remembered the last time she'd been here on a similar evening. Perhaps she was trying to conjure the memory. Bill Cunningham had come riding by unceremoniously on his bicycle in his iconic royal blue jacket. She'd smiled and snapped his picture. To everyone else the image would've looked like a grainy blur of a man on a bike, the blue of his coat being the only distinguishable color among the muddy backdrop of night.

But the most genuine person in the world of fashion photography held a special place in the heart of every lover of Couture, from the Anna Wintours to the average New Yorker. They all coveted the honor of being photographed by him. And here he'd been unobserved by everyone but her.

But she knew she would never see him again. He'd died and left a huge hole. She'd seen a documentary about him once, and as much as he was endearing, he had seemed sad. There was something unresolved within him, and she hoped he'd been able to make peace with whatever it was before he died.

This was when New York was at its best—a glamorous night spent with colleagues and beautiful architecture on a tropical-like night. But not unlike Cinderella, she knew she should leave soon as it was approaching the seamier side of the dark hours. She didn't dare enter the park alone and remained on the outskirts where it was well lit. Nothing good happens after midnight, she could hear her mother say. She enjoyed her last remaining minutes until she spied an open cab. She hailed it and headed back to her hotel.

The buzzing of her alarm woke her promptly at seven-thirty, though it took a few seconds for her to remember where she was. She'd had a hard time falling asleep the night before—too much activity did that to her. She reminded herself it only took fifteen minutes of misery to wake up and then she'd be fine. She hated getting up even under the best of circumstances, but she'd learned in college she'd usually rally at the fifteen-minute mark and feel fully awake. It was uncannily true and worked in talking herself out of bed. What was fifteen minutes of misery, she asked? Nothing.

She showered, dressed, and applied a light coat of makeup to her freshly scrubbed skin. As she put the finishing touch of mascara on her lashes, she remembered the magic of the night before and smiled in gratitude for her job. She was finally feeling more comfortable in her new life and it was nice to reap some benefits after all her hard work.

Her euphoria carried her out the door and down toward the elevators for some breakfast, but as she passed Michael's room she heard light feminine laughter and the romantic murmurs of a night spent together. She quickly sped up, as she didn't want him to see her, but heard the door open behind her, which caused her to accelerate even more. She could feel him looking at her, so she normalized her pace to appear unaware. She turned into the bay of elevators and impatiently pressed the down button a couple times, willing it to go faster. Just when she thought it was all in vain it dinged open and she scooted on. She was about to make her escape when an arm stopped the door from closing, and the rep from Calvin Klein hopped on.

"Oh, hi, Kirsten."

"Hi, Kyra." She felt like an awkward schoolgirl who didn't know how to behave.

Kyra didn't seem to notice and chatted with Kirsten like a kindred spirit, a fellow woman of fashion and one-night stands. "You're up early," Kyra said.

"I'm getting some breakfast. I'm starving." The minute she said it, she regretted it. She wasn't supposed to say that, was she? She was supposed to be insanely skinny and not eat breakfast like Kyra.

"I could use a cup of coffee myself. There's a great place up the block. Can I join you?" she asked.

"Sure." Kirsten tried not to sound surprised as she didn't want to offend or make Kyra feel bad, so she went along amiably.

She admired Kyra for her confidence and verve, though she found her a bit bossy, or perhaps it was her New Yorker coming out. They walked into the nearest coffee shop two doors up from the hotel. It was one of those chain places. Kirsten would've preferred a local, independent shop but expressed no protest at Kyra's suggestion.

Kirsten began not to mind the intrusion and found it rather amusing instead. She noticed Kyra's stealth in looking business-ready with her lavender-gray shift dress from the night before under her smartly tailored asymmetrical moto-styled jacket in coordinating gray linen with black accents trimming the zipper on the sleeve, collar edge, and front pocket flaps. Her black suede and patent leather heels fabulously completing the look. Kirsten was impressed.

Kirsten couldn't help but wonder if she was going to wear the outfit all day or head back to her apartment to change. Did she pack a pair of underwear and a toothbrush discreetly in her bag for such possibilities?

Kirsten went to the service bar to get some napkins after her purchase and noticed Kyra had several packets of sugar lined up together to look like one; she tore off their tops to pour into her coffee. Funny, Kirsten thought. They managed to find a corner table for two and sat down. Kirsten didn't really want a bread product and coffee for breakfast because they always made her hungry later. She preferred to have an egg or yogurt, but settled for the most fattening, least sugary item available—a croissant. *What the heck, it's good enough for the French.* It was wonderfully decadent, and as the strands of soft dough pulled apart in her fingers she couldn't resist dipping it into the foam of her latte. Kyra looked a little jealous, but Kirsten wasn't sure the quarter-cup of sugar in her coffee was much better.

"So, is this your first trip to New York?" Kyra asked.

"Uhn-uh. I used to be a buyer for the BP department at Nordstrom."

"Ugh. Juniors!" Kyra said.

"I know, it was crazy. Always going to LA or here. It's so cyclical. Designer couture is much better. How 'bout you?"

"Me? I've always been Calvin Klein. I was in the merchandising program at FIT, got an internship at Calvin, and the rest is history," she said, like she was disgusted with how boring she was.

"Wow! That's really cool. I'd love to live in New York someday." Kirsten tried to sound enthusiastic to encourage her.

"Yeah, it's pretty cool, but it can get ugly here. You have to have really tough skin to make it. I see a lot of people come here and then move back to wherever they're from." She looked out the window and chewed on her plastic stir stick and then turned directly back to Kirsten. "You seem a little different than Michael's regular assistants."

"Really?" Kirsten played dumb, despite continually getting asked the exact same question or, worse, being given a look implying the same thing.

"Yeah. I've been working with him for, God, wow, like twelve years now, so I've seen a few assistants come and go."

Kirsten didn't know what to say and let it her words hang in the air.

"He's great, though. You'll learn a lot, and it'll look really good on your resume," Kyra said.

"That's what I keep hearing, so I feel lucky to have gotten the position."

"Let's just say he possess certain gifts that are rather irresistible," she said, pointing her stir stick at Kirsten with a knowing look and then sticking it back in her mouth.

Kirsten wasn't sure she wanted to know that and just smiled.

Kyra suddenly seemed self-aware and regretful about divulging too much to Kirsten, as she didn't seem to be picking up on her cues. "Well, I have a big day ahead of me. Thanks for joining me for coffee."

"Sure. It's been nice chatting with you." Kirsten lingered as her abbreviated breakfast left her with extra time. She'd spied a diner earlier, a few blocks away, and had planned a hearty breakfast. The café was getting busier, and she felt she should give up her table. She walked the few yards back to the hotel lobby to await the time she was to meet Michael. She chose a chair facing away from the elevators and didn't hear him come up behind her. Her legs were crossed so that she had thoughtlessly forced her skirt to inch up into a seductive line. Her head swung up instinctively, and she nearly jumped at the sense of someone looking down at her.

"Oh, hi. I didn't see you," she said, shutting her computer closed, then sliding it into her bag.

"Sorry, I didn't mean to startle you."

"No. That's fine. I got engrossed in answering emails, apparently."

He walked around and offered a gentlemanly hand to help her up. She accepted, and he pulled her in a little too close, in Kirsten's opinion. She gracefully turned and bent down to pick up her bag in one fluid motion so as not to seem unnatural and to avoid eye contact. She caught a whiff of his cologne. He smelled good. His superior taste evidently expanded to scent. Most men, in her experience, didn't wear cologne and when they did, tended to pick fragrances that were overpowering.

She could feel his eyes on her back again like in the hallway earlier. This time it was laced with sex. She did her best to disregard it, but the headiness got to her, and she clumsily grabbed her bag, nearly dropping it. Michael reached out to prevent it from falling, but Kirsten was able to catch it.

"Oops! Sorry. I almost lost it, didn't I?" she exclaimed. Kirsten suddenly found herself out of her depth and wished she could be more like Kyra.

They made their way out and didn't have to wait too long for a cab. After she sat down she adjusted her skirt to its appropriate length to the top of her knee. Kirsten could feel Michael watching out of the corner of his eye. She willed herself to look straight ahead, and in a desperate act to stop the blush from rising, she involuntarily squeezed the back of her neck with her hand.

How'd he do that? I'm interested in Brian! What the hell is going on? She felt fissures of electricity throughout her body. *He's your boss!* Images of Nicole and Michael flashed through her mind. Comments rang in her ears from greedy gossipers of last night to coworkers back at Dayfield's, and most pointedly, Kyra's words from this morning echoed in her head. *"Certain gifts that are rather irresistible."*

She got through the day by trying to ignore his omnipresence pressing in on her. He was like Kryptonite. Outwardly it looked like business as usual, but the truth lay barely below the surface: it was a seductive dance, and she was being hunted by a master. *Why now?* She tried to steal moments by herself whenever she could and flip her thoughts to Brian, but he wasn't there and she'd ruined her chances of ever being with him. She hated to admit Michael had gotten to her. She knew it could never be real for him. He was addicted to the chase, and she refused to be another casualty. What she couldn't reconcile was that she liked it. It was intoxicating.

It wasn't until after their appointment with the rep from an up-and-coming new designer, Rand, that the demands of work took over. Rand was stunning. Definitely that something new they were looking for. An excited Michael started texting furiously with Lillian about the budget. Kirsten could tell it was getting heated. This was Michael at his best. He had a good eye and excellent intuition. He was tenacious in his pursuit of what he wanted, and he wanted Rand, which took the pressure off Kirsten. His texting signaled disinterest to the rep while masterfully creating a plan with Lillian to make it work. Michael ended the appointment with a casual "We'll be in touch."

Michael talked impatiently with Lillian during the cab ride back to the hotel. "When have I ever been wrong? You know what I mean, about a designer?" He looked over at Kirsten as he listened to Lillian's response. Then guiltily turned to the window and spoke in a lower tone. "Yes. I'm being good. Look, I've done everything you asked, and our numbers are up."

Well, at least someone has some hold over him, Kirsten thought.

"Yeah, okay. We're headed back to the hotel now, and I will send you a revised budget tonight." He ended the call as a text came through. Calv…en was all Kirsten could see as his thumb hovered over the screen. He ignored it.

"Sorry, Kirsten, I'm afraid it's going to be a long night."

"That's okay. I take it you mean we need to revise our budget."

"Yeah, we need to see where we can pull from to fund Rand."

"I'll get right on it," she said, like the good little assistant she was.

Kirsten was exhausted from the emotional drain of the day and wondered how she was going to find the energy for the task at hand. Michael told her he'd give her a couple of hours. She didn't have much time for a run but knew if she could run hard for even twenty minutes, she could stave off an oncoming headache. Kirsten was fairly adept at crunching numbers and knew she could get it all done in the allotted time.

As she waited for Michael's response to her email, which she sent precisely at the two-hour mark as promised, she rewarded herself by enjoying her order from room service. She'd barely gotten started when she heard a knock at the door. She peered through the peephole to see Michael standing there. She opened it, and without even a hello, he walked swiftly in. He was still wearing his suit and smelled of cigarettes. She hadn't known he smoked. She closed the door and watched him pull out the chair opposite of where'd she'd been sitting and sit down. She stayed by the door, a little annoyed and confused. It seemed a bit unprofessional.

He gave her sweats and ponytail appearance a quizzical look as she joined him at the table where her dinner was getting cold.

"We need to pull more. What about Donna Karan?" he asked.

"I know, but she's one of our best sellers. I don't think we can afford to," Kirsten said, trying to sooth.

"Why! She's not that good," Michael said in frustration.

Kirsten didn't know what to say, but numbers didn't lie. He sat looking defeated across from her. Kirsten pulled her chair and computer over so they could both look at the screen.

"I think you're absolutely right about Rand. He's fantastic, but unfortunately it doesn't always translate to revenue. Look, Minneapolis isn't New York. It's going to take them longer to jump on board. There's enough here to get a nice

ensemble of pieces so Aric can do a special trunk show to
introduce him. Maybe we could even get him to come out in
person. Aric knows which customers need to be there. He'll
make it work. And if we do well with it, which I'm sure we
will, we can buy more next season."

Eyes downcast, he sat lightly drumming his fingers against
the table. He knew she was right but wasn't ready to admit
it. "What are you wearing?" he asked teasingly to change the
subject.

"Sweats. Why? Don't you ever wear sweats?" Kirsten
was unable to picture him in anything other than a perfectly
tailored suit, maybe a nice cashmere sweater over a collared
shirt, but definitely not sweats.

"Not at work. What is it, casual Friday?" Michael asked,
unable to completely contain his frustration.

"No. It's my working-at-home look where no one usually
sees me. Would you like some wine?" Kirsten didn't know
what possessed her to cross what needed to remain a very
clear line, but she suddenly felt empowered by his change in
demeanor. The sexual undertone was gone. He was no longer
Kryptonite.

"Sure, why not?"

"It's red." She smiled and he laughed.

Kirsten poured from a full carafe, the size of a bottle of
wine, and felt the need to explain. "I thought I'd ordered a
glass, but there was some confusion and they brought me a
whole carafe. They took it off my bill, so now I have a lot of
free wine."

She looked directly at him, without wavering, and handed
him a glass. Their fingers brushed and she felt a low spark,
but this time she was ready.

"Cheers!" he said, holding up his glass to clink with hers.

"Cheers," Kirsten returned, lifting her glass to meet his.

"Mmm, it's good; what kind of red is it?"

"I don't know, it's the house red."

He took another sip and looked at her thoughtfully. "You know, I didn't really hire you."

"I know." She hadn't known for sure until he said it but had suspected.

He raised a brow. "Really?"

"It's sort of unusual to interview first and almost exclusively with the VP."

Michael laughed, impressed by her prowess. "Why'd you take it, then?"

"I wanted it," Kirsten shot back.

"Are you sorry you took it?"

"No. Are you sorry it's me?"

"No. No, I'm not." He looked up to cement the fact.

His veneer was starting to peel; she liked that. She took another sip of her wine and finished her dinner. Her gaze wandered the cityscape beyond the window. The room darkened as the night sky crept over the city and sparkles of light began to pop up. The mood started to change, and they talked in tones of truth as two colleagues doing their best to navigate the life they'd been given. The wine and conversation wove an air of intimacy she was afraid to break, but soon they'd be in complete darkness if she didn't turn on a light. She hated to do it and reached behind her to turn on the floor lamp. Shocking at first, as they had both adjusted to the dimness, it also had the exact effect she was afraid of.

Michael looked at his phone and set his glass on the table, then rose to leave, buttoning his jacket.

Kirsten stood in response. "So, we'll keep the budget as is?"

Michael nodded in reluctant agreement.

"Sounds good," she said.

He walked to the door but stopped and turned back toward her. "Lillian was right about you." He reached up and affectionately stroked her cheek, then spun on his heels and left.

Kirsten locked herself in, turned her back to the door, and stood unmoving. She was more confused than ever.

The trip back to Minneapolis was uneventful and already seemed routine, like she'd been traveling for Couture for years. The first day back was busy with all the catching up, and she hardly talked to anyone all day. She pretty much stayed in her office, partly because, unlike before, she didn't want to see Brian. She couldn't handle more of his cold shoulder. It was mid-afternoon by the time she ventured out for lunch, and she opted to go up to the tenth floor to dine at Christine's casual counterpart, Christy's Café.

Fortuitously, she was asked to join a couple of assistants who were lunching late. Time and patience had led to her co-workers slowly but surely deciding she was worthy of their inclusion even though she enjoyed more perks than them. She was beginning to feel like she belonged.

"So, how was New York?" Leah asked.

"Good," Kirsten said in a nondescript tone.

"You don't sound like you mean it. What was Michael like?" Tiffany asked.

Kirsten laughed.

"No, it was good, just exhausting. So, what's new around here? Anything?" Kirsten looked from one girl to the other as she spoke.

"No, not really," they said, shaking their heads in unison.

"Jasmine is leaving," Tiffany said.

"Where's she going?" Kirsten asked.

"Nowhere, she wants to stay home with her kids for a while," Tiffany replied.

"Hmm." Kirsten nodded in understanding.

All three were still mostly single, young, and childless, but knew one day they might have to wrestle with the same decision. Marissa Mayer, the now ex-CEO of Yahoo, not taking much maternity leave, and the advent of Sheryl Sandberg's *Lean In* book had definitely made it a hot-button issue. Maybe Marissa isn't able to have it all, Kirsten wondered, plus she was well aware of the effects of a parent's work taking precedence over the welfare of their child. She felt corporate America still had a long way to go in truly embracing work and family.

"It's not like we can all build nurseries next to our cubicle," Leah said, punctuating their thoughts.

The girls laughed.

"Although," Tiffany piped in, "I saw this news story about this woman who started a WeWork-like space for parents. It's a super smart idea. Basically, you can get up to three hours of childcare while you work. So your kid is near you, but you can have uninterrupted time to work. I mean, it's not a full day, but it's something, like if you wanted to work part-time. It's a step in the right direction."

"I like it!" Kirsten said. "We need to think of something like that. There has to be a better way."

"Hey, Randi," Leah yelled, waving her hand to flag her down. "So, who is going to do our insert now that Brian's gone?"

Kirsten's posture shot to attention and then quickly corrected to hide her surprise. *Brian's gone? Where'd he go?* Kirsten leaned toward Tiffany and whispered, "Where's Brian?" while Randi and Leah talked.

"You don't know?" Tiffany asked.

"No. Know what?" Kirsten asked impatiently.

"He got some really great job in San Francisco, I guess," Tiffany explained.

"You're kidding!" Kirsten didn't attempt to hide her surprise this time. Her heart pounded while her mind raced. *I'm going to have to go by his house and resolve this now. Maybe he's already left? No, there is no way he could have left already, could he?* Kirsten needed more information. "When did this happen?"

"A couple weeks ago. I can't believe you didn't know." Tiffany looked puzzled.

"Welcome back, Kirsten. How was your trip?" Randi asked, wrapping up her conversation with Leah.

"Thanks. It was really good. Better than I thought it'd be. Michael invited me to an industry party so it wasn't all work." She smiled. The moment she said industry party she regretted it. She felt it stabbed Leah and Tiffany a little, which was the last thing she wanted to do, but she'd forgotten for a moment because it was Randi.

"Well, I'm gonna get something to go as I'm a little shorthanded with Brian gone," Randi said, leaving.

"I'm in shock. I can't believe I didn't know this." Kirsten sat, letting it sink in.

"Yeah, supposedly he gave his two-week notice, but then at the last minute he had to change his plans and left after only a week. We all met at Murphy's on Friday to say goodbye,"

Leah said.

"Well, he is very talented, but I'm sure he'll be much happier working for an agency than in-house," Tiffany added.

"Yeah, I guess that's what he always wanted," Kirsten said.

Kirsten forced herself to remain part of the conversation as they finished their lunch. She was flummoxed. If he were still here, she'd want to run to him and explain, but it was surely too late. It was over before it had begun, and she'd probably never see him again.

Kirsten was quiet as they took the escalators back down to their cubicle city. Leah and Tiffany didn't notice and said goodbye as they peeled off to their individual lab rat homes. Kirsten continued mutely to her privileged world of Couture in the far corner. She sat down at her computer and stared blankly. Kirsten was thankful it was quiet. Michael and Aric were gone, and she hoped they weren't coming back for a while. She thought she might cry, but the tears wouldn't come. Probably because it wasn't a deep enough relationship, she concluded. The thought gave her some comfort—further deducing her feelings for Brian would quickly fade. She tapped her keyboard to wake up her computer and went back to work with a confident resolve.

The afternoon started to fly as she became engrossed in answering emails and analyzing last week's sales. Michael and Aric eventually returned and the sound of their voices jarred her back to reality. They poked their heads into her office, and she swiveled her chair around to greet them.

"Hey. Look. We finally got that Thierry Mugler piece for Mrs. Ridenour; isn't it fabulous?" Aric said, holding out the suit.

"Wow, yeah, it really is amazing, isn't it?" Kirsten stood to finger the heathered wool crepe. The mix of gray and black threads gave the classic weave a smart update. Kirsten loved the elegance of wool crepe.

"Look at these pocket flaps. Aren't they wild?" Aric said, turning the suit so Kirsten could see better.

"Yeah, they don't even look like pockets, more like a piece of appliqué. Say, Michael, did you know Brian left?" Kirsten asked, keeping a tight rein on her emotions.

"You're kidding, right?" Michael answered.

"No, I'm not. I just found out."

"Well, yeah, everyone knows. Aric told me before we left for New York so I went up and said goodbye."

"No way! How come you didn't tell me?" Dropping the reins on her feelings, she looked at Aric. Michael seemed a little puzzled by her tone, and Kirsten kicked herself for reacting so strongly.

"I don't know. I assumed you knew," he said, with a hint of deception in his eyes.

"Hmm." He shrugged, sweeping the suit away as he headed back to his cubicle.

Michael, a bit uncertain of the change in mood, went back to his office. "Well, I'm gonna go write more orders."

That little jerk, Kirsten thought. *He purposely didn't tell me and knew I probably wouldn't find out until we got back.*

LAKE OF THE ISLES

It was a gray Saturday morning that looked like it wanted to snow but wasn't sure it was cold enough. The trees were full of buds waiting for the silent call of spring. Kirsten wanted to go to the lake. Normally, she would walk but she had been meaning to check out a quaint-looking bakery cafe she'd driven by a few weeks ago, and it was further than she was willing to walk. As she made her way through the side streets, she felt herself steering toward Brian's house. This is ridiculous! She chided herself and focused on going directly to the coffee shop and even avoided looking down his street as she passed. Yes! She smiled at her little victory.

She found a parking spot right in front, which she decided was a reward for her restraint and therefore didn't mind the long line. It gave her time to reflect and enjoy one of her favorite pastimes: people watching. Her eyes landed on two separate men who reminded her of Brian and Michael. How quickly she backslid. The unsuspecting gentlemen were giving signs she might be flirting with them, so she stopped.

She considered her feelings for the umpteenth time. Brian was long gone, and she found it perplexing a sudden flicker of emotion could have such a firm hold on her. He'd been out of her life longer than he'd been in it. Wasn't there some sort of math problem proving the feelings should have ceased by now? Michael, on the other hand, should not be crossing her mind at all except for work reasons, since he was never boyfriend material to begin with.

There was definitely something about him, though, she couldn't quite excuse—Kyra had been right. They'd settled into a comfortable rhythm of work colleagues with mutual respect, but there were those times, those days, when she felt like he could split her open—like that day in New York. But she knew if he tried, she would stop it. She couldn't help but be a little naughty at times and wear a slightly shorter skirt, letting it hike farther up her thigh by crossing her legs when she sat. Intentionally evoking a memory. Her boldness felt visceral. She took advantage of moments to stand a little closer to him while appearing to have no choice. Kirsten was surprised by her stealth and wondered if it were woven into her DNA. Was she her father's daughter? Sometimes she would get so caught up in her lustful desire for Michael and her feelings for Brian their images and personalities would intertwine in her dreams and fantasies. It was exhilarating and thrilling. Like Anne in *Anne of Green Gables*, she didn't want a man "who was really wicked," just one who "could be wicked and wouldn't."

Moving to Minneapolis gave her newfound confidence. The mere fact she was able to relocate her entire life halfway across the country caused her to discover parts of herself she didn't know existed. It felt powerful and she began to realize it in her sexuality. She wasn't so afraid of male attention and actually welcomed it. It was bringing her closer to letting her virginity go, although she knew it would have to be with a Brian-type. As much as she wanted to see herself as free as the Kyras of the world, she knew she wasn't. Perhaps that's why she felt she wanted to play with Michael a little. She could explore without fear of retribution. He was her boss and there had been an incident, and she knew he couldn't and therefore wouldn't.

"Kirsten!" the barista yelled.

"Thanks." Kirsten smiled and took the hot cup into her cold hands. She sipped the warm velvety liquid while studying the view through the arched brick-framed windows. She'd been right about its charm and discovered it was known for its cinnamon buns, as the case was filled with several variations of frosted, plain, fruit, and nut buns. If it were warmer, she'd sit outside at one of the bistro tables running along the façade, tucked under the wide-striped bumble bee awnings. Their regal colors created a striking balance against the brick. A rectangular parking lot lay across the street for what appeared to be an apartment complex. It was trimmed with big beautiful trees and lawns that spread under their branches. It was fairly picturesque for a car park. The grass was beginning to green up, and she imagined the leafy canopy about to burst subduing the harsh asphalt.

Kirsten was falling more in love with this part of Minneapolis and enjoyed being out among its beautiful old homes. She was a few blocks from the lake where the street narrowed in the distance and the residences grew larger. She wandered out of the café precisely as the sun exposed itself from behind a passing cloud—its warming rays felt heavenly after a long cold winter. Perhaps it had decided not to snow after all.

And it had been a long hard winter, as she reflected back on the last months. She definitely understood why they called it Sprinter. Back home the grass had been green for months, and the tulips and daffodils had already bloomed and died. The weather patterns moved swiftly in the plains with no mountains to stop them. She kept being surprised by how quickly the clouds came and went. When it was cloudy in Seattle, which was often, it stayed. The moisture from Puget Sound with the Olympic Mountains to the west and the Cascade Mountains to the east kept them trapped in a heavy mist. It was like living in a cloud. There were no claps of thunder preceding torrential downpours like in the movies.

She continued toward the lake, pondering how different her life was compared to fourteen months ago. There had been the accident in the mountains of Montana delaying her passage and she'd felt very alone. There was that guy Ryan who'd flirted with her, which made her smile. She'd gone home for Christmas and connected with Michelle but didn't ask about him or even friend him on Facebook.

Work had fallen into a familiar pattern despite Aric's continued coldness, but she'd come to accept it. Leah and Tiffany had become her friends, and they often went out for drinks and dinner after work with the occasional weekend event or excursion. Randi would often include her whenever the ad department went out, but she found it hard without Brian, which seemed true for Randi too, and increasingly the two of them would go out separately instead of with the whole group. Kirsten carefully avoided talking about Brian with her. Besides, wasn't that what Facebook was for? She needed the anonymity, and of course, she still had Sten, her Dad, and Carol. Her life had definitely become less lonely. Somewhere along the way she'd settled into her new life—bit by bit, until her old life had become papered over and even a little foreign, which she found hard to believe. Fourteen months wasn't that long.

She arrived at the lake as the road teed into a parkway bordering it. She spied a stairway leading down to a path paralleling the shoreline. Picnic tables and benches were scattered on the wider grassy patches along the bank. She meandered until she found a place to her liking, letting her mind unwind. She found a bench facing the sun and sat, sipping her latte as she watched the weekenders run and walk by.

There were dogs, kids, strollers, and all kinds of people enjoying the possibility of winter being over. There were plenty of good-looking men too, so Brian didn't have the market on that. A tall man who was a little on the lean side but had thick dark reddish hair like Brian's passed by. Like Brian's, his hair had no choice but to be sculpted to his head with the precision of a military cut. Another guy rode by on a bicycle and had similar features to Brian with his athletic build and longer face—a very attractive man of about the same age, but then he stopped and embraced a young woman in a way that clearly said they were together.

Okay, it's official, she thought, I'm pathetic! I'm sitting on a park bench checking out men. No more, she thought, as she noticed a father steadying his little girl as the training wheels of her perfectly pink bike precariously rocked her side to side. She looked terrified, but he patiently coaxed her by telling her how great she was doing. She went a few more feet, then, feeling the lag of the training wheels, panicked and twisted her handlebars to overcorrect and started to fall. He caught her, but it didn't stop her fear-filled tears. He held her tightly as she clung to him and he stroked her hair, telling her how proud he was of her and how well she was doing. She calmed down and pulled back to smile at him but refused to get back on the bike. He moved them off the path, and they sat on the grass. He held her in his lap, and she burrowed herself into his chest. Kirsten felt a lump rise in her throat as her eyes watered.

She discreetly brushed her tears away, turning her attention back toward the lake. Out of the corner of her eye she glimpsed a guy jogging in her direction. He was cute. Why does every male at the lake seem attractive today, Kirsten teased herself. As he got closer her heart started pounding. She felt like she might know him. Was it déjà vu or only another reminder? He came further into view, and she realized she did know him. It was Brian! She sat upright on instinct, then slumped back down to avoid appearing like she'd seen him first. He wasn't looking her way so she snuck a peek, then turned her head in the direction he was headed in hopes he would see her and have to be the one to say hello. But he didn't see her. He passed by without recognition. She sat feeling helpless as she stared at his back fading around the bend, fearing she'd lost her chance.

Her mind flitted. Did that just happen? What was he doing here? Did San Francisco not work out? She looked around to ascertain where she was. She'd walked further than she'd thought. Her bench was near another entrance to the park, which must be the one closest to Brian's house. She found it difficult to discern the layout of the surrounding neighborhood and their proximity to the curvy circle of the lake, which was more the shape of one of the many geese inhabiting it. She was unfamiliar with the area from this perspective, as the entrance near her apartment was further north of where she was. She calculated how long it would take; having run here herself many a time, she knew it was a little under three miles.

He probably ran a seven- or eight-minute mile. So, twenty to twenty-four minutes, she guessed.

Kirsten began to fidget—crossing and uncrossing her legs as naturally as one should while sitting on a park bench sipping a latte. Though she was out of latte, nevertheless, it seemed to soothe her, so she kept drinking from the empty cup and pulling out her phone to see the time, which crept by ever so slowly.

When it'd finally been twenty minutes, she considered moving to a bench adjacent to where she estimated his entrance. Rational and ridiculous thoughts continued their conflict as she gathered her courage and made her way closer. Her stomach was in knots, and she felt her legs would collapse at any moment, making it difficult for her to walk. She approached the bench and panicked as a couple of teenagers emerged and commandeered it. Quick thinking sent her toward the next one out, but still in the direction he'd be coming. The diversion allowed her to notice him stretching on the grass slightly off the path ahead. He's already done, she thought. He must run a seven-minute mile or the distance is way under three miles. Determined to put her inner conflict to rest, she kept her course despite her body fighting every step.

"Brian?" He didn't see her approaching, so she was practically bending over him to get his attention. "Hello," she said as evenly and cheerfully as possible.

He looked up while pulling his earbuds out. It seemed like he didn't recognize her for a moment, but when he did, he didn't exactly break into a friendly "Oh, hi, haven't seen you for a long time" kind of smile—it was more of a guarded, uncertain "Hey."

"Hi, I thought that was you," Kirsten replied, ignoring any

bad vibes. "How are you?"

"Good," he said, standing up and wiping his sweaty forehead on his sleeve. "How's the fashion biz?"

"Good. I got back and you were like, gone. I had no idea you were about to leave."

"Yeah, it happened super-fast. I didn't even have time to pack much of my house."

"Sooo…is that why you're back?" Kirsten asked. "Packing up your house?" She didn't want him to have an excuse to leave before she was able to guess his mood. It was hard to judge.

"Yeah, I'm taking a long weekend to get it all done."

"Well, we've missed your art direction. The new gal isn't as good, but I also think she's not as ambitious, so a safer choice for stability's sake." Kirsten kept it light and friendly; she could tell he was relaxing some but still withholding.

He chuckled and gently kicked the grass a few times, which signaled to Kirsten he didn't want to talk to her but was trying to be polite.

"Well, I'd better head back," he said, as he started to turn toward the road.

"Yeah, okay, good to see ya!" Kirsten desperately wanted to get him to stay. Facing his back again, she panicked and almost shouted, "Uh, Brian?"

"Yeah," he said, turning around.

"Um, there's something I'd like to talk to you about if you have a minute."

He looked a bit surprised and unsure, but came back to where she stood ringing her cup nervously. "Sure, what's up? Done with that?" he asked, reaching for her cup.

"Uh, yeah." Kirsten offered it to him, and he threw it in

the garbage as if it were the most normal thing between them.

"Do you mind if we keep walking? I need to cool down," he asked.

"Sure." They walked back to the trail and walked side-by-side at a leisurely pace while Kirsten tried to remain composed. "I know this is going to probably sound strange to you"—she laughed a little—"but it's been bothering me, and since you're here, well, the only way to find out is to ask."

Their eyes met briefly, his not giving anything away.

"Before you left it seemed as if maybe I'd done something to offend you because you seemed, maybe, a little aloof toward me. I don't know if I saw something that wasn't there or if maybe there was. I wanted to know because, well, I'd want to know if I'd done something to make you mad."

They continued walking and looking straight ahead in what seemed an interminable silence, but it was much more comfortable than standing face to face.

Brian stopped, spun at her, and said, "What do you mean?" He was looking her dead in the eye as if there was something and he thought she should know what it was.

"I don't know," Kirsten replied. "Maybe it was during the Midsummer Gala that something happened?" She tried to read his eyes as she waited for him to respond and caught a glint of pain, not anger. She felt terrible.

He shrugged and continued to walk again.

She stepped up her pace to keep up with him. He wasn't going to reveal anything. She didn't know what to do, but someone needed to show some courage. He should be more mature, she argued inside her head, but she knew he was hurt. She stopped and crossed her arms tightly while he kept going a couple more steps, then he turned and mindlessly kicked some pebbles on the path. One skittered across the pavement unnoticed as some weekend runners went by.

"Okay, it isn't that I may have ignored you at the gala, is it?"

Silence and more pebble kicking. Really, she thought, still nothing.

Kirsten felt her frustration ignite and leveled her eyes at him.

Her rising conflagration triggered Brian, and he finally confessed. "Yes! I was upset by how you treated me that night. You looked right at me and then looked away. Then, as if to save yourself, you made a last-ditch effort to acknowledge my presence by looking up and whispering a hello. How could you do that? Knowing I was desperate to get into a design shop and there was the creative director at Bloedel Kirkpatrick standing right next to you, and you wouldn't even introduce me! Am I not good enough for all you fancy, high-fashion gurus? You knew it and I knew it, so why are you standing here asking me if I was mad at you? I didn't think you were the type, Kirsten."

"I'm not the type; that wasn't why I acted that way, and I tried to make amends several times. You went on vacation, then I had to go out of town, and then you were gone, and in between you went out of your way to avoid me, so how was I to explain? I realize what I did was inconsiderate and rude, but you didn't have to return the favor. I tried, but you wouldn't have it." The last eight months of angst poured out of her. She knew she shouldn't be irritated with him, it was her mistake, but she couldn't help being hurt by his avoidance of her.

A strained quiet fell between them which felt good for

once; at least there would be fewer questions to answer. A runner with a baby jogger was coming toward them, and they scooted off the path to an enclave of shrubs for more privacy. She knew he was wondering when she was going to explain herself or *if* she was going to explain herself, and the firm line of doubt about her having a rational explanation for her actions was more than obvious across his face. He wasn't going to say anything more. He was waiting.

"Brian," she began tentatively, "I know this is going to sound bizarre, and you probably won't believe me, and please bear in mind this is really difficult for me to say."

He crossed his arms against his chest.

"I didn't know it was you at first. Honestly, I didn't recognize you in that suit. You looked different. A good different, not a bad different." She added quickly to assure him. "You looked good—really, really good, actually…" She looked at the ground as if it might hold a clue for her to know what to say next.

When he didn't say anything she looked up. He was waiting for more.

She didn't have more. She didn't know how to say, "I suddenly had the hots for you and didn't want you to know, so I looked away."

"What? You looked away because you didn't recognize me and were surprised I could look good in a suit?" he said in disbelief.

"No. You don't understand. I'd never seen you dressed up before. I mean, you're always so casual, you know. I wasn't surprised you *could* look good in a suit. I thought you looked good. You know, you looked good," she said with emphasis, turning her head away and hoping for some miracle.

"Oh?" he finally said.

She looked up hesitantly and watched his face as the truth started to sink in.

He let out a laugh in relief.

Embarrassed, Kirsten rolled her eyes and gave him an uncomfortable smile.

"Ohhh!" he said.

"Oh?" Kirsten said.

He became serious, realizing what she meant. He couldn't stop looking at her. It weakened Kirsten, and she looked away. "Kirsten, I'm sorry. I had no idea."

"I know. I feel silly. I'm sorry," she said, looking back. "Look, I'm glad you know. It was eating at me. I didn't want you to think I didn't like you and I was a snob."

"Yeah, no, it makes sense." He didn't want her to go. Reaching out his hand, he pulled her close by the neck. She could feel his breath on her skin, and he smelled of minerals from the drying sweat on his body. He leaned down and kissed her gently on the lips. It was heady and disorientating. Kirsten felt dizzy. She thought this only happened in romance novels.

Brian pulled away and slid his hand down over hers. "I'm sorry I shut you out. I was just so mad you'd do that to me and, at the time, I wasn't getting any response from San Francisco."

"It's okay. I'm glad I finally got a chance to clear it up. I felt bad and you wouldn't let me explain. You were gone, then I was gone, and then you were gone forever."

"I'm not gonna be gone forever; this is my home," he said resolutely. "Hey, why don't you walk me back? Maybe we could talk. Catch up." He didn't let go of her hand, letting it linger lightly in his palm.

"Sure, I'd like that," Kirsten said, still spinning.

They turned to exit the park, and Kirsten let him lead the way, their hands naturally slipping apart. A shyness overcame them, and Brian attempted to brush it away. "How's Randi?"

"Good. Same old Randi. We've actually been hanging out more."

"Yeah? I miss working with her. She makes things easy. I'm dealing with a lot of egos at my new job, and it can be exhausting."

"Yeah? I'm sorry. It must be nice to live in San Francisco, though?"

"It is. The bay is amazing. A guy I work with invited me out on his family's sailboat and I got a tour. Kind of awesome. Makes one feel quite small. Not like the lakes here."

Kirsten laughed. "I bet."

As they neared his house, its familiarity brought trepidation. Kirsten would die if he ever found out how many times she'd driven by in his absence. What came next was uncharted. Anxiety filled her as she crossed the threshold of a place she thought she'd never see again.

"I'm sorry to leave you alone, but I really need to take a shower. I promise I'll be quick. Please make yourself at home," Brian said as he turned to go upstairs. "Oh, there are some sodas in the fridge if you want anything."

"Okay, thanks." She wandered into the kitchen. The table was covered with pizza boxes and magazines and dishes filled the sink. She opened the fridge and saw it only contained a few basics, the modern essentials like soda and beer, and lots of different hot sauces and salsa.

The place seemed colder and messier compared to the last

time she'd been there, probably because Brian had been gone and, if he still had renters, they more than likely didn't take as much care as he would. She cleared a spot at the table, sat down, and slowly nursed a soda she didn't really want. There was an issue of *Fast Company* with a tech icon on the cover staring at her. She needed to not think about what had just happened or what her next moves would be—if this scenario or that scenario played out. All reasoning vanished.

Brian came downstairs and hurried through the kitchen and into the laundry room half-dressed. He came back out and finished pulling down his shirt while he sat down to put on his socks. Kirsten stole a quick glance before he pulled his shirt completely down and felt the need to caution herself.

He turned and rested his elbows on the table and looked at Kirsten sitting diagonally across from him. This wasn't exactly what he had ever expected to happen and the worst possible timing, but what could he do? While hurrying through his shower, he'd battled to reconcile his desire with reality. Kirsten Swenson wanted him. Well, she'd said he looked good. Looked really good, if he recalled correctly. And he'd kissed her. He'd never thought in a million years that would ever be a possibility, and now here she was. Her snubbing him was the only thing that had propelled him away from her, but now to find out it wasn't a snub at all, but the exact opposite.... As he toweled off, he'd wondered if she even still liked him, and if so, would she be willing to start anything given the distance standing between them. It wasn't like he was going to stay away forever. Minneapolis was his home. He had every intention of coming back. He'd already put in six months, so what was another year or so? Or would she consider moving away from her job at Dayfield's? She was from the West Coast. He'd shut the water off and resolved not to get ahead of himself.

"Well, hmm." Brian smiled sheepishly.

"Well, hmmm." Kirsten smiled back.

"Well?" Brian said.

"Well?" Kirsten parroted again. This was why she liked Brian; he made her laugh no matter how anxious she felt.

"Sooo, what's next?" Brian finally asked.

"I don't know. The truth is, I don't know what it means, and it's been so long ago now."

"Well, there's only one way to find out," Brian heard himself say. There was no denying anymore what he really wanted to happen. He would not have the strength to decide any other way. He knew he'd be able to find an acceptable rationalization later; what it would entail was beyond him for the moment.

"What?" Kirsten asked naively.

Brian stood up, walked over to her, and held out his hands for her to pull herself up.

As she stood, she realized what he meant. Shyness overcame her again, and she looked down. What gave guys the guts to be so bold in this arena? She could never do it.

He ran his hand gently up the side of her arm, his touch encouraging her to tilt her head up. Holding her there, he leaned in and kissed her softly. Her hands found their way to his shoulders, then as the kiss deepened and became more urgent, her arms embraced his neck.

She pulled back with her eyes still closed, and her hands slid down his chest over his freshly laundered shirt. She found the scent of the laundry soap mixed with the newly applied deodorant to be strangely comforting and better than any cologne. She could feel his warmth come through the fabric as she pressed against him. His head rested on top of hers, and she knew all she had to do was look up and he'd kiss her again.

She was at a crossroads and in a position she'd never been in before. She'd never wanted to be with a man like this. She felt excited and nervous, yet terrified of letting Brian know she was a virgin. Maybe he wouldn't be able to tell. She wanted to be daring and throw caution to the wind.

He sensed her indecision and gently lifted her head at the back of her neck. She liked he was taking control and let him guide her. She no longer cared if the whole world was watching, if her emotions were taking over, or if he was taking advantage of her and she couldn't tell. She'd wanted this for such a long time that no matter the outcome, she was willing to accept it—even if it was a disaster.

Then as quickly as it had begun, it stopped, and they pulled away from each other, knowing they needed to catch their breaths. He took her hand and led her upstairs to his bedroom.

The bed wasn't made and there were boxes everywhere, but she didn't mind—all she wanted was him. God help her, she didn't have the strength to resist. He took off his shirt, and Kirsten began to unbutton hers.

This is it. I'm finally going to do it.

Realizing she couldn't be totally reckless, she stopped when he brought her toward him again. "I don't have anything, and I'm not on anything. Do you have something?" He nodded in understanding and went into the bathroom.

She could hear him rummaging around. I guess it's a good sign, Kirsten thought. I'd hate to think he knew exactly where they were. She started having misgivings and wondered how many times he'd done this with how many other women.

He came out, opened his dresser drawer, and fished around to no avail. Now *he* was getting nervous and uncomfortable.

He was in the middle of moving, which could be the reason for the search. Given the present circumstances, there was no way for her to know for sure.

Brian's thoughts raced while his frustration mounted at not being able to find a condom. He felt stupid and afraid he'd lose his chance if he didn't find one soon.

He never would've guessed she was attracted to him. Of course, he'd known he was attracted to her from the first time he saw her outside his cubicle. She'd been all business and completely unaware of the effect she had on those around her. She didn't flirt or wield her looks to win favor, which, ironically, is precisely what they did. She tried so hard to be professional and grown-up, and Brian had found it completely alluring. He'd decided immediately to do everything he could to get to know her better, but his efforts had gone unnoticed. He'd worked long enough at Dayfield's to know most buyers weren't as accommodating or forgiving as she'd been upon their first encounter and wondered if it was because she'd liked him even then. He'd been elated when he'd seen her sitting at Half-Time but played it cool until he'd learned they lived by each other and then made sure he gave her a ride home. She was an intoxicating combination of strength and vulnerability.

He finally found one in a miscellaneous box and threw it up onto the pillows.

He moved in close again, wrapped his arm around her, and caressed her cheek with his other hand. "Are you sure this is what you want?"

"Yes," she said without breaking their locked gaze. He slowly pushed her shirt off and kissed her shoulders and neck. Kirsten couldn't believe how composed she was. She fell so easily into him, wanting more. They moved to the bed and lay down together. Boxes lined the wall next to the right side of the bed, leaving a narrow margin of empty space between them and the bed. The same side of the bed had a few boxes carelessly placed on top as well as the headboard above. It was an obviously king-sized bed; otherwise, there wouldn't've been room for both of them. "Sorry, I can move the boxes," Brian said.

"No, that's okay," Kirsten answered, feeling a little wild because of the incongruity. She started to lose herself again, and Brian tried nudging the boxes out of the way. She reconsidered his question, as it must be bothering him, or perhaps they were both afraid of making another condom-like stop. It was too late, however; her indecision had prompted her brain to signal her body before she'd fully signed off, and she abruptly pressed up against his shoulder with her hand to sit up. The sudden gesture caused him to overreact, afraid he was hurting her; his head swung up and caught the edge of a box on the headboard. It startled him, and in his effort to right the box he knocked an object next to it, and it crashed down on Kirsten.

Wham! Kirsten screamed in excruciating pain and bolted upright. Overwhelmed by her throbbing forehead, she lay back down, placing her hand against the wound.

"Oh, my God!" Brian exclaimed. "You're bleeding!" He jumped up and ran to the bathroom.

Kirsten pulled her hand away, revealing blood on her fingers, and stared in disbelief.

Brian dashed back to her side, dabbing her forehead with the only thing he could find, a hand towel, and applied pressure to stop the bleeding.

"What was that?" Kirsten said.

"I don't know. This looks bad, and it's really bleeding. You're going to need stitches."

"Stitches?! I've never had stitches in my life. What was it?"

"This," Brian said, holding up some weird mass of jagged metal.

"What is that?" she asked.

"This would be a paperweight. I'm so sorry; I had no idea. Are you sure you're going to be okay?"

"Well, I'd feel a lot better if I didn't have to have stitches. I'm pretty much a wimp."

"Well, this bleeding isn't slowing, but head wounds usually gush a lot. I'm afraid I'd better take you to the hospital or urgent care, because I have had stitches and I know."

"Great!"

Kirsten held the hand towel tightly to her head while Brian put his shirt back on. She didn't know if she should laugh or cry. The strange turn of events had her lying half-naked with a bloody gash on her forehead—she pictured telling Sten. If he could see her now he'd get quite the laugh.

Brian helped her up to a sitting position so he could help her on with her shirt. "How do you feel?" he asked.

"A little lightheaded. Don't feel bad; it's not your fault." The situation was a bit awkward to make a joke out of, and Kirsten could tell he was feeling rather responsible, so she refrained from being flippant.

She allowed Brian to steady her on the way to his car even

though she was perfectly capable of doing it herself. They rode in silence for the short trip to urgent care while Kirsten kept the towel pressed to her forehead. The waiting area was fortunately not too busy, but it still seemed to take way too long. She finally got called and asked Brian to go with her.

"So, what happened?" the nurse asked.

"Uhm, paperweight," was all Kirsten could get out. Brian tried to help.

"Yeah, it got knocked off a shelf and landed on her."

The nurse seemed suspicious. "Are you her husband?"

"Uh, no. No, he's moving. We were packing." Kirsten explained to stop the questions.

"Sorry, but if you're not married, I'll have to ask you to sit out in the waiting area," the nurse said to Brian.

"Oh? Yeah, sure, no problem," Brian said and got up and left. "I'll be right outside if you need anything."

"Okay, thanks." Kirsten tried not to panic; she'd managed to avoid major physical injury her entire life and didn't want to get stitches without someone there to hold her hand. She knew it was silly, but she couldn't help it.

"When was your last tetanus shot?"

"Uhm, seven years ago. I do it every decade." She was relieved she could skip that; still, a needle was unavoidable as they needed to numb the area first. Kirsten focused on reading a leaflet pinned to the wall talking about the importance of vaccinations and quickly reconsidered, but the nurse was adept and had already injected her. She'd forgotten his name and tried to remember as she quietly observed his tatted-up arms. The jumble of competing images ended in a perfect line around his wrist like a cuff. Unlike Kirsten, nurses weren't afraid of needles. He was a large man, and the tattoos made him appear more intimidating than he was. Kirsten sensed a sweet demeanor underneath and began to feel less nervous in his hands. That, and she'd survived the shot, which was starting to do its job.

"Okay, I'm gonna step out while this takes effect, and then the doctor will be in to give you the stitches."

"Awesome," Kirsten said, giving him a wry smile.

Her legs dangled from her perch on the doctor's table, wondering what Brian could be thinking and feeling, because she definitely didn't know what she thought or felt. She decompartmentalized as she knew she only had enough energy to get through her stitches, and she hoped the doctor wouldn't be too long. She finally decided to brave a look, slid off the table onto the floor, and walked over to the mirror.

It was a high gash near the hairline favoring her right side. It was short, maybe three-quarters of an inch long. It looked fairly deep but was hard to tell from the blood. The skin was ragged and chewed like a scrape around the edges. Kirsten didn't like seeing that part. She gently touched around it and didn't feel anything—a good sign. She heard a knock on the door and scrambled back up on the table.

"Come in."

"Hi, I'm Dr. Ahja." Kirsten was relieved to see what appeared to be a younger version of Sanjay Gupta. Who didn't like Sanjay? She was afraid to say he looked like him, because A, he might get that all the time, and B, he might think she's racist for assuming every male Indian doctor looked like a CNN correspondent. Nevertheless, she found his bedside manner comforting.

"So, you need some stitches, huh?" he said, coming over and taking a look with his doctor light.

"Yeah, I'm afraid so."

"Well, you're in luck. I was considered the best in my class at suturing."

"Oh, good. I was hoping," Kirsten said.

"It says in your chart you're allergic to penicillin?"

"Yes. Do I need to take antibiotics?"

"No, not unless it gets infected. So, how did this happen?"

"A paperweight. I was helping a friend pack, and it got knocked off the shelf and hit me," Kirsten said, looking into his neutral face, replaying what really happened and feeling the embarrassment all over again. Her registering emotion unintentionally signaled a lie.

"Are you sure?" he asked. "This is a safe place, Kirsten. Are you safe?"

"No! I mean, yes! I'm safe. I think you're misunderstanding. I just feel really stupid, because I was lying on the floor taking a break and my friend, Brian, was taking stuff off the shelf, and it got knocked and fell on me." Kirsten was impressed with her quick thinking. All those years of watching crime shows were paying off. The height and angle of her description lined up with the actual events. "I shouldn't have lay there."

"Okay," he said, "you understand I have to ask."

"No. No, of course." Kirsten became very emphatic, realizing she couldn't afford to let her emotions muddle the truth.

"Okay, let's get this done," he said, turning to prepare the necessary instruments and astringents. It became quiet, and he worked in silence while Kirsten followed his instructions to a tee and remained still as a statue. It wasn't too bad; even though she was numbed, she could still feel the pressure from the prick and tug of each stitch and the imagined pain coming with each.

She left with a handful of instructions and a prescription should she need it. Brian was patiently sitting in the waiting room, his concern for her showed on his face. How ridiculous to think Brian could ever be an abuser.

"How'd it go?" he asked.

"Not too bad." She smiled, trying to make him feel better. They got back into his car and sat there, not knowing what to do next.

"I thought you might be hungry. Would you like to get a bite to eat?" Brian asked.

"Uhm, yeah, that would be good. Maybe a late lunch?"

"There's an excellent brewpub up back by your place. The Kenwood Brewery?"

"Oh, yeah, I've been meaning to go there."

It was a perfect fusion of rustic charm and European flair. Kirsten felt like they were having a first date, which suited her just fine. It was a limited menu since they were between meals, but still boasted a choice of traditional brew fare with a nod toward fine dining. Kirsten was famished and settled on a turkey panini with a rhubarb mostarda. Upon Googling the word, she learned *mostarda* was an Italian condiment made of candied fruit and a mustard-flavored syrup—*just like it sounds*, she thought. Brian ordered classic pulled-pork sliders.

It was busy for the time of day, and the hubbub cheered Kirsten up. She would've loved to have a beer but was afraid the alcohol would mix badly with her numbing meds. Brian followed her lead and refrained as well.

Her wound wasn't too big and required only a small bandage. Kirsten hoped its smallness wouldn't provoke too many questions.

Brian asked if it hurt.

"No, not really, but I think I'm still under the effects of the medicine. Tomorrow will probably be more telling," she said with a twisted smile.

"I'm *so* sorry," he said again. "I feel terrible."

"I know. It was an accident. Just glad it's over and it wasn't worse. It could always be worse, right?"

"Right." He laughed. "But it could always be better." Their eyes met, remembering what had almost been. It all seemed inconceivable at the moment and much more than either had bargained for—a simple Saturday morning in the park.

AFTER

Okay, so this isn't your typical morning after, Kirsten thought as she lay in bed—or almost morning after, she corrected. The sun streamed through the window as if to say it finally had decided it would be spring. Her wound was rather tender, and the trauma left her feeling a bit hungover. Brian had been very sweet and walked her all the way into her apartment. She'd have to get her car later.

What time is it? She rolled slowly over so as not to jar her head. *Ten!* She still was unable to rouse herself. Eventually, her need to pee overruled and she gingerly sat up, stood, and headed for the bathroom. Her morning routine remained the same, except it was executed with much greater care. She took her time getting ready, not one to push the envelope when it came to physical injury, no matter how minor. She looked at her forehead in the mirror but decided not to look under the bandage and give it more time to heal. She could see some yellow and purple bruising beginning to emerge outside the dressing. *Great!* It was going to be more difficult to hide.

She sat at her table sipping her coffee and reliving the previous afternoon. Relieved about finally fixing things between her and Brian, she savored the memory of his kissing her. It reminded her of a couple she'd seen kissing once on Houston Street in New York. It was more like a highway than a street.

Loud, busy, and very wide by any city's standards, but there they were in the middle of the afternoon. She'd never seen such surrender and abandon in a kiss. They looked to be of college age, and the girl was giving him everything in that one kiss. Kirsten was struck by how fragile and sensuous it was. She'd wondered if the guy appreciated it or if one day soon he'd leave her, and she'd be devastated because she was so young and defenseless.

The phone rang. "Oh, no, not yet," she cried. It was Brian. "I'm not ready." She let it ring a few times before she picked it up, preparing herself to sound as normal as possible. "Hello."

"Kirsten?" Brian asked.

"Yes, hi."

"Hi. How are you feeling?"

"Like I have five stitches in my head," she said sarcastically.

He laughed tentatively. "How 'bout if I bring over some coffee and muffins?"

"Yeah, that'd be great. I'll text you the code," Kirsten said.

"See you in a few."

She decided to spruce up a bit and changed out of her joggers into jeggings and a casual yet funky sweatshirt she finally settled on after changing her mind three times, finalizing her look by quickly applying a light veneer of makeup. She heard a knock and swiftly dumped her coffee. She peered through the peephole before opening the door.

Brian entered her simple yet feminine apartment, trying to take in all the details he'd missed the night before. Not knick-knacky, which he liked. Surprisingly comfy and floral for a connoisseur of high fashion. "Nice place," he said.

"Thanks," she replied, and led the way to her kitchen.

The events of the previous day seemed to have created

a slight discomfort between them. He worried about how to begin again and thought maybe there was no point and she'd changed her mind. He did live nearly two thousand miles away; not exactly convenient. He only knew deep inside he didn't want to blow it. He wasn't sure he was ready for something like this, but he didn't want to end up with regrets.

"Have a seat," Kirsten said, while indicating the chair opposite her favorite spot at the table. Sensing the awkwardness, Kirsten refused to let it become real. She had nearly slept with the guy.

"Coffee and muffins as promised," Brian said, setting a bag and drink carrier on the table.

"Great, I'm starving." She got plates from the cupboard and set a muffin on each. "Actually, how 'bout we sit in the living room; it's more comfortable in there," Kirsten offered, thinking the table wouldn't be conversational enough.

"Okay, sure." Brian picked up the coffees and followed her into the next room.

They sat on the couch and began to eat their muffins and sip their coffees. Normally she would be the first one to talk about the hard stuff to control the situation, but instead she felt uncharacteristically shy.

"I guess we should talk about what almost happened yesterday," Brian said.

"Yeah." Kirsten smiled with relief, despite the blush she felt spreading over her cheeks.

"I'm really sorry. I feel so dumb for causing it."

"I know. It really isn't your fault, though, you know. It's actually kind of funny if you think about it. I mean, do you really think anyone is going to believe me?"

Brian laughed. "Uh, yeah: I, uh, had an accident with a

paperweight."

Kirsten laughed too. "I think I'm just going to make some-thing up for tomorrow they'll believe." They started to get comfortable again. "The truth is, Brian, I'm not so sure it was a bad thing it happened. It was kind of fast. I wasn't thinking too clearly."

Brian didn't know where he wanted to go with this, so he followed where he thought she was going. "I know what you mean. I don't live here anymore, so it probably wouldn't be such a good idea."

"I do like you, and I hope you don't think I was leading you on. Seeing you was such a shock and to finally be able to tell you what had really happened...I don't know...I feel like it went a little crazy. Do you forgive me about Bloedel Kirkpatrick?"

"Yeah. It all doesn't seem to matter now. I should've let you explain, but at the time I was too upset."

"I'm usually much better on my feet. I'm really sorry. I'm glad the truth is finally out; it had really been bothering me. I didn't know if I should get ahold of you, and I worried if I did I might make it worse. It just needed to be done in person, I guess."

Brian sat contemplating whether he should say something more, but all he could do was think about how much he want-ed her and how beautiful she was and how she had been in his room wanting him. He could still see her patiently waiting for him to find that stupid condom. How her Nordic blonde hair had gleamed in the light, her brilliant blue eyes looking like they could hold a multitude of sins. He didn't think he could give her up, and it wasn't like she was saying no. She did admit to still liking him, it was merely a matter of distance. Okay, so it was a large distance, but he didn't plan on being there forever. Couldn't they enjoy the time they had? It seemed unfair to discover this now only to let it go.

He reached across the couch and took her hand. "I'm glad it's finally out too. The thing is, I've liked you from the first time I saw you. I just never thought you'd think I was your type."

"My type? What is my type, then?"

"I don't know...maybe more like Michael...a little more suit-like."

"Michael?" She laughed to shrug it off but was knocked down a bit by his accuracy. "I may love the fashion biz but I'm not much like the people who work in it."

"Could've fooled me with all those savvy clothes and your chic business style."

"Hey, you make it sound like I'm a snob. I'm not thought of in that way, am I?" Kirsten exclaimed.

"No—well, maybe a little, but in a good way," Brian said.

"I don't see how it could be in a good way," Kirsten said.

"I can see that," Brian said jokingly while he stroked her hand and continued to look steadily at her.

Kirsten began to feel uneasy. The distance thing wasn't going to be enough to help her bow out gracefully.

Brian leaned in while pulling her within kissing range.

Kirsten tried to not look away, to meet him honestly, but uncontrollably looked down briefly before she met his eyes again. "Brian, no; we can't."

"We almost did."

"I know, but we didn't. And as hard as this is, I really think it's for the best."

"I'm not going to stay in San Francisco forever, you

know."

"Brian… Then we'll discuss it when you get back."

"I just moved there. I don't think I can wait that long."
Brian couldn't believe what was coming out of his mouth. He
desperately wanted her and would do anything to get her to
agree. "I just found you when I thought there would never be
a chance. I don't think I can let it go, and I don't think you can
either." He closed the gap and kissed her.

Kirsten started breaking apart. She was helpless. His kiss-
es became more urgent, and his hands began slipping under
her sweatshirt.

"Brian, stop!" Kirsten yelled while jumping up from the
couch. Something had snapped in her, and even she was surprised at her strong reaction. She didn't know what it meant,
but knew she was scared. She hated her fear was coming back.
It'd never mattered before because she hadn't really liked the
other guys, but Brian she liked. She got off the couch and
walked into the kitchen.

Brian was confused and didn't know what to make of
her reaction; he only knew he shouldn't push it. He knew he
was right about the way they both felt about each other but
couldn't grasp the full meaning of her withdrawal. He got
up from the couch and walked up to the bar counter jetting
out from the open kitchen where Kirsten stood. "I'm sorry.
I don't understand why anything else should matter. If we
want to be together, we should be together. Time and distance
aren't going to change that."

"How do you know?" Kirsten replied. "All of this is based
on emotion instead of reality. I don't know if what I feel was
made stronger by your leaving so suddenly, or if maybe if
you'd never left I'd feel differently."

"Why would you feel differently?" Brian said.

"I don't know. Maybe if I'd spent more time with you after behaving so foolishly at the gala, I would have more perspective, but now all I've had for the last six months is speculation gone wild."

"You don't strike me as one to create false innuendos, Kirsten."

"How do you know? This has all taken me by surprise."

"You think it hasn't for me too? I'm supposed to be getting on a plane next week, and maybe I wouldn't have to if I'd only known!"

"What are you saying? That you wouldn't have taken this job if you'd known how I felt?"

"Maybe. I don't know."

"Well, it's futile to argue about it because you are getting on a plane and will be gone for who knows how long."

"Well, I don't want to now. I don't want to lose you."

"You won't be losing me, Brian."

"How come I don't believe you?" Brian said dejectedly.

Kirsten let the silence lengthen. She didn't know what to say and was desperate to end the gap. She couldn't lie, and the longer the silence grew, the more it confirmed the truth.

"Brian, why would I lie to you?" Kirsten pleaded.

"I don't know. I sense there is something you're not telling me."

"Well, I don't know what more I can say. It really is about the distance and the suddenness of it all. I need time to think." Kirsten found herself buying time to make it work. Maybe she could make it work. Maybe having it be a long-distance thing would take the pressure off. I'm such a pig; he deserves the truth, Kirsten's conscience bothered her. Why do I keep lying to him? I don't want to. She was terrified.

"Think about what? There isn't anything to think about. Either you want to be with someone or you don't." Brian couldn't help being frustrated despite wanting to be patient and understanding.

Kirsten realized as much as she didn't want to agree, he was right. Why did he have to put it into an either-or situation? Why couldn't it stay muddled a while longer? She guessed it'd be asking too much to see each other platonically until he left. "I guess you're right. I wish it didn't have to be this way."

Brian sat there hoping she'd change her mind. He knew what he saw and felt and couldn't decipher her refusal. He rose from the couch, looked at her, and started to speak, then shrugged his shoulders and headed for the door. She wanted to run and grab him and tell him not to leave, that she wanted him more than anything, but her legs wouldn't budge and she stood motionless. He reached the door by the time she was able to move, and she came up behind him as he reached for the knob. Sensing her closeness, he slowly turned back halfway to say goodbye. He looked defeated.

"Brian, I'm so sorry. Please try to understand."

"I do," he lied.

Kirsten hugged him with more reassurance than she had to give and felt his resignation. She briefly clasped his face with one hand and tried to communicate all her emotions with her eyes, but could see it wasn't going to work. She wanted to kiss him lightly on the lips but knew he would refuse. She couldn't give him what he wanted.

He slipped away from her and out the door. She pushed the door closed and leaned into it, unable to step away. She stood there a long time before finally turning her back against the door. Reaching her hand around, she turned the deadbolt and slid to the floor. She sat until the sun entered through the opposite windows, piercing her eyes. Its constant counting of time was indifferent to her distress. She turned away from it and brushed her lips with her fingers, remembering his taste and touch with regret.

She desperately needed to cry, but nothing would come out. She decided staying locked up in her apartment all day wasn't going to improve anything. In a frenetic state, she jumped to her feet and ran to get her coat and purse. Kirsten wanted to go for a drive; she did not know where. When she got outside, she suddenly realized she didn't have her car. It was still parked in front of the cinnamon bun café. She started walking to the Lake of the Isles, going faster and faster until she was running as if trying to catch a bus. Her purse bounced up and down against her side, so she pulled it over her head to wear it crosswise. For the briefest moment, she worried about how ridiculous she looked, then rationalized there was no one around to take notice and she couldn't do anything but run. She ran and ran until she couldn't run anymore, then walked the rest of the way, desperately wanting to reach her car so she could get in and cry. She'd run farther than she'd thought and walked the few blocks back to the café and away from the lake. Once inside her car, she drove away from the activity of the Sunday brunch crowd to a quiet side street and sobbed uncontrollably.

The rest of the day was a blur. She finally went to bed way too late because she couldn't pull herself off the couch. Watching TV all evening had done little to keep her mind occupied and distracted from Brian. Getting to work tomorrow was going to be a challenge. She already knew she was going to be late but didn't care and knew Michael wouldn't say anything even if he did mind, which he wouldn't.

Kirsten wandered into her office about nine-thirty and sat quietly down to work on some easy paperwork. She avoided human contact of any kind. It was one-thirty before Michael poked his head in.

"Aren't you going to go to lunch?" he asked.

"Um, yeah, I guess, I'm not really hungry. Why? Are you?" Kirsten replied.

"No, I just got back," Michael looked confused.

"Oh." Kirsten attempted to sound casual. Sometimes it was nice to work with only men because they knew when not to ask what was wrong even with a bandage on her forehead. He headed back to his office, and she breathed a sigh of relief.

Michael popped his head back in. "I forgot to tell you Brian is back in town, and he's having a thing at his house tomorrow night for whoever."

Kirsten never had found out why he'd chosen now to pack up his house, so she decided to play dumb to get some info. "What's he doing back? Did he get a job here or something?"

"No, I think he's decided to put his stuff in storage so he can rent out more of his house. I guess things are going well for him out in San Francisco."

"Oh, yeah, that's great," she said.

Kirsten did go to lunch, but only to clear her head. It was the perfect time because most people were done with lunch by two, and she could sit quietly in the back of a deli and eat her small salad.

She didn't like how things had been left because it wasn't clean. But life is messy—not everything can be wrapped up with a little bow on top, and this was going to be one of those times. She'd promised herself she'd live with integrity. If she didn't have that then how could she expect people to trust her, and she wanted to be trustworthy. Something she'd never gotten from her father.

Hard as she tried, she couldn't get much work done. Fortunately, there was nothing urgent. She wandered into Michael's office and sat down. He looked up in his slow casual manner and sat back in his chair, looking at her. "What's going on with you today? Are you okay?"

"No, but I will be. Is it all right if I go home?"

"Yeah, sure."

She felt silly for ever having worn a short skirt to the office. Michael was more like a big brother, which was what she needed more than anything at the moment. And just like that, she felt their relationship shift. It felt right, like it was exactly what it should be.

Aric made his way in and took the chair next to her. "So, what's with the bandage on your forehead?"

"Well, you probably wouldn't believe me if I told you, but I was doing a little rearranging over the weekend and a bookend fell on me, and well, I had to get stitches."

They laughed and conviviality filled the room. They talked about the spring lines, what they loved about fashion, and shared titillating tales from days gone by at Dayfield's. Kirsten was finally being let in, and the timing was perfect, given her state. It was what she'd always wanted from her work. People she liked, doing what they loved. And she'd finally won Aric over, which was huge.

It'd only taken a year, but oh, what a year it had been. She felt lighter as she opted for the slower elevator. The doors opened, and she hopped onto the car full of people from the advertising department.

"Hey, Kirsten," everyone said.

"Hey, guys, what's up?"

"We're going to go to Murphy's for some beer," Will said.

"That bad already, huh? It's only Monday, guys."

"Yeah? Well, we're going to have to come back. We'll be here all night thanks to the buying department."

"Hey, it wasn't me. I'm not making any changes, I promise."

"We should see if Brian can meet us. He could probably use some cheering up," Randi suggested. "I swung by last night and he looked like hell."

Kirsten cringed.

It was a beautiful afternoon as the sun tried its best to rid Minneapolis of winter. *Like it could?* But on this particular afternoon she felt it might actually succeed. She decided to forgo the bus and walk home. She recalled the words of Carrie Bradshaw about how we're always in search of the perfect apartment, job, and boyfriend. And if we have two out of the three, why do we let that one other thing rob us of our happiness and make us feel inadequate, or something like that. *She was right. Why do we do this?*

She had a fantastic apartment and as of today, an excellent job. She just didn't have the perfect boyfriend. Well, she had the perfect boyfriend; she was the imperfect girlfriend. *Why?* She couldn't answer. *I need to talk to Sten—he'll know.* She situated herself on a bench at a little park near her building and called him.

"Hell-o," he said in surprise.

"Sten! Can you talk?"

"Yeah, sure. I'm working from home today."

"I've missed you. Where have you been?"

"Where have I been?"

"Okay, fine, so I've been a little busy. It's just payback for you ignoring me over the holidays."

"I wasn't ignoring you."

"I know. How're things with Michelle?"

"Good."

"Really good or just good?"

"They're good."

"Wow, Sten, I hope you're a lot more enthusiastic with her about it."

"What's up?"

"Mmmm, I think I need to see a counselor."

"Why?"

"Because I just passed up an opportunity to have a really great boyfriend."

"Who?"

"Brian."

"Brian? I thought he'd moved away."

"He did. He still is. He was here this weekend to move some stuff out of his house, and I happened to run into him accidentally."

"Accidentally? You aren't still stalking him, are you?"

"No. I saw him running at the lakes and, well, I finally told him why I'd snubbed him."

"You did?"

"I did."

"And how'd that go?"

"It went really well, actually. I was absolutely terrified at first, but then I was finally able to find a way to get it out in a subtle way. After a few tries he finally got it."

"Wow, good for you. Feel better now?"

"Yes. Well, I did, but then it went downhill again."

"What happened?"

"Well, I'm not sure exactly. It was going well, and we went back to his house to talk and, well, one thing led to another, and I really thought *it* was going to happen. I was surprisingly calm—not like all the other times—so I really thought I was finally gonna, you know, be able to do it."

"But you couldn't."

"No, I could, but then I got hit in the head with this paper-weight and was bleeding, and we had to go to urgent care to get stitches."

"What?! Where'd this paperweight come from? I don't understand."

"I know; it's hard to explain. But he's moving and there were boxes everywhere, and one fell and this weird crumpled up piece of metal flew out and hit me."

"Wow."

"I know, crazy, huh? You can't make this stuff up. Anyway, it didn't happen, obviously, and now I have this bandage on my forehead because I had to have five stitches."

"Are you okay?"

"Yeah, yeah, I'm fine. Just a little sore. Anyway, the next day he comes over to see how I'm doing and we start talking and we really like each other, but he lives so far away and who knows when he'll come back. I don't know, I started to panic and I couldn't do it."

"Well, maybe that's why? Long-distance relationships don't usually work out."

"Yeah, I know, but I don't think so. It was weird. So now

I don't know what to do because I always thought it was because I never really liked the other guys, and I really like Brian. Like a *lot*. I mean, I think I might even be in love with him."

"Yeah?"

"Yeah."

They sat there for a minute letting it hang.

"Sten?"

"Yeah?"

"What's wrong with me?"

"I don't know, Kirsten. I think you have to have everything perfect before you'll do it, and, well, nothing is ever going to be perfect. You need to find a way to let go."

"I know. I don't know how, though, that's why I'm thinking of seeing a counselor. What do you think? Do you think it would help?"

"I don't know. I saw one after Sofie died, but he didn't do anything. He just sat there while I talked. Then a few years later, I learned he'd had an affair with one of his patients. I think most counselors become counselors because they're trying to figure out their own demons and don't know any better than the rest of us."

"Great! I'm screwed."

"Maybe you should just tell him."

"Tell him? I can't do that. What guy wants to be with a girl he can't have sex with?"

"I don't know, but maybe if he really loves you it won't matter."

"Seriously, Sten? Would you be with someone like that?"

"I don't know. I might if I really loved her."

"Yeah, maybe at first, but what if I'm never able to do it.

Ever! What if I have the perfect wedding and we're married and I still can't do it?"

"I don't know. I think you should tell him. If he knew, maybe he could help you."

Kirsten was silent.

"I'm sorry, Kirsten. I wish I could be more help."

"I know. It helps being able to talk about it. Thanks, Sten."

"Sure thing, 'cuz."

"Okay, I'm gonna go now."

"You sure?"

"Yeah. Thanks for listening and say hi to Michelle for me."

"I will."

"Bye."

"Bye."

She sat on the bench, taking in the beauty of the day and feeling much better than she had twenty-four hours ago. *Is that Nicole?* Kirsten saw a lithe blonde step out of a silver sports car at the edge of the park. *It was Nicole! Wonder what she's doing here?*

She wore a drapey dark cream blouse with dolman sleeves and a deep pleated vee in front. It was tucked into a white pencil skirt that stopped just below her knees. A floral pattern was sprinkled across it in the same color as the blouse. Her golden blonde hair was wrapped up into a messy bun in the back, and she walked effortlessly in her slingback pumps of the same shade. A coordinating handbag hung over her arm and her phone in hand.

She walked onto the path and headed Kirsten's way, her large dark glasses shading her eyes. She stopped cold upon seeing Kirsten.

"Kirsten? What are you doing here?"

"I live nearby and decided to walk."

"Why?!"

"I don't know, it's such a rare day and I needed the fresh air."

"Are you okay?" Nicole said, sitting down next to her.

"Yeah, why?"

Nicole pointed to her bandage.

"Oh?" Kirsten lightly touched it, having momentarily forgotten. "No. This was a freak accident."

"Who's the freak?"

Kirsten laughed. "No, really it was."

Nicole took off her glasses, revealing a bruise on the side of her left eye.

"Are you sure?"

"Oh, my God, Nicole! Are you okay?"

"I will be. I guess I finally got what I deserve."

"Huh? Why would you ever deserve that?"

"I don't know. I'm sure you've heard the rumors."

Kirsten played dumb. She felt sorry for Nicole. Perfect Nicole with a bruise on her face suddenly looked defenseless.

"No. Was it that guy who just dropped you off?" Kirsten deflected.

Nicole started to cry, her shoulders shaking with her silent sobs. Kirsten scooted over and put her arm around her while Nicole rummaged in her bag for a tissue to dab her eyes and blow her nose. She nodded her head yes.

"I don't even like him that much. I only went out with him to move on and make someone jealous." Kirsten wondered if it was Michael she was trying to make jealous.

"I'm so sorry," Kirsten comforted.

"Oh, God! I'm so embarrassed. What you must think of

me."

"I don't think of you in any way," Kirsten lied. "Relationships are complicated. Who am I to judge?" Flashes of Brian and Michael exposed themselves in her head. Despite the friendly tone she'd exchanged with Michael a little earlier, she felt her shame rise again and was even more glad she'd never acted on it. Kirsten could empathize with Nicole regarding Michael—he was an anomaly.

"What do people say about me?" Nicole stopped, red-eyed and puffy, to look at Kirsten.

"I really haven't heard anything, honest," which was true, Kirsten told herself. No one had come out and told her point-blank, there had only been a few strange comments, like the time at the sports bar. "I got the sense something had maybe gone on between you and Michael, but not because anyone said anything. I promise," Kirsten answered.

"Yeah? No, I'm sure not, but yes, there was something between us, but I can't talk about it. I'm legally bound."

"Legally bound?" Kirsten didn't like the sound of that.

"It's not what you think. Michael is not like that. I promise!"

Kirsten gave Nicole a stern questioning look.

"It's complicated. You have nothing to worry about. The thing is, I like Michael and I know he likes me. He's just not capable of commitment." Nicole paused and sat quietly on the bench before deciding to divulge more. "It was my fault. I got angry and punished him. I couldn't accept him for who he is. The thing is, I know who he is and I took advantage of it. I thought I could be the one to change him."

Kirsten didn't need to ask anyone any more about what had happened. Without Nicole giving specifics, Kirsten knew what she meant, and Nicole could see Kirsten understood.

"You and Michael aren't...?" Nicole suddenly asked, waving her phone at Kirsten.

"No! No." Kirsten was startled by the question.

"No. No, of course not. I mean, I didn't think so. You don't seem like the type. I don't know, he's just very. Uhm. He's very—"

"Sexual." Kirsten finished for her.

"Yes! That's it." Nicole looked at Kirsten with a raised eyebrow, and Kirsten blushed a little and started laughing.

"Really? You're sure you don't fancy him?" Nicole chided her.

"No. No, but I get it. I've seen him in action, let's just say," Kirsten said, smiling.

"Yeah, no, if he lasers in on someone there is no hope. They're gone! And if he doesn't, then women throw themselves at him—either way he wins."

"Yeah, that sounds about right," Kirsten agreed.

"Well, good for you for not getting taken in by him, or maybe just a little?" Nicole couldn't help pressing.

"No, but there was a rep in New York."

"Kyra!"

Kirsten laughed. "Yes, Kyra."

"I knew it!"

Kirsten didn't feel comfortable admitting her lustful fantasies about Michael, particularly since nothing had ever happened. Hearing Nicole only cemented her resolve to keep her relationship with Michael professional.

"Well, I have to get back to the office and unlike you, I'm not walking," Nicole said, tapping her phone to summon an Uber.

"Sorry."

"Thanks, but I won't be there long. I'm glad I ran into you, Kirsten. It's been good talking to you."

"Yeah, me too. And please stay away from men who drive silver sports cars."

Nicole laughed. "I promise."

Beautiful, perfect Nicole who had no problem having sex. It was easy to be intimidated by her. However, on what was otherwise going to be a terrible day, they were merely two young women sitting on a sunny park bench, each with facial wounds resulting from interactions with men, their pain diminished by their newly formed solidarity. Their worlds didn't seem so far apart after all.

THE BALL

Kirsten stared at herself in the mirror, studying the lines of her face as she turned her head from side to side. A bit of acne would require some cover-up, and her brow showed faint permanent lines that would eventually deepen as she aged. She tried to imagine what she'd look like when she was eighty and hoped she'd have the courage to embrace it. There was nothing more unattractive than a woman trying to overcome her age with a bad dye job, plastic surgery, and too much makeup.

Her phone rang. "Hey, Sten! What's up?" she chimed playfully.

"Hey. I'm really sorry, but I can't be your buffer tonight. I'm really sick."

"Really?" Kirsten said.

"Yeah, I know. I was hoping I'd get better, but I'm just not. I'm really sorry. It's not very symptomatic except I'm super tired and all I do is sleep," he explained.

"I know you are. I'm sorry you're feeling so bad. I guess I'll have to deal with Gus all by myself for once. Maybe it's a sign I need to grow up. It's all right. You get better," Kirsten sang in a motherly tone.

"'K. Thanks. Have fun."

"Yeah, right. Bye, sweetie."

"Bye." *Crap!* She really didn't want to go now. She'd

turned the invitation down last year; she hadn't thought she could again and had convinced Sten to be her date.

She glanced at the gown lying on her bed. It was a barely damaged return sitting off the sales floor collecting dust and waiting to be sent to a discounter. She felt like Cinderella again and couldn't believe her luck. It was an Elie Saab—a Lebanese designer who she absolutely adored for his formal wear. It was ice blue in the most delicate body-hugging silk chiffon with elegant crystal beadwork. Its butterfly thin layers flowed out of the skirt around her legs, swooshing luxuriantly. Oh, how she loved the feel of silk against her skin; nothing could compare, and she was increasingly horrified at the use of synthetics in higher-end clothing. They were rougher and didn't let the body breathe, plus they made it difficult to get stains out, especially oil stains, unlike natural fibers.

Normally she didn't care for a lot of beadwork, but he was a magician, and she'd never seen the likes of it. It was going to look stunning with her pale features and blue eyes. It was the perfect dress for a winter ball. However, she had yet to find the right shade of lipstick. She'd looked all over the cosmetic counters at Dayfield's with no luck. Sometimes cheaper was better, and she never had qualms about buying cheap if it looked good and wore well. Form must meet function.

She headed out to the local drugstore to see what she could find.

"Kirsten?" She turned toward the unfamiliar voice.

"Derek? Oh, my gosh. Hi." She couldn't believe it was him.

"Hi. How are you?" he returned.

"Good, good. Buying girl stuff," she said, waving a wand of lipstick. "So, are you a lawyer yet?"

"Yeah, I am. I passed the bar last summer, and I'm working for a firm downtown."

"No more bartending, huh?"

"Well, only once in a while when they get desperate. I actually kind of miss it."

"Yeah? So did you have to tame your 'fro for the new job?"

He laughed at being caught in his conformity, patting his much shorter hair. "Well, maybe a little. So, what are you up to besides buying lipstick?"

"Not much. Going to this cancer ball tonight, hence the lipstick."

"Oh, yeah, I'm going to that. The Legacy Ball, right?"

"Yeah." Kirsten was surprised.

"Yeah, it's for a friend of mine…well, Brian. His dad died of lung cancer—the nonsmoker kind—and, well, he can't make it so I'm filling in." Kirsten felt a pang upon learning Brian had already lost his father and remembered the drive home in his dad's old BMW, it seemed forever ago. She realized it must be more than his dad's car. It was probably his last car. He'd looked a little embarrassed by the small luxury at the time and to understand the meaning behind it made her ache for him all the more. *Dang it!*

"Filling in? You must be really close."

"Yeah, hard to say if I spent more time at his house or mine growing up. His dad was like a father to me."

"That's really sweet."

"Say, I could pick you up, if you like. There's a bunch of us going. I mean if you don't have a date or anything."

"Oh? Yeah. I'm going 'cause my dad invited me, but I'm meeting him there."

"Oh! Forget it then."

Kirsten felt bad for putting him off and since it was with a group and not only him, she decided to say yes.

"No. Yes, I'd love to. My cousin was gonna be my date and then he got sick, so yes, that'd be great. Thanks."

They exchanged contact info and set up a time.

Derek never ceased to surprise her with his sense of humor. He pulled up in an old Cadillac and honked the horn when she emerged from her building. It was hilarious. There were four in the back and a space saved for her upfront with Derek and some petite mousy thing in between. She recognized a few of the faces—one, in particular, was from the drinking competition that seemed a lifetime ago.

"Everybody, this is Kirsten."

"Hi," they greeted in synchronicity.

"Hey." Kirsten waved, turning her head back.

It was another arctic evening in January, the kind that took your breath away and froze the hair in your nostrils. Kirsten felt unsafe in her glittery silver strappy pumps and was thankful she only had to navigate the de-iced path in front of her complex. *How is a girl ever to feel fancy in such a climate?* She imagined her toes turning blue from frostbite and recalled a story she'd heard once about an Alaskan whose wet hair had broken off like icicles upon being exposed to the outdoors.

Hopping into the car, she'd noticed the other girls were dressed similarly and had forgone their fur-lined, calf-length boots. The steel beast, anticipating her concern, blasted divine heat, and Kirsten quickly forgot she was cold.

The ride was filled with happy chatter, and before long Derek kindly dropped everyone off in front of the hotel before he parked. The mousy girl, Emily, smiled a silent invi-

tation to Kirsten to be friends for the evening as the other
two girls, Chrissy and Megan, coupled off with their backseat
boys, Sean and Tyler. They made their way toward the Great
Hall, where the Legacy Ball was being held, but Emily and
Kirsten hung back in the lobby waiting for Derek to catch up
as promised.

Kirsten felt strange socializing with Brian's circle of
friends and wondered if he'd find out. She hoped not but
couldn't help letting it happen. It was another way to stay
close to him—even better than Facebook.

Facebook had become her obsession for most of the last
year. There she could keep tabs on him. What was he up to?
Where was he and, more importantly, who was he with? Was
it a girl? He was always one for posting funny quips or ironic
news worth sharing. She was careful not to like anything too
often and only when their mutual friends liked it too. They
had never unfriended each other after she'd rejected him. She
chastised herself for not being stronger. She should've asked
Facebook to hide his posts, but never did. Every like or comment sent an underlying message, leaving the other unsure
what it meant. Was he/she just being nice or were they trying to encourage progress in their relationship? Facebook had
a strange way of maintaining ties that otherwise would slip
away. Facebook was emotional meth, Kirsten concluded.

Derek was able to park fairly quickly and then ushered
them into the hall. The building suddenly opened up to a
three-storied height to signify its grandeur. It harkened back
to the early twentieth century. The walls of the ballroom were
covered in small subway-sized stone tile and had three arched
openings on the short-sided walls and four on the longer sides.
The dome of the arches reached a floor-and-a-half upwards.

The glass interior was separated by darkly varnished wood mullions imitating spokes on a wagon wheel. Two matching French doors spanned the width below, each with its own glass sidelight. Large coordinating stone chair-rail moldings framed and ran between the half-moon-shaped arches, imposing a vision reminiscent of a Roman bridge, its heft anchoring the tall room.

The top third of the room supported the magnificently skylighted ceiling with painted trusses and old-time starburst windows. Carefully placed lighting along the floor cascaded up the wall. Its phosphorescence softened the bright crystal chandeliers hanging from the high ceiling, creating a warmer and more inviting space.

Kirsten discreetly searched out Gus and politely excused herself. Relieved August accepted the change better than she thought he would, she rejoined Derek and his friends at a back corner table.

They were all old childhood friends, and Derek noticed her isolation and whisked her away for some dancing, with which Kirsten confessed her unfamiliarity.

"Not to worry," Derek said with fun and confidence. "I've been doing it since I was a kid, you're in good hands."

"I hope I don't step on your toes." Kirsten laughed.

"My mother was a dance instructor. She taught me well."

"I see." Kirsten let him guide her, and he overlooked her clumsiness.

He was good, and after he gave her a few pointers, she felt like for first time in her life she could dance. Derek was impressing Kirsten with his eclectic abilities, putting her at ease. She found herself letting go and forgetting he was Brian's best friend. They danced two fun waltzes and ended with a swing number, which Kirsten decided was her favorite. They headed back to their table in the corner, where she could see everyone congregating around a newcomer. Tyler's head moved enough to reveal it was Brian.

She nearly gasped out loud. Kirsten stopped in her tracks and exclaimed without hesitation, "I thought he wasn't coming. What is he doing here?"

"Yeah, I don't know." Derek was puzzled by the look on her face.

"I have to go, Derek. I'm sorry." She was about to turn and leave when Chrissy started waving Derek down and pointing at Brian as if to say, "Look who's here."

"Kirsten, wait. Don't go! What's this all about?" he said, grabbing her arm.

It was too late. Chrissy had dragged Brian over to meet them.

Derek greeted Brian with a manly, brotherly hug. "Brian, buddy, welcome home. Glad you made it."

"Yeah, I decided I'd better come or Jessica would never let me hear the end of it. I came straight from the airport. I almost didn't get a flight."

How he managed to get the words out so easily, Kirsten would never know. She could tell he'd seen her as soon as Chrissy escorted him over. Surprise and the ensuing emotion had registered as plainly on his face as her own and were equally difficult for him to hide. As he spoke, he tried to catch her eye.

She chose to halfway hide behind Derek—fortunately, he was really tall. Brian bent his head down and stepped out to greet her while Derek simultaneously moved away so he could.

The pit in her stomach began to grow and pulse. She felt every cell in her body opening up. Her lips parted slightly, and she sucked her breath into a shallow hold in her throat. She felt caught in a lie, but more importantly didn't want anyone to suspect there was anything between them. She desperately wanted to make them believe they were nothing more than old colleagues.

She played offensively by greeting him first. "Brian, hello," she said as she reached out to shake his hand. She could tell he was a little unhappy about the tack she was taking but nonetheless gave in.

"Hello, Kirsten. How are you?"

"Great, thank you." She smiled again. "Small world, isn't it? I ran into Derek at the drugstore of all places, and we both realized we were coming to the Legacy Ball."

"Yes, that's exactly what happened," Derek said, feeling the need to confirm the innocent facts while giving Kirsten a quizzical look. He wasn't sure what to make of her one-eighty turn in behavior.

Kirsten could feel Chrissy studying them carefully.

"How do you two know each other?" she said wagging her finger back and forth between Kirsten and Brian—apparently having forgotten the barbecue.

"Dayfield's," they said in unison too quickly.

Kirsten smiled and gave her a funny "oops" face.

Derek skillfully interjected and suggested they sit down. Kirsten was relieved.

Brian had no choice but to catch up with his friends, which allowed Kirsten to sink into her chair next to Derek with Brian on his other side. She slowly regained her strength from its support. Emily sat on her right, with the other four filling out the circle.

She half listened to their friendly banter as she contemplated her next move. She avoided his eyes as much as possible while attempting to keep up appearances. Occasionally, their eyes would meet exchanging messages. He was being good and minding her wishes with only a glimmer of frustration. Conversations wound down and Sean and Megan left to dance, while Tyler tried to get Chrissy to keep him company while he had a smoke.

"Geez, Tyler! Really? Here?"

"What? I vape."

"So? No. It's too cold," she said, maintaining her post next to Brian.

An acquaintance of Emily's came over and asked her to dance, which warmed Kirsten's heart. She protested because of her inability to dance, but he cleverly asked her, "Then why are you here?"

Kirsten applauded his effort as he insisted she go. "I don't know how either but did it anyway. Right, Derek?" she said to enlist his help.

"That is exactly right. And except for a few broken toes, I'm fine," Derek teased.

"Hey. Be nice." Kirsten slapped him lightly on the arm.

Brian felt a flash of pain at seeing such playfulness between them. What had happened in his absence? He tried not to surmise. It felt like punishment for his moving away.

Emily finally accepted, leaving the four of them at the table. Brian watched Kirsten smile at them and couldn't help but soften his eyes on her. He knew it made her happy to see Emily get asked to dance. This was the constant tug on his heart. She could seem so impenetrable, like tonight when they first saw each other again, and then totally surprise him with her compassion.

Kirsten couldn't avoid looking at him since he was nearly across from her. She could see his façade had fallen, and he was looking at her with his steady, heart-melting Brian look. God help her cellophane heart. She could feel Chrissy taking it all in and didn't know why it bothered her; it just did. Derek felt the need to keep it light and took on the role of comedian. Kirsten stood up and excused herself to the ladies' room.

"Yeah, me too," Chrissy said, getting up with her.

Kirsten could feel Brian's eyes burning a hole in her back as she left. Once she disappeared from view, Derek turned to Brian and said, "What was that all about? I'm sorry. I had no idea."

"It's nothing, really. Don't worry about it. It never went anywhere and it's over."

"I swear I haven't seen her since the barbecue. I always liked her and thought, why not? That's it, I promise."

"Derek, really, it's okay, man."

"You're positive? She sure seemed upset to see you, though. She was going to leave."

"She was?"

"Yeah, but Chrissy pulled you over before she could."

Brian's body tensed and he squared his jaw.

Kirsten felt ambushed by Chrissy tagging along and more so when she insisted on small talk.

"So, what do you do at Dayfield's?" Chrissy asked.

"I work in the buying office."

"Oh, so what department do you buy for?"

"I'm not the buyer, I'm the Associate Buyer for Women's Designer Couture," Kirsten said.

"Wow, that must be a lot of fun."

Kirsten faked a smile of surprise at her enthusiasm, still not trusting its meaning. "Yes, it is. How 'bout you. What do you do?"

"Oh, I'm a graphic designer. I work for a little firm in the North Loop," Chrissy said, while holding the bathroom door open for them.

"Oh, so is that how you know Brian?"

"Brian?" she laughed. "No, Brian and I go way back. We went to grade school together."

"Really? Wow, I can't imagine knowing someone for that long."

"Yeah, it's hard to believe, but we used to make out behind the bushes at the edge of the playground."

"Well, I guess he won't ever double-cross you with all the insider information you must have," Kirsten teased.

"Yup." Chrissy swung the stall door closed behind her.

Kirsten no longer cared what Chrissy thought as she stared back at herself in the mirror. She ran the hottest water she could stand to warm her hands and then freshened her makeup.

Chrissy came back out to do the same and surreptitiously gave her the once-over. "That is such a beautiful dress."

"Thank you. It's not really mine."

"Dayfield's?"

Kirsten nodded yes.

"Must be nice."

"It does have its perks sometimes." Kirsten smiled, and they left together.

"Hey, you girls are finally back?" Derek said.

"Well, you know how those ladies' rooms can be," Chrissy joked.

"How 'bout a spin on the dance floor, Chrissy?" Derek said, standing up.

"Love to, darling."

Derek gave Brian a meaningful glance in Kirsten's direction as he left.

"Are you going to eat with your family tonight, Brian?" Emily had returned and asked as Kirsten sat down.

"Yes."

"Good, because Jessica would have your hide if you didn't."

"Well, why wouldn't I?" he said trying to deflect the conversation.

Emily, being polite, engaged Kirsten in conversation, and Brian tried to be patient. His eyes never left her.

As she spoke with Emily about how she knew Brian and what she did for a living, she felt Brian's eyes moving over her, from her hands as they gestured and fiddled around her neck like she was playing with a necklace which wasn't there, to her eyes, to her lips. She began to feel weaker and weaker but resolved to act like she didn't notice and continued her conversation. When she couldn't stand it anymore, she pushed back by looking directly at him and asking, "How's San Francisco? Do you miss the snow?"

"Well, I don't miss the long winters, but actually I do miss the snow." He leaned toward her and volleyed back. He'd play her game and be all cool and casual if that's what she wanted.

"Come on, Kirsten, what do you say we take a turn on the dance floor?" he asked, calling her bluff.

She didn't know what to say.

"I promise I won't bite if you promise not to break my

toes." Interpreting her hesitation to mean yes, he stood up and extended his hand to her.

"All right, if you promise not to bite," she said, relenting and taking his hand to lift her up.

They walked out to the closest edge of the floor and slipped into each other's arms. He was careful not to bring her in too close, but enough so it wouldn't look stiff. They didn't say anything for a while, both waiting for the other to speak.

Kirsten finally broke the silence. "So does everyone know about us?"

"What do you mean?"

"I mean like Derek and Chrissy and everybody?"

"No, no…well, Derek knows some, but that's it, I promise."

"How much is some? Does he know about my stitches?"

"No. Derek was as surprised as we were. He wouldn't have invited you if he'd known, trust me. How are your stitches, by the way?" he asked, looking down to take a peek. "I don't see anything. It looks like it healed nicely." His eyes rested on hers, eliciting the memory of what almost was. She bit her lip and her eyes glossed as she averted them away. She became weightless in his arms like a thin piece of blown glass.

"Yes," she whispered.

They continued dancing in silence to the soft lilt of a waltz, afraid to make any changes in posture in case either should misunderstand its meaning. Kirsten was surprised at the number of people dancing. Balls seemed passé to her.

The regular stream of his breath on her neck kept time like a metronome. Its constant rush demanded she not lose step. She began to cramp because of her unease and knew she'd have to make concessions soon or she'd crack like the frozen trees outside.

She focused her attention on her breathing and took deeper and longer breaths, slowly calming herself down. She noticed his scent. He smelled good.

I love that smell, what is it? It's like fresh laundry. Kirsten almost exclaimed, it's Tide! They should bottle it and sell it as cologne; they'd make a killing.

He felt her relax a little and bent his head down to maneuver his hand across her back a few more centimeters, pulling her closer.

"Is your dress from The Couture Shop?" he asked, afraid to tell her the truth of what he felt.

"Yes."

"It's beautiful."

She sensed his fear and knew—no, had seen—how beautiful she looked in his eyes. If they weren't surrounded by people she'd want him to kiss her; she couldn't help it. Her dress, his suit, the dancing…it was all too much. It had been a tortuous year trying to forget him. She realized she couldn't. The memory of him was omnipresent. His steady blue eyes and boyishly long lashes softened her core. His kiss, his touch, his wit always made her laugh. How many times she'd wanted to send a quick text or call him, but what would she have said?

Nothing. She couldn't—wouldn't—reveal her secret.

"Thank you," she barely mouthed. She was trying desperately to look normal and in control. She didn't want to expose her emotions in public.

They needed some time and privacy to figure things out. The Ball had cornered them. She wished they could disappear. Instead, Michael danced by like a reminder she'd forgotten on her calendar. He was with a gorgeous brunette in emerald green, who was nearly falling out of her dress. The design she'd chosen was clearly meant to highlight her best features without looking slutty, but Kirsten wasn't sure it successfully achieved either objective. His standards were slipping.

She knew he could see her as their eyes locked briefly as he swept by. There was no hiding lust or the subtlest attractions from him. Michael was a chemist of these alchemies.

Seeing her with Brian only affirmed the beast he thought himself to be. He was forever the man with yet another woman, and Kirsten would not be with a man like that.

The music ended, but Kirsten didn't notice and was momentarily confused when Brian stopped their dance.

"Was that Michael going by?"

"Um, yes, I believe it was," she said, trying not to be distracted by Michael's sudden presence.

They smiled shyly at each other, and he led her off the dance floor.

Kirsten, feeling disorientated and weak, worried she'd trip and fall. His hand was low on her back—almost too low—as she let him guide her. She had no fight left, and Brian refused to keep the pretense any longer.

The gesture would've gone unnoticed had they been an established couple, but seeing as they weren't, his hand was like a branding iron, and Kirsten felt the stares.

Brian steered her toward a couple of women talking on the outskirts of the dance floor diagonally opposite their table. A very lovely woman with stunning auburn hair and sparkling blue eyes turned, hugged Brian, and gave him a kiss on the cheek. She looked to be in her fifties.

"Hello. Are you coming in for dinner?"

"Yes. Mom, this is a coworker from Dayfield's. Kirsten, this is my mother, Elin."

"Hello, it's lovely to meet you, Kirsten," she said, reaching out her hand.

"Hello," a stunned Kirsten said, taking her hand to shake.

"Hi. I'm Jessica, Brian's sister," said the other woman, reaching across Elin to take Kirsten's hand. Her smile showed the kind of mischievousness that can only come from a sibling who had the power to embarrass.

"Hi." Kirsten smiled, pretending not to notice the eye ribbing Jessica was giving Brian.

Brian's mother was someone you immediately warmed to, and Kirsten was thankful she didn't respond like Chrissy had upon first seeing her with Brian. The elegant matriarch, being much wiser and more sensitive, would wait until the appropriate time.

"There's room for Kirsten to join us, if you'd like," Elin offered.

"Oh, no, thank you," Kirsten said.

"That'd be great," Brian said at the same time.

Flustered, Kirsten explained, "I don't want to intrude. You must want to have Brian all to yourselves now since he lives so far away." Kirsten turned so only Brian could see her face and said, "I should probably keep Derek company."

Elin insisted, "Don't be ridiculous! Bring Derek too; he's practically my second son. There're two extra spots since Matthew and Katie aren't here."

"Oh." Kirsten looked from Elin to Brian.

Brian shrugged and smiled. "I guess it's settled then."

"Yes, thank you, Elin," she said, trying to figure out what Brian was up to.

"There he is," Elin said, waving Derek over. "Why don't you and Kirsten sit with us tonight? I have two extra spots because Matthew and Katie are gone. I'm feeling abandoned enough as it is."

"Sure. Is that okay with you, Kirsten?"

"Yes. That'd be fine."

Elin and Jessica led them back to their table, and Kirsten stopped abruptly as she saw her father sitting there.

"Kirsten! You're going to come sit with us after all," August nearly bellowed as he stood. Jessica and Elin were pulled aside by an official event-looking person who needed to speak with them.

"Dad?!" Kirsten said. She was immovable, and August had to come around to kiss her on the cheek. So many things raced through her head. *Like, be nice. You don't want anyone to notice your strained relationship.* She managed a nice daughterly hug but couldn't find a way to bridge her two colliding worlds, which resulted in a bit of awkwardness between Brian and August as they waited for an introduction.

"Hi. I'm Brian," he said, realizing he'd need to act as emissary. "Kirsten and I used to work together at Dayfield's." His eyes looked back at Kirsten, hoping the look would spark some help, but it didn't. She must be mad at me, he thought. It was like the universe was forcing them together. While Brian was thankful for the push, he wasn't sure Kirsten appreciated it.

Derek, having been waylaid, sidled up beside Kirsten and said hello.

"I'm Derek," he said, reaching his hand out to August.

"August. Nice to meet you, Derek. You work at Dayfields's too?"

"Me? No. I'm a friend of the family." There was another painful pause as Kirsten was still unable to make conversation.

"So, how do you know the McNeills?" Derek asked.

"I just met them tonight. I'm Kirsten's father." Kirsten was relieved to learn they didn't already know each other.

"Oh, that's right, Kirsten said you were here."

Great, Kirsten thought. She could see Gus's curiosity rise at her not one, but two supposed escorts.

Elin finished her conversation and turned back toward them. "August, this must be your daughter." She laughed lightly at the coincidence. "I guess our table won't be empty after all. Kirsten, why don't you sit next to your father?" Elin suggested; August was sitting opposite her. "Jessica and Brian, why don't you take either side of me. There, that should work to everyone's advantage." The remaining nonimmediate family members filled the space between the McNeills and the Swensons. Kirsten could feel Brian's gaze across from her in his perfectly placed seat. She met his eyes briefly in a moment of transparency, revealing her resignation to her helpless state, fueling his need for her.

Carol returned, surprised to see Kirsten. She said hello and took her place on the other side of August.

Dinner was served, and Kirsten was grateful for the diversion. She learned Brian had two older sisters: Jessica, who was married to John, and the oldest Katie, who was married to Matthew and lived in Chicago. Katie would soon be giving birth to their first baby, and was, therefore, unable to come.

"What do you do at Dayfield's, Brian?" August asked.

"I used to work in the advertising department, but moved to San Francisco about a year and a half ago to work at an agency there."

"Well, that's a long way from Minneapolis," Carol said.

"Yes, it is. I don't plan on being there forever, though."

Brian looked at Kirsten. "Minneapolis is my home."

"And what about you, Derek?" August asked.

"Me? I recently passed the bar, and I'm working at a local law firm."

Kirsten couldn't help feeling like she was sixteen. August never had the opportunity to interrogate any of her dates before and was now taking full advantage. She tried to imagine what he was thinking. Brian and Derek suddenly seemed so young and polite.

"Kirsten, what is it you do at Dayfield's?" Elin said.

"I work in the buying office."

"She's the Associate Buyer for Women's Designer Couture," August added, too proudly.

Kirsten winced inside.

"Really?" Elin said in polite surprise. "You must work with little Michael Warner—well, I should stop saying that; he's not so little anymore, is he?"

"Yes." Kirsten chuckled in surprise.

"Gosh, I've known Michael's mother since before we had babies. You let me know if he gives you any grief," Elin said with a wink and a smile.

Kirsten smiled right back. "Oh, I will." *Wow, could the evening get any more incestuous?*

"Well, Gus, there you are." Lillian appeared suddenly from Carol's direction, her distinctively formal, almost British voice whipping Kirsten's head around.

"How were your holidays?" Lillian's elegant snow-white gown set her olive skin aglow. She was simply effervescent making her important social rounds, but why would they include her father, Kirsten wondered.

"Good, and you?" said August, dabbing his napkin on his

mouth before he stood to greet her with a kiss on the cheek. "Wonderful."

"Lillian, this is my wife, Carol." August leaned back and put his arm on the back of Carol's chair. Carol pushed away from the table so she could turn and greet Lillian. August sat back down.

"Hello, Carol. It's lovely to meet you."

"And, of course, you know Kirsten." August turned his head toward her.

"Well, of course. Hello, Kirsten. How wonderful your father gets more time with you since you've moved back."

"Hello, Lillian, long time no see." Kirsten gave a little laugh to overcome her shock. *Apparently, it could get more incestuous.*

"Now, Gus, I have to thank you. Hiring Kirsten here has been the best thing we ever did; even Michael can't disagree."

Hiring me? Kirsten sat perplexed. What did her dad have to do with this? She started to fume. *It would be so like him to have set me up. Why couldn't he tell me he knew Lillian? Why did he always have to go behind my back and manipulate the situation?*

Lillian moved along, intending to greet everyone. "Hello, Elin. You look beautiful in that Couture Shop original, I hope?"

"Yes, of course it is. Good to see you, Lillian," Elin returned warmly.

"I see you got most everyone here tonight."

"Yes, except Katie and Matthew. Katie is due any minute with their first."

"Oh, really?!" She clapped her hands together lightly. "Congratulations! I didn't know. Well, enjoy your evening, everyone," Lillian said, and floated gracefully away.

Kirsten's head snapped over to Gus. "Dad, what was that all about?"

"Oh, nothing. I just put in a good word for you."

"But..." Kirsten refrained from having a family argument in front of everyone. Her eyes met Brian's, and she read the question in his eyes but couldn't answer. She had her hands full stemming the tide around her. Never had the precarious strands of her life come so dangerously close to colliding.

Elin asked, "So, Gus, how is it you know Lillian?"

"Well, it's hard to say; we go a-ways back."

Yeah, I bet, Kirsten thought in disgust.

"She was very helpful in the research for my last book."

Oh, boy, here we go. Great segue, Dad. Kirsten's back stiffened in preparation for the self-promoting liturgy.

"Book?" Elin said.

"Yes, yes! I wrote a book called the *Scandinavian Crossing* a few years back, and Lillian shared some fascinating resources about the history of Scandinavians moving to America. Her family had preserved photos and diaries I found very useful."

"Really?" Elin seemed genuinely interested.

"Yes."

"Well, you know, I read that book and found it to be very fascinating. I'm of Swedish descent myself," Elin said.

"I thought you might be! I've been trying to figure out where I've seen you before. I thought perhaps you were part of Andersson Publishing."

"Yes, yes, I am. My grandfather is Oskar Andersson."

"I think I saw your painting hanging in the lobby when I was there trying to get my book published." August had a proud way of presenting himself, creating discomfort across the table.

Kirsten waited patiently for an appropriate moment to steer the conversation elsewhere, afraid of where he might go with it.

"You probably saw my grandmother. I look a lot like her, minus the red hair." Elin offered an explanation. "Did Andersson publish your book?"

"No. I was hoping they would, being Scandinavian like myself, but it didn't work out. Maybe next time."

"Well, I apologize. I'm afraid my brother's branch of the family has been managing the business, and I'm not aware of their business dealings."

"Oh, no, no, of course not."

Kirsten seized the moment to avoid an awkward silence. "So, Brian, how long will you be home before you have to go back?"

Surprised by her abruptness and formality, Brian succinctly answered. "Tomorrow night. I couldn't take any more time off than that."

"Yes, he came to surprise us," Jessica said affectionately.

The dinner conversation transitioned to lighter subjects, and Kirsten was able to fall silent, then quietly excused herself to go to the ladies' room. Fortunately, there was no Chrissy to follow her. She thought she was going to die if she spent another minute at the table. She walked the length of the lobby, spying a private corner hidden by some tall plants. She settled on a bench placed behind the foliage and was startled by the sound of her name.

"Kirsten? Are you all right?" Brian had followed her.

"I don't think I can take one more surprise tonight. I hardly know anyone in this city, let alone this state or this side of the

Rockies, for that matter, but somehow I've managed to run into all six of them tonight."

"Look, I'm sorry if you feel I've forced you into an uncomfortable situation," he said, sitting down next to her.

"It's not your fault. Your mother was just being nice."

They sat in silence for several seconds.

"Kirsten?" he said tentatively.

"Yes?" she returned hesitantly.

"I've missed you."

"I've missed you too," she said quietly, unable to completely face him.

"Kirsten," he said with rising confidence, covering her hand in her lap with his.

"Yes?" She shyly looked back at him.

Brian moved in closer and kissed her.

He pulled back partway, caressed her cheek, and pushed a strand of hair away from her face. "You sure are full of surprises. I didn't even know you had family here."

"I'm full of surprises? How about you? Everything is a complete and utter mess."

"Why?"

"I don't know. It's my father, I guess. I don't want to go into the particulars, but let's just say he drives me completely nuts."

"I'm sorry." He stroked her cheek and kissed her again.

This time she gave in fully. They were practically making out when Derek came running up to them.

"Brian, come on, it's time."

Brian stood abruptly in reaction to being caught, and Kirsten attempted to regain her composure in his shadow.

"Oh, yeah. C'mon." He grabbed her hand and pulled her

back down the hall as fast as he could without running.

The threesome entered the ballroom as the MC began and stood in the back so as not to intrude on the moment.

"Every year we commemorate those we have lost to renew our commitment to fighting this disease. We at the American Cancer Society do not differentiate; we want to find a cure for all cancers! Please join me in welcoming Elin McNeill tonight. She is going to read the list of those we have lost in the past year to this insidious disease. Elin holds a special candle for this vigil as she lost her own dear husband nearly five years ago to lung cancer. Elin."

The room filled with clapping. Kirsten suddenly realized the meaning of Brian's entire family being there tonight.

"Brian, I'm so sorry. I had no idea," she whispered in his ear and squeezed his arm.

He squeezed her arm back, but kept his gaze fixed on his mother walking across the stage to the podium.

She could see the emotion in his eyes, and it only made her love him more.

"Thank you. I'm very honored to be here tonight. Having lost a loved one, I know how much it means to the families and friends of those names I will be reading that you are all here supporting the fight against cancer."

As she proceeded to read the names, Kirsten was amazed at how many names there were, despite all the supposed advances in medicine. She felt the enormity of it.

The MC retook the podium while Elin stepped back to her table. "Thank you, Elin, and to the entire McNeill family."

He continued to talk, and Kirsten tuned him out and looked at Brian, wishing he was sitting with his family instead of standing next to her. He should be sharing this moment with his mother and sister. Sympathy filled her as she remembered Elin's earlier words: "abandoned enough as it is."

The music started up again and people started to mingle.

"Brian, you should ask your mother to dance or something. I feel bad you were back here with me."

"Yeah, it's okay." He slipped his hand around hers and brought it to his lips, kissed it gently, then began to lead her through the crowded ballroom.

They headed back to the table where everyone was sipping coffee over partially finished dessert plates. Kirsten returned to her spot next to Gus, and Brian went over to his mother and asked her to dance. Elin was touched by his invitation.

As the evening came to a close Kirsten's anxiety crept back. She felt like she was about to turn into a pumpkin. Brian, too, was wondering how to end the evening—weighing family obligations with his desire to be with Kirsten.

"So, I assume you're staying at your house?" Jessica asked.

"Uh, yes, I dropped my bag off there on the way here." He turned toward Derek. "Can you give me a lift?"

"Not sure, my friend, we were overstuffed on the way in."

"I can Uber home," Kirsten volunteered.

"Oh, yeah, good idea. I'll share it with you," Brian said firmly.

No! That's not what I meant.

Kirsten scanned their faces, realizing no one cared. It was understood. There was no more fight in her. Brian and Kirsten were the ingenues. They would eventually be together, end of story. She took her wine glass and finished the remaining sips in one large gulp.

"That solves it, then," Derek said.

Kirsten saw Brian pull out his phone to summon the Uber.

"Looks like there's one twelve minutes out. Should I get it?" he asked, looking at Kirsten, making sure she wouldn't back out.

"Sure. Yeah. We should go now, though, because I need to get my coat." She hugged Gus and kissed him on the cheek. "Goodnight, Dad." Gus looked like he realized for the first time his little girl was all grown up. It made Kirsten uncomfortable. She didn't know what to do with it.

It aggravated her his sadness would touch her. She felt guilty and annoyed at the same time. It wasn't her fault he'd been absent. Why did she still have to pay the price of being his daughter? No amount of time or distance changed any of it.

She stood and said goodnight to Carol and turned toward Brian's family, wishing she could've grown up in a family like his. "It was nice to meet all of you, and thank you for including me on your important night."

"It was our pleasure." Elin smiled and came over to give Kirsten a hug. "We'll have to do it again sometime, perhaps not on such a formal occasion."

"Yes." Kirsten smiled. "Goodnight." She looked at Derek. "Thanks for the ride here."

"My pleasure," he said.

Kirsten and Brian left and kept to the opposite side from where Brian's friends had been sitting. It was a sea of people as the evening came to a close, keeping them hidden.

Kirsten could tell he didn't want to take the time to say goodbye—which was fine with her.

They went straight to the coat check, and Brian helped her into her long fluffy down coat. She turned to face him as he stepped forward to receive his coat from the attendant. The sea parted, momentarily, and her eyes brushed with Chrissy's in the distance. It was unavoidable. She saw. She knew. Kirsten felt the pang of her disappointment.

He finished putting on his hat and gloves and grabbed her hand while she rotated around, leaving Chrissy to watch them diminish into the dark night.

Despite her long down coat, hat, and gloves, Kirsten was freezing. The cold air blew over her exposed feet in their strappy heels and up her dress. She should've worn her long underwear, no one would've seen.

Seeing her shiver, Brian put his arms around her from behind and pulled her back to his chest, rubbing her arms up and down in an effort to warm her. "I don't know as I'll ever get used to these below-freezing temperatures. It's very unladylike," she said and they laughed.

A blue Prius pulled up, and Brian opened the door for her to get in.

It was a short drive to her apartment, and he helped her out past the old snow and ice piled up on the sidewalk. They hurried into her building, and he tipped the driver on his app.

Kirsten brooked no protest as her desire mingled with the effects of the wine. She led him up the four flights of stairs in silence. She unlocked her door and a pleasant glow emerged. She had several thoughtfully placed candles sprinkled throughout her apartment set to timers. She turned on her electric stove she'd bought for her nonworking fireplace. Brian took off his coat and laid it over the back of her overstuffed Shabby Chic chair. "Nice. I forgot how cozy your apartment is."

"Thanks," she said, as she reached to turn on a low lamp next to her couch across from her chair.

He came up behind her. She stood, afraid to face him, and unzipped her coat. He turned her around and kissed her. Their lips met slowly and parted softly. The kiss deepened with growing intensity. Their arms embraced and hands caressed as they melted into each other. He moved his lips down her neck to the nape and pushed her coat off, letting it slide to the floor. He pulled her in again and pressed even closer. She let out an involuntary whimper. This time she was ready and led him into her bedroom where more of the same candles cast a soft light.

She couldn't have planned it better; everything was perfect, she even had a pack of condoms in her nightstand.

They helped each other slip out of their clothes. To feel his skin against hers was more luxuriant than any silk gown. Brian was of average build but had broad shoulders. He looked strong, and she felt smaller than she thought she was in his hands.

He stopped to put on a condom. She hated the interruption; it ruined the sanctity of their ephemeral voyage. He kissed her stomach on bent knees, bowing over her. His need was great, and he wouldn't be able to contain himself much longer. She stroked his head.

The delay caused a shift within Kirsten. He moved up to kiss her mouth and noticed her reticence. He hovered over her, waiting for what he did not know. Did he not have her permission?

A tear rolled silently out the side of her eye. Brian didn't know what to make of it. He'd heard some women cried when they had sex, but he'd yet to experience it. "Kirsten, are you okay?" he asked. She turned her head away, unable to speak.

He watched the tear pool on the side of her face, unable to

continue its journey because it was sitting at the wrong angle. She finally spoke. "I can't. I'm sorry; I can't." It felt wrong. Something deep within her said no.

"What?" He continued holding himself over her in disbelief and hope.

"I can't. I can't. I'm sorry."

"Okay. Uhm." Brian was trying his best to collect himself and not get ruffled. He finally slumped off of her and dropped heavily next to her.

They lay side by side in uncomfortable silence, staring up at the candlelight flickers on the ceiling.

Kirsten sat up and covered herself with the extra blanket she kept on her bed. She found it hard to look at him. She felt terrible. How could she want something so much and have it feel so wrong? It sounded like bad lyrics to a pop song.

"I'm sorry."

"What's wrong? I don't understand," he said, sitting up and putting his boxer briefs back on.

"I just can't." Kirsten sat with her back to him as her feet dangled off the side of the bed.

"Is it the distance thing, because I'm already applying to agencies here in Minneapolis so I can come back."

"Brian, please." Her voice cracked. "I just can't. It won't work."

She started to cry. She didn't want to cry, but she couldn't help it. "Brian, please just go."

"No! I'm not going to go." He gently turned her back toward him and wiped her tears away with a tissue from her nightstand. "Kirsten, what is it?" he asked, craning his head down and trying to meet her eyes.

"I don't know. There's something wrong with me. It may

never get fixed, and you don't want to be with someone like that. You deserve better," she said finally, looking at him.

He couldn't believe what he was hearing. "I don't want anyone but you. I'm not leaving." He pulled her in to hold her, and she let him for a minute before she turned away again.

"Brian, please just go. Please!" They sat in silence. Kirsten refused to turn around and could feel Brian pleading with her to. "Brian, please just go," she said gently but firmly, her tears diminishing. "Please."

"Okay. Okay, if that's what you want," he said, fighting his surrender. She sat mutely on the edge of the bed as he got his clothes back on—staring into the unblinking eyes of her Kirsten doll sitting on a chair in the corner of her bedroom.

He was dressed but couldn't bring himself to leave. He stood looking at her, helplessly hoping she'd change her mind, but she wouldn't acquiesce. "Brian, please. I'm sorry. I really need to be alone right now."

"Okay." He sighed in disbelief, unable to reconcile what he believed to be true with what she was saying. He stopped in the doorway to speak one more time. She still wouldn't look at him. "God, Kirsten, who hurt you?" Kirsten's eyes widened and shot up in confirmation. His head dropped; he slowly turned and punctuated his retreat by the rap of his fingertips on the door frame.

Who hurt me? No one.

Click.

She heard her front door close.

LOVE

Kirsten cried until she was dry as desert sand. She tossed and turned while the echo of Brian's words lolled around in her head.

God, Kirsten, who hurt you?

No one. No one hurt me. I've never been molested or raped...or have I? She'd heard of people who repressed the memories of bad things happening to them. That'd be an easy answer to her own question of what was wrong with her, but somehow it didn't feel right.

Who hurt me? My dad, I guess. But so have many daughters been hurt by their dads. That doesn't render one an eternal virgin.

But the seed was planted: August. August Spencer Swenson, father of one Kirsten Dianne Swenson. She suddenly remembered his exchange with Lillian.

What has he done? Kirsten started to get angry. *Who the hell does he think he is manipulating my life? Always doing as he pleases without regard for my feelings or what I want. It was like I was brought into the world for his own means, to use as he sees fit. I didn't even get my job on my own merit! Here I thought I was so fortunate; all my years of hard work and planning starting to come to fruition. I am a twenty-seven-year-old woman. I am not anyone's puppet!*

Her whole life with her dad started to flash before her: every disappointment, every wrong, every unhappy memory. *Do I even have a happy memory of him? Has there ever been a time where I actually had fun with him?*

Her Kirsten doll continued to sit unblinking in mock rebuke. *I need to move her; she's no help.*

She ran to her closet and grabbed the shoebox full of her most memorable photos. She sifted through them looking for any sign, any picture with only him and her. There were a few: one of him feeding her a bottle. His gaze was somewhere else, and he looked unhappy. She wasn't being held. Her infant self appeared placed in his arms like an object of duty. She wasn't being loved. She wasn't loved. He didn't love her. It was all empty words and presentation. The picture was worth a thousand words.

She wept uncontrollably.

At 2:33 a.m. she finally crawled into bed and fell asleep. When she awoke around ten she felt hungover. The night before seemed like a dream. The only reminder was the anger still churning in her body. She threw off her covers and got in the shower. The warm soapy water invigorated her. As she scrubbed and scrubbed, she got angrier and angrier. She needed to ask and needed to hear him say the words. It was an awakening. Why had she never asked him point blank before? Why had she never called him on his behavior? Why? Why? It was a form of abuse, and she no longer was willing to let this continue to happen to her.

It was midday before she made it out to Northfield, and she was relieved to see August's car in the drive. It hadn't occurred to her he might not be home. —

She burst into the house yelling, "Dad?! Dad!"

Carol came running into the living room to meet her. "Hi, Kirsten. Is something wrong? I didn't know you were coming over."

"I wasn't. Where is he?"

Carol was startled.

"Well, your aunt is here, and they're talking in the kitchen." She moved into the dining room next to the living room and instinctively stood guard to the entrance of the kitchen that sat in the back of the house. She didn't know what to make of Kirsten's intrusion and had always been unsure of how Kirsten felt about her.

Conversely, Kirsten had always wondered if push came to shove if Carol would take his side. It was understandable if she did, but Kirsten felt it was disrespectful and shortsighted for a stepparent to stand between two people with a blood relationship. Particularly since she was an adult.

If Carol ever wanted to have a good relationship with her, she'd need to understand this. There are always two sides to every story, and steps usually only get one side.

Kirsten knew Carol wouldn't enter into a physical altercation and shot past her into the kitchen.

Seeing her aunt was such a pleasant surprise Kirsten couldn't help but tamp down her anger. "Aunt Anne, what are you doing here?"

The kitchen was L-shaped with a rectangular-shaped island in the middle with the long side facing the dining room entrance. A partially consumed coffee cake sat in its pan on the island, along with a couple of mugs of coffee being drunk by her dad and aunt. The sunroom was off to Kirsten's right, where it looked like they'd been having brunch.

The kitchen was influenced by French provincial textile

designs with the Mediterranean blue cupboards and classic French tiles filling the backsplash. Large terracotta tiles surfaced the countertops with the more French tiles trimming the counters' edge. More terracotta tiles covered the floor. It was a bit heavy for Kirsten but seemed to fit Carol.

Her aunt came around the island to give Kirsten a hug. August was at the far end of the island near where they'd been eating. Kirsten was afraid he'd come in for a hug, but she was thankful he stayed put.

"I could say the same thing to you. Gosh, what a beautiful young woman you've turned into." Kirsten smiled at her warmth and words of love. "Was that you yelling? I couldn't quite make it out."

"Yes. I didn't know if anyone was home." Kirsten faked a cover story, as her aunt was the last person in the world she'd want to hurt.

"I wasn't planning on being here, but I needed to talk to my dad."

"Is everything all right? What's wrong?" Gus asked, setting his mug back down on the island.

Kirsten's fury having been subdued by encountering her aunt caused her to pause. "Uhm," she said collecting her thoughts. She renewed her resolve by remembering how many times she'd never said anything or did anything. She didn't want to be that person anymore. He'd lied to her. It wasn't nothing.

"What's wrong?" She started quietly and got louder. "What's wrong?! Did you ask Lillian to hire me?"

He was a bit shocked at her tenor. "Well, no. I mean, I put a good word in for you."

"You put in a good word for me? You never told her about

me? How did she know to inquire about me?"

August stood like a deer in the headlights.

"How did *you* know to put a good word in for me?"

August dropped his gaze to the floor.

"So, my getting this job was all a sham. It was a way for you to get me back to Minnesota."

"Gus, you didn't?" Anne asked.

August shifted his weight and cleared his throat.

"Everyone likes you, and you're doing well. Why does it matter?" he finally spoke.

"Why does it matter? That's your answer for everything, isn't it? It *matters*. It *always* matters, just not to you. As long as you're getting your way, it doesn't matter. But what about me? I am your *daughter*. Do you even love me?"

"Of course I do. I will always love you! Don't be silly."

"This isn't love, Gus. You have no idea what love is. You are the most oblivious, self-centered person I know. You have no idea the havoc you've created in my life. I can't even let myself get close enough to a guy to have a real relationship. Did you know after every summer visit I would go home and cry for weeks? Weeks! Aunt Anne and Uncle Bill were my parents every summer, not you. Not you! It was always about your work and your women."

Gus was ashen.

"Yes, your women. You think I didn't know? You think I still don't know? Let me guess: you and Lillian, right? By the way, were you married to Carol yet when all that started going down?"

"Kirsten, please..." Carol had been hiding in the doorway of the dining room and looked horrified.

"No, Carol." Kirsten turned to look at her. "I'm not shutting up about this anymore. I will no longer live a lie." Carol shrunk like a frightened chipmunk.

A fragile quiet lay over the room. Kirsten turned back to look at her father, waiting for him to speak, apologize, something. Kirsten found his silence infuriating. How could he not try to comfort his only child, his daughter? It was then she realized he never would, and no amount of anger would change that.

"I'm done with you. I don't want to see you. I don't want to talk to you. I don't want to see your name on my caller ID. If you ever have a change of heart and want to treat me with real love and respect, then I am here. But until then, don't even bother."

You could hear a pin drop, Gus continued to stand in frozen fear, his empty gaze fixed on Kirsten.

"Really? You have nothing to say to that?"

"I'm sorry. I can't right now," he muttered, then walked out past her through the dining entrance. Carol retreated to a corner in the dining room visibly shaken.

Trembling and not sure what to do next, Kirsten raced out of the house, angrier than when she'd arrived—leaving the same way she'd come in. She climbed back into her car and sat. Anne followed soon after and got into the passenger seat.

"Sorry we had to get reacquainted like this," Kirsten said, feeling guilt creep in.

"Me too. Look, I'm not gonna defend my brother, but he is family, and I think one day you'll regret this."

"Yeah? You're that sure he'll never change." Kirsten said sarcastically.

"Ha. You always were too smart for your own good." Anne smiled.

"How are you? Sten tells me you haven't ever gone back to the lake house." Kirsten said, hoping to steer the conversation away from her.

"No. No, I guess I haven't, but he did tell me you were there and about the lanterns you set off from the dock."

"Yeah, we did. It was good. You would've liked it. She would've liked it." Kirsten turned to look at her aunt in time to see tears fill her eyes, which made Kirsten well up too.

"Oh, Kirsten, I've made such a mess of things. I've let my grief cheat me out of life, and Sofie had so much life. She was the best part of life. She would not be happy with me and seeing you now with your dad, I realized how ashamed I'd be if she could see me now."

"It's okay," Kirsten soothed.

Crying, they held each other for comfort, then burst out laughing. It'd been so long since they'd seen each other and to have their first meeting be so emotional suddenly seemed ridiculous. "I'm sorry," Kirsten said, wiping tears away from her eyes. Anne was doing the same, and Kirsten reached for some tissues she kept in the glove compartment.

"It's freezing in here," Kirsten said, turning the car on to get the heat going.

"You know what I can't reconcile?" Kirsten asked, blowing her nose. "I'm here, and he treats me like crap. You were the best mom anyone could ask for. I don't blame you for your grief. At least it makes sense. I don't understand why he even had a kid in the first place," Kirsten blurted.

"Do you regret your life?" Anne asked.

"No."

"It's not so simple, sweetie." Anne patted her hand.

"I know. I know. You had a terrible father yada-yada-yada, but you'd think it would make you want to be the best parent you could be—like you."

"Gus did the best he could. He was never able to face his pain, and it poisoned him," Anne said.

Kirsten wasn't satisfied. "Yeah, and he's poisoned me. But at some point, you have to grow up and at least try not to damage your children."

"I'm sorry," she said, squeezing Kirsten's hand.

"What are you doing here, anyway?" Kirsten asked.

"Well, I needed to talk to your father about the lake house. It's time to pass it on,"

"So you're going to keep it?"

"Yeah. I can't sell it, and although he won't admit it, he can't either."

"So Sten will be the executor because he's the oldest, right?"

"Technically, yes, but I've been neglectful, and your dad has been the one taking care of it and paying the property taxes, so he wants it to go to you."

Kirsten's anger fired up again. "Seriously? I thought there was a trust for all that."

"Ugh! I shouldn't have said anything, and yes, there is. I'm sorry. Look, don't worry about it; we'll work it out. We always do, and he does have a point."

Kirsten was still disgusted. "Wow! He really is unbelievable. It's not like Sten, or I care. Fortunately, we get along."

"People change, and life happens, and it's wise to have it written legally because you never know."

Kirsten's phone rang. She checked the caller ID and saw it was Derek. Derek?! She exclaimed in her head. She couldn't deal with whatever he had to say and made it go to voicemail.

"Kirsten?"

"Yes."

"Not all men are your father. You're your own person and can make your own decisions. Don't give your dad the power to take that away from you."

"I know, but it's complicated. It's so deeply psychologically rooted. I don't even understand why I behave the way I behave." As soon as she said it the truth unveiled itself— Gus probably felt the same way. She needed to forgive him. Somehow, some way, she needed to forgive him, or she'd end up like him. Her phone dinged, signifying Derek must've left a message. She didn't look at it.

"I know. It never is. It's a process, and you'll need to be patient with yourself. I know this may sound strange, but have you ever grieved your dad?"

"Huh? He's not dead."

"No, I know. I've read a lot about grief and gone to a lot of counseling about it, and it's not reserved exclusively for the dead. Life is full of all kinds of loss. Maybe you need to grieve the loss of not having the father you wanted or thought you should've had. Sometimes we hold onto things we will never have, and it can be just as crippling. It sounds crazy, but in a way, I refused to grieve Sofie, because I couldn't forgive God for taking her away. I wouldn't allow it because I was too angry."

"Yeah?"

"Yeah. Maybe you should get away from here. Go to the lake house or some lake, there's a few around here"—she winked—"and write a letter to your dad telling him all the things you've been afraid to say and burn it. Heck, roast some marshmallows over the flames. Make s'mores out of 'em. Do your own grief ceremony." She patted Kirsten's hand and gave her an encouraging smile.

"Well, it's gonna be one hell of a fire. I should be able to make a lot of s'mores." Kirsten snickered.

"I think the more marshmallows you roast, the greater the joys you'll start to experience."

"Thanks." Kirsten gave her aunt a hug.

"Sure thing, pumpkin." Kirsten's phone rang again. It was Derek! She panicked, thinking something awful had happened to Brian, and answered it. She mouthed the word 'sorry' to Anne. "Derek!? Is everything all right?"

"No." Derek's voice was strange.

Kirsten's heart began to pound.

"It's Elin; she was in a bad car accident last night, and they don't think she's going to make it."

"Oh, no!" Kirsten was relieved it wasn't Brian, but the thought of Brian losing his mother and becoming parentless pained her.

"Could you please come to the hospital? I think Brian would really appreciate it." Derek's tone was surprisingly resolute.

"Uhm, I don't know. I'm not sure it's a good idea," Kirsten said.

"I know it didn't go well last night between you two, but I think he could really use your support. We're at Hennepin County in Intensive Care." Derek remained unwavering.

Kirsten's thoughts spun, but she felt she couldn't say no. "Okay, okay. I'll leave right now. I'm in Northfield."

"Okay. Bye."

"Bye," Kirsten whispered in shock.

Kirsten turned to Anne with a ghostly, confused look. "I

have to go. I'm sorry, but my sort of boyfriend's mom was in an accident, and I need to go to the hospital."

"Oh, my gosh. Yes, go. We'll catch up later, 'kay?" Anne gave her a big hug and a kiss on the cheek. She climbed out and stood in the driveway, pulling her coat tight around her, and waved goodbye as Kirsten backed out and turned the car to leave.

Hennepin County Hospital? Kirsten had no idea where that was but knew enough to know it wasn't good. It was the one always on the news because it took all the trauma cases. She pulled over to input the location into her phone and let AVA (Automated Voice Activation) guide her.

AVA did a good job, and she was able to get there in little less than an hour. She walked into the emergency room entrance and asked for ICU. Despite hospitals always seeming to be well signed, she usually succeeded in getting lost. She finally found the waiting area for ICU and scanned the room before entering.

She spied Jessica and John first; they were sitting off in a corner using their phones. Brian's back faced her as he looked out the window opposite her with a cup of coffee in his hand. He was still wearing the same suit from the night before. She tried to blink away the image of him leaving her bedroom. He looked awful. She didn't see Derek and felt uneasy without him around to explain. She had no right to be there.

Kirsten tentatively made her entrance, feeling like an intruder and far too assuming to tread upon the grief of people she hardly knew. Where was Derek?! Brian turned away from the window and noticed her standing there; his face radiated relief. "Kirsten!"

"Brian," she said, moving toward him.

They embraced, and Kirsten was glad she'd come.

"Hi." She kissed his cheek while he tried to stop tears from forming with the heels of his hands. "I just found out. Derek called me."

"He did?" Brian was surprised and touched.

"Yeah," Kirsten intoned comfortingly.

"Thanks for coming. She was in surgery all night and hasn't woken up yet, so they're starting to get concerned. If she doesn't wake up soon, she may never."

"I'm so sorry, Brian."

"I can't believe it. She can't die." Brian's fear was undeniable.

Kirsten saw Jessica look up and walked toward her. "Jessica, I'm so sorry. I just heard."

Jessica stood, and they hugged like they'd been family forever.

It should seem odd, Kirsten thought, but it didn't. Tragedy had a way of bringing people together.

Derek came in with a tray of coffee drinks and handed two of them to John and Jessica. He stopped to kiss Kirsten on the cheek. "Thanks for coming," he whispered.

"Of course," she returned.

They sat with Jessica and John, Brian next to John, taking one wing of the corner, and Derek next to Jessica on the other wing. Kirsten assumed her place next to Brian. "Kirsten, would you like some coffee or a latte?" Derek asked.

"No. No, thank you. I've got my water." She waved her water bottle.

A grandparent-like couple sat across from them and gave Kirsten a friendly smile.

"Kirsten, these are my mom's parents, Henrik and Judy."

"Oh, hello." Kirsten scooted forward on her chair to shake their hands. It seemed it was inevitable Kirsten would be meeting Brian's entire family in one weekend—no dating for months first. She didn't know what else to say or if she should say more. 'So sorry about your daughter,' came to mind but didn't feel quite right. The mood was solemn and had no room for comforting words.

A few more family members showed up and filled the seats around them. There were Brian's paternal grandparents, Jim and Linda, and Elin's brothers, Lawrence and Todd, along with their wives and another aunt who was Brian's dad's sister. Kirsten wanted to remember their names. It was the least she could do, plus she had the time. She played a memory game by going around the room and saying each person's name in her head and taking a mental picture of them when she said it. For example, Todd green sweater who's next to Lisa with the cool boots.

Kirsten became their distraction. It was easier to talk to a stranger than amongst themselves. They all wanted to know about her and how she knew Brian. She felt like an imposter, and Brian gladly played along. The events of the night before became a mirage. They felt like the family she'd always wanted, and she reveled in their attention.

Kirsten found the waiting fatiguing but refused to leave Brian's side. Finally, the doctor came out with good news. Elin had finally woken up, and everyone breathed a sigh of relief.

Only immediate family were allowed to see her and only briefly. While Brian went to her side, Kirsten meandered out of the waiting room and down the hall. The weight of the last twenty-two hours had taken their toll, and she looked for a quiet place to unload. She spotted a chapel and walked in.

It was small, serene, and empty. She sat down on one of the pews close to the front near the altar. About half the candles were flickering and casting shadows on the wall. She wasn't Catholic and didn't feel compelled to light one, nor did she know why or when to light one. A peace enveloped her. Surprising, since she'd never felt at peace in a church before, but somehow in this little chapel, it seemed real and sacred. This close to death, how could it not?

"Excuse me," a voice said from behind.

She jumped a little at learning someone was there.

"Sorry, I didn't mean to frighten you."

There was a wide column coming down from the ceiling, separating the pew a few rows back, and it had hidden a man wearing a clerical collar. He looked like Santa Claus with his white hair, full beard, and protruding stomach.

"That's okay. I didn't see you." Kirsten turned back to face him.

"If you don't mind my asking, who are you here for?"

"I don't know."

"You don't know?"

"No. I mean, yes. It's a friend's mom. I don't really know her; I met her last night for the first time."

"You must be a really good friend."

"Not really. He's more than a friend, I guess. I don't know. He might be my boyfriend...we can't seem to figure that part out."

"So, it's complicated," he said.

Kirsten tried a little sarcasm. "Yeah. Isn't it always?"

"It can be, but only if you make it. Death or potential death can be very crystallizing."

"Yes, I bet you see that a lot here." Kirsten laughed a little at his acuity.

"What would make it uncomplicated?"

"If I could have sex." Kirsten surprised herself at how easily she let it slip out. "Oops, sorry, I shouldn't have said that."

"No, not at all. Why can't you have sex?"

"I don't know. I can't bring myself to do it. I want to, but at the last minute I can't, even though I really love him." The flickering light cast a spell of warmth and love, illuminating the chaplain as a kindred spirit. She knew she could tell him anything and he would understand. Perhaps this was the attraction to religion that had always eluded her.

"I think there are certain things written on our souls by our Creator, and no matter how hard we try, we can't bring ourselves to ignore them. Perhaps this is one of those things for you. It's not a bad thing; it's who you are. You need to embrace it. It's when we don't we cause ourselves to live in a state of anxiety, sometimes for a lifetime."

How easily he was able to solve her quandary. Why couldn't she do that?

"Yeah, that's kind of what my cousin said."

"Have you told him? Your kind-of boyfriend," he asked gently.

"Essentially."

"And he didn't run?"

"No. No, he didn't." She laughed.

"He must really love you."

"Yeah, I think he does. I've never seen real love, so it's hard to believe, I guess."

"It does make it harder, for sure, but you'll never have it if you don't try. There are no guarantees in this life."

"There aren't, huh? Kind of thought that's what you guys were all about," Kirsten joked.

"Yeah, we get that a lot." He smiled at her. "I can guarantee God loves you very much, but there will be suffering."

Kirsten smiled and pivoted back to meditate on his words. They fell silent. "Well, it's getting late, and the wife is expecting me. It was nice talking to you. I hope you figure it out."

Kirsten turned to see him put his arms into forearm crutches and clumsily struggle to get up.

She hadn't noticed his disability. "Thanks. Thanks, I will." She watched as he started to walk out at a stilted lumber. "What happened to you?" Kirsten couldn't help but ask.

"Polio. I had it as a child, and then it came back."

Kirsten was drawn to him. She was awash with a deep peace and resonating love from this man. This man who had obviously endured much. He had a reassuring acceptance of himself like he knew something about the divine. It was real to him, not a myth conjured up to make you feel better.

"Thank you for talking to me. It helped." Her words sounded hollow compared to what he'd given her.

"Glad I could help."

Kirsten lingered a little longer, enjoying the solitude and letting the peace seep in. When she left the chapel, she noticed some framed pictures of chaplains past on the wall. There was her chaplain.

What? Died August 14th, 2007—the day Sofie died. She didn't know what to make of it. She felt her skin prickle in a way she'd never experienced before. It wasn't scary or ghostly. Had she just witnessed her first miracle? No one would believe her. She looked up and smiled. "That's how miracles work, right, Sofie?" she whispered.

Kirsten returned to the ICU waiting room and found Brian sitting in his seat, shaking her back to reality and making her shelve her other-worldly encounter. She sat next to him. "Hey, how is she?"

"Good. She doesn't seem to have any memory loss, and the doctors are saying she should pull through now she's awake. Hey, where were you?"

"Sorry, I was hanging out in the chapel. Have you been back a while?"

"No, only a few minutes. The chapel, huh?"

"Yeah, there was a chaplain and everything." Brian raised a brow and took her hand in his.

Jessica entered and asked about going to dinner.

"Yeah. Where should we go?" Brian asked.

"How 'bout Normandy Kitchen? It's not too far so everyone can walk, good food and can easily accommodate all of us. I made a reservation on Open Table."

"Okay, sounds good." He turned to Kirsten. "Is that okay? Do you have time?"

"Yeah. Yeah, sure." She smiled up at him and squeezed his hand to reassure him.

Brian and Kirsten walked to the restaurant with Jessica and John. Derek left, seeing as Elin was out of the woods. Normandy Kitchen was one of those places that'd been around for nearly a hundred years serving elevated comfort food. The bar and dining furniture were made of darkly varnished wood with contrasting red upholstery. Decorative tin was pressed into the cove ceilings, and live jazz often filled the place. It was a welcoming reprieve from the walls of the ICU waiting room and befittingly less quiet, as it was a Sunday night.

They were seated in a quiet room in the back, where several four-tops were pushed together to form one long table. John and Jessica, along with Kirsten and Brian, sat on one end, with their grandparents bridging the middle between them and their aunts and uncles.

"How long have you lived in the area?" Jessica asked Kirsten, having missed hearing Kirsten answer the same questions earlier.

"Um, coming up on two years now," Kirsten politely replied.

"How do you like the cold? You're from Seattle, right?" Jessica continued.

"Yes, you mean the frozen rain?" They smiled at her little joke. "Actually I like being able to get a lot of snow. It doesn't snow much in Seattle, and when it does, it paralyzes the city. I guess you could say it's the summers I mind; all the mosquitoes and humidity. Ten thousand lakes? They should call it ten thousand mosquitoes."

Everyone chuckled, and Kirsten was glad she was able to make them laugh. Food was ordered and eaten, and Brian's family seemed to brighten from the cozy atmosphere and hearty fare.

As the meal drew to a close, his family started to leave in the same groups they'd arrived in, and Kirsten whispered in Brian's ear, "Can you come over for a bit? I'd like to talk to you."

"Yeah, sure," he said, not knowing if he should be surprised, elated, or neither.

Kirsten drove them to her apartment as Derek had driven Brian to the hospital. It was less welcoming than the night before, despite the candles, prompting her to turn her electric stove on.

"I'm going to have a cup of tea. Would you like anything? I can make you coffee if you'd rather. I have one of those Keurigs, so it'd be a snap."

"No. No, thank you." He joined her in the kitchen while she filled her electric teapot.

It was easier to talk with the distraction of making tea. "So, I've been thinking about things and, well, the truth is that I…um…I've never had sex before." Her eyes were unable to meet his.

An audible silence beat between them.

"I kind of figured. It's okay, you know. I'm totally cool with that." He could tell she was embarrassed and uncomfortable and wanted her to know it didn't matter to him in the least. "Hey," he said taking her in his arms to further impress upon her his sincerity. "It really is okay." He stroked her hair and held her for a minute. "I kind of like the fact you're still a virgin."

"You do?" she said in surprise, pulling back to look at him.

"Yeah." He thought about the two times they'd almost had. *What was she thinking not telling me?* So many things made more sense now; her boldness, then her withdrawal. It made him love her all the more. It's not like he'd had a lot of sex either. His dad's cancer had stunted his early adult years, he'd been living at home and taking a few classes when most of his peers were living it up at university, a serious girlfriend in high school had broken off before college, another one had ended a year before he'd met Kirsten, and there was the sad, drunken night with Chrissy after his father died that never should've happened.

"I'll wait as long as it takes. We'll figure it out," he promised her.

"What if it means until we're married? Not that I think we should get married; we still need to get to know each other."

"Even until then."

"Are you sure you can do that?"

"Yes. I mean I'm not happy about it, but I will if that's what you need. I love you, Kirsten. I know it doesn't seem like we should be saying that right now—maybe it's too soon—but I can't help it. I just know I do. It doesn't make sense considering how little time we've spent together, but I've always known it."

He pulled her in tight and closed his eyes, remembering a moment bedside with his dad. His mom had exited the room to get his dad some soup, and his dad's eyes never left her. 'I'm a very lucky man to have married so well,' Brian recalled him saying. 'It's easy to get sucked in by a pretty girl, it's important to find one who has integrity and strength and makes you laugh. Don't settle for anything less. Marriage is a long haul and you need a good partner to get through the hard times.'

Kirsten had all that and more. Julia had broken his heart in high school, so freely giving herself for the right amount of attention showered on her. Kirsten was careful, she didn't give her heart easily.

"Okay." She smiled shyly up at him. "I really like you a lot, and I think I even love you too, but it's hard for me to be sure. I'm sorry I can't give you more right now."

"That's okay."

"You know last night when you asked me who hurt me?"

"Yeah?"

"Well, I couldn't stop thinking about it, and I ended up going to my dad's. That's where I was when Derek called. I kind of had it out with him."

"What do you mean?"

"Well, I told him off, basically. I was suddenly so angry. It was him who hurt me. He hasn't exactly been father of the year."

"I'm sorry. I kind of sensed there was some tension between you, but thought it was about the job thing."

"Well, that didn't help, and that's what I started off with, but then it became a watershed."

"I'm sorry. It's hard to imagine; my dad was the best and I really miss him."

"I'm sorry. What was he like?"

"He was strong. He was a builder."

"Yeah, what was his name?"

"Rob. Robert McNeill of Lakewood Homes. He developed a lot of neighborhoods in the suburbs of Minneapolis, so to see him so weak and sick was really hard. I'd tag along sometimes with my little tool belt and learned how to hammer a nail by the time I was three. Then I'd work summers for him in high school, but I found I didn't like framing much and preferred finish work and designing more and more. I've always loved to draw, and once I discovered computer design, well, the rest is history. I do still love carpentry, but more as a hobby. He was fine with that. In fact, I think he was a little glad. It could be a tough way to make a living; a lot of boom and bust."

They continued to talk into the night about anything and everything despite their lack of sleep. They laughed. They cried. And eventually, they fell asleep in each other's arms.

Brian awoke to the sound of Kirsten talking. She was leaning on her side with her back to him so as not to wake him.

"Hi, Michael. I'm not going to make it into the office today. A friend is in the hospital...Yeah, she's gonna be okay. I'll call you later today, and we can touch base...Thanks."

She didn't want him to know it was Elin, although she remembered Michael knew her and after seeing her and Brian at the ball he would probably eventually guess.

Brian's phone rang and his voice took a professional tone.

"Okay, I'll see you at three o' clock then." He tapped his phone and looked at Kirsten with an impish grin.

"What?" she demanded impatiently.

"Is Michael going to be upset you're not coming in?" Brian stalled.

"No. Tell me. Who was that?" Kirsten demanded.

"Well, it was Bloedel Kirkpatrick. They need another designer, so I'm going to see them at three."

"Really?!" Kirsten clapped her hands in disbelief.

He laughed. "Really."

Their eyes locked in quiet understanding while their hands reached to intertwine. Brian reeled her in and kissed her.

EPILOGUE

The baby's crying. Kirsten pretends not to hear. Brian snuggles up behind her. "It's your turn."

"No, it's not," Kirsten grumbles. "I did it last night."

Silence. "Rock, paper, scissors?" Brian cajoles her into meeting halfway. She raises her hand in agreement.

"One. Two. Three." Kirsten counts, and without looking finds his fist and covers it with her hand. "Paper," she says triumphantly.

"Hey! How'd you know?" Brian is surprised.

"Because you never do rock, and you think I always do scissors." Kirsten laughs.

"That's not true," Brian protests.

"Yeah, it is. Men. You're so easy. I can read you like a book."

Brian leaves and comes back with the baby in his arms, happy to finally be saved. "Good morning, Sofie girl," Kirsten coos. "Are you hungry? Yeah?" Brian settles her in Kirsten's arms to nurse and then climbs back in behind her.

"Easy, huh?" Brian says, kissing her neck.

"Stop." Kirsten laughs.

"You're easy. How do you think we got into this mess?"

"Well, I guess you just had to put a ring on it," Kirsten teases.

"If I'd only known, I'd have done it sooner." He laughs, kissing her neck again.

A NOTE FROM THE AUTHOR

Hello, I'm Tina, and thank you for reading my book! If you liked it, please give it a rating at your favorite online retailer. Like Kirsten, I spent my early career in the apparel industry after receiving my degree in clothing and textiles. I enjoy cooking, mostly because I love food, and I've been an avid moviephile ever since I saw *A Tree Grows in Brooklyn* while home sick from school. This is my first novel. I'm married to my high school sweetheart, and we have two kids. I currently live in Portland Oregon.

CPSIA information can be obtained
at www.ICGtesting.com
Printed in the USA
LVHW091125270219
608762LV00032B/552/P